LOVE ME WILD

CALI MELLE

Edited by Emma Cook | Booktastic Blonde LLC
Proofread by Nicole D'Cruz
Cover Art by @illustrated.by.moon
Cover Design by Cali Melle

CONTENT WARNING

Some content may be sensitive to individuals. This book covers the topics of off-page domestic abuse, emotional abuse (not between main characters), death of parents (off page).

PLAYLIST

The Night We Met - Lord Huron
My Blood - Ellie Goulding
Love Somebody - Morgan Wallen
Say Yes to Heaven - Lana Del Rey
July - Noah Cyrus
Chasin' You - Morgan Wallen
Must Be Doin' Somethin' Right - Billy Currington
Run - George Strait
I Need You - Tim McGraw, Faith Hill

That love that you're looking for? It's out there, I promise…
and sometimes you find it where you least expect to.

PROLOGUE
ELLA

THREE YEARS AGO

"No, no, no."

My hands shake and I stare down at the two pink lines glaring back at me.

This can't be real. Life must have mixed my cards up with someone else's. We buried my parents a few hours ago and I thought that was the worst thing that could ever happen, but here I am facing the one thing I've tried to prevent. My worst fear. The cruelest of jokes.

I'm pregnant by a man who doesn't love me.

A man who could never love anyone more than he loves himself.

"What does it say, El?" My best friend Remi's voice comes from the other side of the door.

My mind shifts into overdrive, running wild with a million possibilities. The man I'm married to isn't the man I fell in love with and we're already on the brink of a separation. The timing of a child could not be worse and now, here I am, pregnant with his child.

"Oh my gosh, Remi."

The test falls from my fingers in a rush, clattering on the floor as I bury my face in my hands. The tears fall from my eyes without any warning and my body begins to shake as my sobs fill the bathroom. He's gone on another business trip for the weekend. My period has been late for a week now, but I waited until he was gone since I was already fearing the worst.

And this is it.

"Oh, El," Remi murmurs softly, remorse hanging in her voice as she slips into the bathroom. She comes over and wraps her arms around me. "It's going to be okay. It's not the end of the world. There are always options, you know?"

A shiver ripples down my spine and my stomach feels empty. Fear floods me, dripping into my veins. I know immediately in my heart, I can't get an abortion. It may be the right solution for some people, but I don't think I would ever be able to forgive myself for it.

"I can't do that, Remi. It's not the baby's fault. It didn't ask for any of this."

She's silent for a moment. "Okay." She lets out a breath. "We will figure this out."

"I have to leave him now," I half whisper the words, the decision weighing heavily on my chest. "I can't stay in a failing, loveless marriage just because I'm pregnant with his child."

"I agree with you," she says, her voice a soft embrace as we break apart. Her hands cup the sides of my face and she swipes the tears away. "You know how I feel about Jacob and the things he has done. You deserve better, Ella."

I swallow roughly, holding back my emotion. "I know I do."

Collecting myself, I rise to my feet, moving away from her as I brush the tears away from my face in a haste. My heart pounds erratically in my chest, the panic settling inside as my flight instincts begin to consume me.

I had already planned on moving out when the timing was right, although I didn't anticipate it happening like this. Jacob has been trying to convince me to stay, even though he's the one who's had a foot out the door for years. He didn't fly back to Silverspur Springs with me for my parents' service. He insisted that his work trip was more important, which gives me the perfect opportunity.

Lifting my hand to my stomach, I flatten my palm over my belly button.

This is mine. The only thing that is mine.

"What's the plan, El?" Remi says, her voice breaking through my thoughts. "Do you want to come home with me?"

"No, I'll be okay," I say in a rush, shaking my head. "I'm flying home tomorrow, but Jacob won't be back for a few days. That gives me enough time to file the divorce papers, pack my things, and return here."

Remi's eyes are soft as they slowly search mine. "How can I help?"

"I don't know yet," I say, my voice cracking around the words. "But I'll let you know when I figure it out."

I glance down at my ring finger, sadness encapsulating me as I stare at the symbolism of the commitment I made to Jacob Evans. I met Jacob two years ago, right after I turned eighteen. He was charismatic and handsome and I was captivated by him when I ran into him at a bar one night. He was passing through town on a business trip and I didn't hesitate when he asked me to dinner.

Three months later, I flew out of the only town I had ever known with nothing more than a suitcase filled with my belongings. I moved in with Jacob on a whim and a hope. A dream of being with someone who valued me for me. I didn't know at the time how wrong I could be. I chose to leave with Jacob instead of staying with the friends and family I knew.

And it was the biggest mistake I had ever made.

Tears fill my eyes and I slide the rings from my fingers, setting them on my nightstand. Even though the love is lost, all of this still hurts.

"I think I just need to be alone, Rem," I say to my best friend, tears burning the corners of my eyes as I stare at her from across the bathroom.

Remi's lips tug downwards into a frown, her eyebrows tugging close together as sympathy washes over her expression. "Okay, girl. I love you so much and I am here. Whatever you need, whenever you need it, okay?"

I close the distance between us, letting her pull me in against her chest. My arms wrap around her tightly and I cling to her for a moment, waves of emotion flowing over me. Releasing her, I take a step back. "Okay. I love you too."

Remi kisses the side of my head before she slowly heads out of the bathroom. She pauses by the door, her eyes finding mine once more. "We'll get you through this, babe."

"I know."

I wait until Remi leaves before I wander out of the house with my thoughts running wild as they chase after me. I walk and walk until the soles of my feet are sore. The lake is just off in the distance and I don't stop until I'm stepping onto one of the public docks, walking until I reach the end and sit down.

My mind is in absolute shambles. Between losing my parents and having to bury them today, and this mess I've gotten myself into with Jacob, I can't think straight. Things with him weren't always bad. He worked a lot, which left me lonely and secluded, but I tried to think of the alone time as a positive and poured myself into my art.

Our relationship moved quickly and within a year and a half after moving in with him, we got married. I don't know where things went wrong, but the first time Jacob cheated on me was right before the wedding. He fed me lies about it never happening again and I chose to believe him. I chose to stay.

Little did I know, it wasn't the first time and it wouldn't be the last.

The dock beneath me gently rocks, the water lapping at my calves from the wake of a passing boat in the distance. My fingers thread through the spaces and I tighten them, wringing them together in my lap. A sob tears through my body, tightening the muscles in my chest, constricting my lungs. I clamp my eyes shut, willing away the tears.

I've been trying to hold in my emotions all day, mainly for the sake of my brother, but I can't anymore. The gaping hole inside my heart continues to weep, the pain washing over me in violent waves. I'm no match against the sadness that encapsulates me and the tears streak down the sides of my cheeks without my permission.

The last week feels like it's aged me twenty years and finding out I'm pregnant is only compounding to the myriad of emotions. It's like my parents were fine and then they were gone. I spoke to my mother a few hours before the accident. I had no idea they would leave for dinner one night, only to be hit head on by a drunk driver.

Life changes in the blink of an eye and this was a change nothing could have prepared me for.

The wooden boards of the dock creak, shifting slightly, most likely from another boat, but I pay it no mind. My nostrils collapse as I suck in the deepest breath I can to calm myself down. Their funeral today gave a sense of closure, although it did nothing to fix the hole the loss left in my chest.

The smell of leather and cedar invades my senses and the dock shifts again. A warm, solid leg brushes against mine and I know it's him before I even open my eyes.

Cole Wild.

The silence settles between us and as I lift my eyelids, I find him sitting with his dress pants rolled up to his knees, his feet tucked beneath the surface of the water. His hands are folded in his lap and the sleeves of his black dress shirt are rolled halfway up his forearms.

"What are you doing out here?" I ask, my voice catching in my throat as I wipe the tears from my face.

Cole slowly turns his head to look at me. His blue eyes land on mine, filled with nothing but sorrow. "Lookin' for you."

"Mission accomplished. You found me." I clear my throat, pulling my gaze from his. I look back out at the crystal-clear lake, not wanting to meet his stare. "I'm fine, Cole."

Cole lets out a soft breath, his eyes still trained on the side of my face. "Okay, El."

Tears burn the corners of my eyes and the pressure along my jaw builds. The heaviness settling inside my chest is crippling. The weight is far too much for me to take and I know I'm going to break. I've been trying so hard to keep it together all day. I've let myself cry, but I've refused to fall apart.

"Please go," I whisper, my voice cracking around my words.

"No can do."

"Goddammit, Cole," I choke out, the pressure building inside my chest. I whip my head to the side, the tears breaking past my lower lids like water crashing through a broken dam. "Just leave."

The inner corners of his eyebrows dip, his perfect lips tugging downward as he slowly shakes his head at me. "You're not fine and I'm not leavin' you like this."

"What the hell do you know?"

"You," he says softly, his voice barely above a whisper. His eyes travel down to my lips, lingering for a second before lifting back to meet my gaze. He stares directly through mine, into that hollow hole in my chest. "I know you, Ella. You always put on a brave face for everyone else, but you don't have to keep doin' that. No one is askin' you to be the strong one here."

That last word falls from his lips and the levees inside me are cracking apart. If only he knew how messed up things are right now.

His hand lifts and he presses it against my cheek, cupping the side of my face as he catches a tear with his thumb. "Oh, El," he murmurs. His palm warms my skin, his stare warming my soul. His gaze drifts back down to my mouth before trailing back to my eyes.

I don't know what the hell I'm doing as my body shifts forward, leaning into him while closing the distance between my face and his. My eyelids flutter shut, my lips seeking his, desperate to feel anything but the pain festering inside my chest, but I never find them.

"Ella, no," he murmurs, his voice laced with pain, his hand pressing firmly against my cheekbone. My eyes flash open and he gazes at me, his expression unreadable as his eyebrows draw together. "Not like this."

Time stops. My breath catches in my throat and I pull back. Heat creeps up my neck, spreading across my face.

"Oh my gosh." I stare at him, eyes wide and face burning from embarrassment. I'm mortified. Why the hell did I think it was okay to kiss him? "I'm so sorry. I don–I don't know what I did that for."

My gaze leaves his in a flash and I turn my head against his hand to look anywhere except at him, but he stops me. He turns me back to face him and his eyes slowly search mine.

"Ella," he says softly, a ragged breath leaving him. "Stop, El. You're going through so much right now, it's normal to be on an emotional roller coaster." His throat bobs as he swallows hard. "Don't shut me out. I'm right here–here for you. You don't have to be strong around me. You don't have to pretend like you're okay."

A sob catches in my throat and I finally break. My ribcage cracks wide open and the tears spill from my eyes, blurring my vision. Cole doesn't say a single word as he reaches for me, pulling me flush against him as sobs tear through my body. My hands curl into fists and I tuck my elbows against my ribs, succumbing to the pain.

His hands are soft and comforting as he runs them over my hair, down my back, over and over again, attempting to sooth me. I bury my face against his chest as he wraps his arms around me, holding me tighter. He rests his head against mine, gentling rubbing my back as whispers fall from his lips.

"Shh," he murmurs into my hair. "I got you. I got you." He holds me close against his body. "It's gonna be okay."

Time ceases to exist and the sun begins to set as he still cradles me against his chest, murmuring those soothing words until they begin to tangle into the fibers of my soul. I know tomorrow he won't be here, so I hold onto the moment; I hold onto him.

Because I know after he leaves, there will be no one else here to hold me together.

CHAPTER ONE

ELLA

PRESENT

The sun peeks through the clouds, its rays casting a blanket of warmth across my face and my arms as my gaze trails along the green grass dancing in the soft breeze. The leaves from the willow tree in the center of the field shift in the air and a smile lifts the corners of my lips as a flash of blonde curls disappear behind the trunk of the tree.

"I can't believe how big she's gotten already."

Turning my head, I glance at my brother as a thoughtful smile dances across his mouth as he watches my daughter, Chloe running around through the meadow at the park. If someone would have told the helpless Ella Daniels three years ago, that this is where she would be, I would have never believed them.

"I swear, I feel like I blinked and the time passed. I still can't wrap my mind around the fact that she'll be turning three already."

Wyatt chuckles softly, turning his head to look at me.

"You've done so well with her, little sis." His gaze shifts back out to the yard, watching Chloe as she bends over and plucks a small purple flower from a patch at the base of the willow tree's trunk. "She's strong and fierce, just like you."

A lump lodges in my throat and I swallow back the emotion that has the corners of my eyes burning. "I only want the best for her. I want to give her the entire world."

I know I'm doing the best I can, but I also know I could be doing better. Working a dead-end job as a bartender isn't exactly what I had planned for my career. A starving artist isn't an option, either, although I know that is where my heart truly is.

Wyatt reaches over, his hand finding mine as he gives me a gentle squeeze. He turns to look at me, his eyes slowly searching mine. "You are, Ella. You're an amazing mother to her."

"Wy-Wy!" Chloe calls out as she comes running through the grass, toward the bench we're sitting on. "Wook!" She raises her arm, waving her hand around as her little fingers tighten around the stems of the flowers she's been gathering.

Mixed in with the flowers are three dandelions that have lost their yellow petals. Instead, they've changed into fluffy, white balls—the kind you blow on while you make a wish.

"He-uh," she says, handing one to Wyatt and me as she sets her others down on the grass. She closes her eyes, her face scrunching up as she puckers her pink lips. I bite back a grin and watch the determination on my daughter's face. The whimsy and magic as she makes a silent wish. Her eyelids lift, her bright blue eyes shining as she blows on the puff ball.

The seeds lift into the air, the light breeze carrying them away and she erupts with giggles, bouncing up onto her toes and back onto her heels. "You do, mama!" She exclaims, pointing at the one I'm holding.

I let my eyes close, sucking in a deep breath as my mind wanders. I wish for nothing but happiness for my little girl. I never want her to experience the dark. Only the light of the world. I wish for her to be safe and happy.

I open my eyes and find Chloe watching me expectantly. I look over at my brother and see he's still finalizing his wish as I begin to blow on the seeds, watching them float away. Wyatt does the same and the breeze catches Chloe's giggles, carrying the sounds along with the pieces of the dandelions.

"Fa you," Chloe says, handing me a flower before giving one to Wyatt. She looks back and forth between the two of us, her cheeks pink with excitement. Her blonde curls bounce as she spins on her heel and takes off back over toward the willow tree.

"She's like a little fairy," Wyatt chuckles, shaking his head as he looks down at the flower she gave him. "I hope she holds on tight to the magic in life."

"Me too." I look over at my brother as he rests his hands in his lap, his back pressed against the bench. He's heading back to Cheyenne in a few hours and sadness presses against my chest at the thought. I know Wyatt has his own life there, but sometimes I just wish he would move home.

"Guess who I talked to last week?

My eyebrows cinch closer. "Who?"

"Cole." He pauses. "You remember him, right?"

My breath catches and my heart skips a beat at the mention of his name. "Cole Wild?"

The cobwebs sway around my heart, a few breaking away as it begins to beat a little wilder. Cole Wild—the middle Wild child—was a pillar from my childhood. He was my brother's best friend and was everywhere I turned.

"The one and only."

As if I could ever forget him.

A girl never forgets the first boy who brought life to the butterflies inside her stomach.

"I do. How is he doing?"

"He's okay, I think," Wyatt says with a shrug. "It was the first I've heard from him in months, but we've both been so busy. He said he was thinking about hanging up his glove and cleats. He's been having a lot of problems with his shoulder and it's beginning to affect his ability to pitch."

"Oh no," I murmur, glancing down at the flower in my hands, unaware until now that I had been absentmindedly picking the petals off one by one. Cole left Silverspur Springs eight years ago after he was drafted to a professional baseball team in Texas fresh out of high school.

I last saw him three years ago, when he came back for our parents' funeral. That was the day my entire life changed–the day that propelled my life into a completely different direction. I spent that day in a daze, trying to hold myself together for the sake of my brother, but I'll never forget the kindness he showed me that day—even though I ended up completely embarrassing myself.

"El, did you hear me?"

I blink rapidly, forcing away the memory as my vision focuses back on my brother. "No, I'm sorry." I shake my head. "I got a little lost in my head for a second."

Wyatt nods in understanding. "I was just saying that he didn't seem upset like I thought he would be, but I think it's been a long time coming. He's been having issues for a few years now."

"Do you know what he's going to do after he retires?"

Wyatt shrugs. "I don't know. He didn't really say." He lets out a sigh. "I just hope everything ends up working out for him."

Even though I embarrassed the hell out of myself that day, I still have a soft spot for Cole Wild. He is a good guy and I'll always hold onto the good parts of that last memory I have with him. The day he was there for me in a way no one else could be. The day he watched me fall apart and refused to leave my side.

I swallow hard, looking back out at Chloe as she comes running over.

"Me too."

CHAPTER TWO

COLE

"Your new tenants are planning on moving in on the first. Does that date still work for you?"

Balancing my phone on my shoulder, I scroll through the available flights, finding one for the thirtieth. Tomorrow. "That works." I select the earliest flight I can find, not minding that it has a three-hour layover in Chicago.

"Okay," Missy, the woman from the property management company says. "If you can drop off the keys and garage door opener along with any pertinent information, we will make sure it gets to the tenants."

"I'll drop it off tomorrow on my way to the airport."

"That's perfect. Save travels, Mr. Wild. I'll be in touch if needed."

"Thanks again, Missy," I say, typing in my payment information, ending the call with her. The transaction is complete and I stare at the screen for a moment, a contradictory sense of overwhelm mixing with the simultaneous relief I feel.

These last two weeks have been a complete whirlwind.

After dealing with injury after injury for the last two years, I was planning on making this upcoming season my last with the Titans. My contract was set to end then, but life has a funny way of shaking things up every now and then.

Two seasons ago, I tore my rotator cuff in my right shoulder and had to have it surgically repaired. The damage was more extensive than they thought and the surgeons did the best they could. I went through intense rehabilitation and physical therapy to try and get my shoulder back to where it was before my injury, but I never achieved that.

Since then, I've sustained other minor injuries, but each one has taken longer to rehab and only created more instability within the joint. I've been gritting my teeth, pushing through the pain, but after speaking with the team doctors, physical therapist, and the rest of the executives, it was determined best if I retired a year early.

The team can't afford to have a liability for a pitcher and I can't risk losing all function of my shoulder if I keep injuring it.

It wasn't an easy decision to make, although it was a necessary one. I'm grateful for getting the opportunity to play professionally, for getting the chance to live out my dreams, but I know my time here in Texas has come to an end. It's time I close this chapter and head back to where I belong.

Back to Silverspur Springs, to my family's ranch.

Closing my laptop, I tuck my phone into my front pocket and head over to the front door where the last two boxes of my belongings are. I downsized considerably and dropped a lot off at the local donation center since I'm moving back into the main house on our ranch. Everything else I'm taking with me has been packed up and I've been loading them into a shipping pod all afternoon. I have been renting the house fully furnished, so all my furniture and decorations are staying for the new tenants.

I grab the last two boxes, put them on the dolly that came with the shipping pod, and head out to the driveway. Lifting the remaining boxes, I stack them inside and tuck the dolly in the corner before I shut the doors.

"It's going to be weird having new neighbors."

I turn around and see Tucker, one of my teammates and closest friend I have in Texas, standing at the end of my driveway. His wife stands behind him on the sidewalk, pushing the stroller back and forth, most likely to keep their four-month-old son content in the carriage.

"Hey Tuck," I say, nodding my head at him before looking at his wife. "Hey Payton."

"Hey Cole," she says, waving as she smiles brightly. She glances down at the stroller and stops rocking it as she looks back at me. "Did you end up having any luck with flights?"

Tucker and Payton were the first to hear about my early retirement, along with the news of me heading back to Silverspur Springs.

I nod, shifting my weight on my feet and tucking my hands into my jean pockets. "The best option was tomorrow, which works since your new neighbors will be moving in soon."

Tucker groans, a frown tugging his lips downward. "Don't remind me."

"Tuck, be nice," Payton scolds him, cutting her eyes at the back of his head. "The new neighbors might be nice."

"The keyword is might, Pay."

Payton rolls her eyes and begins to push the stroller

away from my driveway. "I'm taking Brody home so I can get started on dinner. Bring Cole back with you."

Tucker stares at me for a moment as Payton walks away and heads onto their property that sits right next to mine. "Do you really have to go?"

I chew on the inside of my cheek, dipping my chin. "I gotta get back home. My brothers need me." I pause, my eyes trailing over the grass that covers the sandy soil and the palm trees that loom above. I've always missed the fresh mountain air. The smell of dust, hay and leather. "You know this place was never for me."

Tucker walks over, his shoulders falling as a sigh escapes him. "I know. You've done nothing but complain about the humidity and stale air since you got here." A smile cracks on Tucker's face. "It's been eight damn years of hearing you talk about how the weather is so much nicer in Wyoming."

A chuckle rumbles in my chest. "I promise you; it is."

"I'll have to take your word for it," Tucker says. "Payton refuses to go anywhere that doesn't have a beach."

"There's a lake," I offer, shrugging my shoulders. "That kinda counts for a beach, right?"

Tucker laughs. "Not the kind of beach Payton likes, but nice try." He lifts his arm, wrapping it around the tops of my shoulders. "Come on, she's going to be annoyed if we're late for dinner."

"I thought she said she was going to make it?" I question him as we fall in step together and head across my yard and into his.

"By making it, she meant turning off the crockpot."

I follow Tucker onto his front porch and he pulls open the front door, holding it for me to step in first. I kick my shoes off in the foyer and he does too. The smell of paprika and onions wafts through the air, immediately grabbing my attention and pulling me down the hall into the kitchen.

"What did you make, Payton?" I ask, strolling into the kitchen with Tucker behind me. "It smells delicious." Payton turns around from the stove with Brody strapped to the front of her torso and smiles at the two of us.

"Tacos!"

"Let me take him," Tucker says as he closes the distance between them. I step farther into the kitchen, stopping by the island in the center of the room as I watch them. There's a twinge of jealousy in my chest as Payton smiles at Tucker while he undoes the straps and cradles Brody in his arms. Payton rests her hands on his forearms, staring down at their little guy for a moment.

A relationship was not a priority for me these past eight years. Baseball was my sole focus and it left little time to get involved with anyone. I knew as soon as my baseball career was over that I'd be heading home to shift into my new focus—the ranch.

But watching the two of them together with the life they share and the life they created, stirs up a sense of longing deep inside my chest. It's something that might not be for me, although it's something I find myself wanting more these days.

Maybe it has to do with the changing seasons of my life. Maybe this retirement and moving has awakened a part of me that I didn't know was inside before.

Or maybe it's because I've been alone for so long... and I don't think I want to be alone forever.

"Come sit," Payton says, waving me over to the dining area. Tucker carries three plates over, setting them all on the table before he starts to bop Brody up and down. He stirs in Tucker's arms, his mouth widening as he yawns. "Would you like me to make yours?"

Tucker shakes his head at her. "You eat first, then I'll get mine."

I take a seat across from Payton, next to Tucker, and she motions for me to help myself. Grabbing a tortilla, I fill it with some chicken and then move onto the toppings, loading up my shell.

"Are you excited to get back to your hometown?"

I chew a bite of my taco, swallowing it back down as Tucker stands near Payton, rocking Brody as they both wait for my response. "I am. I miss it there."

"He hates it here, babe," Tucker laughs, his face lighting up.

"That's true," Payton giggles. "I'm sure you'll be much happier there."

"I think I will be," I say after swallowing another bite. It's not that I've been unhappy here, it's just not what I grew up with. Even after being here for as long as I have been, it still has never truly felt like home. "It's home, ya know?"

Payton nods and so does Tucker.

"You'll come back to visit sometime though, won't you?" Payton questions me as the two of us finish eating and Tucker continues to rock Brody.

"You guys can't get rid of me that easily."

Payton laughs softly and Tucker's chest rumbles with a chuckle. I pop the last of my taco into my mouth, rising to my feet before Payton gets the chance to. I step over to Tucker, holding my hands out.

"Here, I'll take him so you can eat."

Tucker raises an eyebrow. "You sure about that?"

"I'm not allergic to kids," I laugh, taking the baby from him. "And it's not my first time holding him."

"Fair enough," Tucker nods, smiling as he quickly sits down in his seat and wastes no time piling taco meat onto a tortilla. I shift my weight from leg to leg, swaying back and forth, staring at Brody's soft features while he sleeps.

"Do you think you want any?"

I adjust Brody in my arms, my eyes slicing to Payton's as she looks over at me. "What?"

"Kids," she smiles, looking at Brody, Tucker and then back to me. "Do you think you want any?"

"Oh, I dunno," I admit, shrugging my shoulders as I'm careful not to disturb the baby. He's warm in my arms, tucked in against my chest. "I haven't thought much about it."

"You're good with them," Tucker chimes in, shrugging his shoulders. "Well, you're good with Brody."

"I think good things are going to happen for you back in Wyoming." Payton gives me a dreamy smile, her eyes filled with hope. "Maybe you'll find the woman of your dreams and finally settle down. And who knows...maybe you'll even have kids of your own."

Tucker snorts. "I don't think I'd hold my breath if I were you."

"Oh, stop that," Payton scolds him, pursing her lips. "Everyone deserves to have a happily ever after."

Tucker's lips lift into a grin. "Did you get that with me?"

"Yes, babe," she murmurs as she stares back at him with nothing but adoration.

I can't help but feel as though I'm intruding so I quietly shift my body, pulling my gaze away from the two of them, looking back at their son nestled in my arms. His lips part again and he yawns in his sleep, his body stretching in my arms.

Contentment washes over me and warmth spreads through my chest. I used to think I didn't want any of this, but now I'm not so sure.

And maybe—*just maybe*—I want exactly what they have one day.

CHAPTER THREE

ELLA

"Grammy!"

A warmth washes over my chest as Chloe breaks into a run as she speeds toward Iris.

Iris lets out a hearty laugh, her body crouching at the end of the walkway as she stretches her arms out to Chloe. She runs right to Iris, her little arms snaking around her neck as they embrace one another.

Iris isn't Chloe's biological grandmother, but she's the only one she's ever known. She's the only one she'll ever know.

"There's my favorite little sweet pea," Iris says as she presses her lips to the side of Chloe's head. Chloe giggles as Iris lifts her into her arms as she stands upright. "Are you going to help Grandma Iris in the garden today?"

Chloe claps her hands, her little body wiggling in Iris' arms. "Yes!" Chloe turns in Iris' arms and waves at me. "Bye Mama!"

My shoulders shake with laughter and Iris joins in, her cheeks lifting towards her eyes as she shakes her head.

"Jeez, Clo," I say, lifting my eyebrows at her. "Way to get rid of me."

"You know she loves her time with me," Iris smiles as she sets Chloe down onto the ground.

"She does," I smile back at her, nodding my head in agreement. Bending my knees, I crouch down. "Give me a hug, babe. Mama has to head to work."

Chloe comes over to me, wrapping her little arms around my neck as she places a sloppy kiss on my cheek. "Love you."

"Love you too," I murmur, kissing the top of her head before releasing her. She gives me another wave, walking past Iris as she guides her up the steps onto the front porch.

"Go get your gardening gloves, sweet pea." Iris turns to me as Chloe walks into the house. "Thanks again for covering for Maisie tonight. Her not feeling well was unexpected and my knees haven't been cooperative with me standing for long periods of time."

"I'm always here to help in any way I can." I step to Iris, reaching for her hand and give it a gentle squeeze. "It's the least I can do for everything you've done to help me."

"Oh, honey," she says, abruptly pulling me in for a hug. "You know you've always been like a second daughter to me. That's what family does. We help each other when we need it."

"I can never thank you enough," I say, my voice cracking around my words as emotion floods me. In addition to my brother, Iris and Remi were the two people who were there for me in the lowest point of my life. They helped me crawl my way out of the darkness and get back on my feet.

Iris releases me, but she takes my hands in hers, staring

at me with her eyes shining brightly. "You bringing that darling little angel into my life is the greatest gift."

Tears burn the corners of my eyes and I give her hands a gentle squeeze before taking a step back. I love Iris dearly. She's the closest thing I have to a motherly figure. Her daughter, Remi, has been my best friend for as long as I can remember. The two of them are my family, but the emotions still make me feel uncomfortable.

Crying in front of others isn't something I tend to do often and I'm not about to do it now on a random Tuesday evening.

"I'll be back later tonight to get her."

"See you then," Iris smiles, lifting her hand in a small wave before retreating back into the house.

My footsteps are quick as I head to my car, pushing the mix of emotions into the small box I keep locked away inside. My life isn't perfect, but it's good.

And that's enough for me right now.

"I swear to God, if I catch that creep looking at you again, I'm kicking him out."

Remi steps up beside me, letting out a sigh of annoyance as she grabs a glass and pours beer from the tap into it. I glance back over my shoulder at the older man sitting there, his eyes now on the back of Remi, looking her up and down.

This is one of the reasons why my life isn't perfect. I never imagined I'd be working as a bartender to support my daughter and I. Hell, I don't know what I really had planned, but I know it wasn't this.

It's a job I'm so grateful for, though, because without

this, I don't know what I would be doing. I didn't get a college degree and I have no other experience. The only thing I've ever been good at is painting. It's what I had hoped I'd do as a career one day. However, the starving artist's life as a single mom is not something I'm interested in.

"I've never seen him here before," I say to Remi, keeping my voice low. "I just saw him checking you out now."

"What a weirdo," she mutters, shaking her head as she fills another glass. "Has he said anything weird to you?"

I shake my head at her, grabbing a glass to make a cocktail. "I've only taken his drink order so far."

"Shit. Did he say he wanted food too?"

"He said he needed a moment to check out what we have."

Remi scoffs. "I bet he did." She spins on her heel, her gaze shifting directly to him. "Fucking creep."

"Ignore him," I wave my hand dismissively. "He's my problem."

"Wrong," she says, glancing at me as she purses her lips. "If someone is a problem for you, they're immediately a problem for me."

A smile cracks across my lips. "Same goes for you too, you know."

"Oh, I know," she nods, smiling back at me as she starts to walk over to the couple who ordered the beers. "Besties for the resties."

"Always!"

I finish mixing the cocktail and grab a bottle of beer from the fridge, taking it over to two other people sitting near the strange man. Dread rolls in the pit of my stomach and I walk back to him, plastering the fakest smile I can muster on my lips.

"Have you decided what you want to order?"

A smirk tugs on his lips and his oily cheeks lift. "I'm good with my drink. I think I'll just hang out and enjoy the view."

The hairs stand on the back of my neck. "Okay."

"What time do you get off tonight?"

My stomach drops and my heart pounds erratically against my ribcage. "That's none of your business."

His smirk doesn't falter. "Oh, come on. I don't see a ring on your finger. We could have some fun."

I swallow hard, resisting the urge to shrink back into myself. "Sir, I'm going to have to ask you to stop. I'm not interested and you're making me uncomfortable."

His mood changes. "Excuse me?" He snarls, narrowing his eyes at me. "There was nothing I said to make you feel uncomfortable."

"Is everything okay over here?" Remi asks as she immediately appears beside me. She pins her gaze on the man as he abruptly gets up from his barstool and drains his drink.

"That one is on the house for poor customer service," he snaps at her with a lingering warning in his tone. "I'd suggest you reevaluate your waitstaff here."

"I think it's time for you to leave."

"Oh, I have no intention of staying, nor will I be bringing my business back to this piece of shit establishment."

Remi raises her eyebrows and points to the exit. "Okay, buddy. Door is that way."

He slams his glass down onto the bar, his eyes immediately meeting mine again as he stares me down for a moment. My heart beats erratically as my flight instincts engage, my body ready to run if I need to. He spins on his heel without another word, striding directly out of the bar.

Remi immediately turns to face me. "Are you okay?" She asks as her eyes scan my face. "What happened?"

"I'm okay," I say, letting out a breath and nodding my head. "He was asking when I got off work, made comments about me not having a ring on my finger and how we could have fun. I told him he was making me uncomfortable and that he needed to stop."

Remi shakes her head, her jaw clenching momentarily. "What a disgusting pig. If I don't leave the same time you do, someone else will walk with you to your car. I don't need him lurking around the parking lot, waiting."

"I'll be okay, Rem, I promise."

"I'm not taking any chances," she says, shaking her head at me. "People are too unpredictable and that man is exactly the reason why us girls have to stick together."

Stepping back to the bar, I lean forward and grab his empty glass before setting it along with the other dirty dishes to go into the dishwasher. "I'm so glad I have you," I say, turning back to her.

Remi grabs a rag and cleaner with a smile tugging on her lips. "Same, girl. Besties for the resties, remember?"

Warmth settles in my chest and I smile back at my best friend. "Always."

Remi is one of the only people who has always been there for me, standing by my side, even when I tried to push her away. There aren't many people I trust with my life or with my daughter, but Remi is someone I know will always make sure the two of us are safe.

And I wouldn't be where I am today without her.

CHAPTER FOUR

COLE

The familiar smell of hay and leather infiltrates my senses as I step into the barn. Dust kicks up from the concrete floor and I glance down the aisle of stalls, looking for either of my brother's. They aren't expecting me here—hell, I wasn't even expecting to be back home this early into my career, but it's impossible to predict how your life will go.

I left Silverspur Springs eight years ago when I was eighteen and fresh out of high school. College was originally my plan, but only because I received a full ride scholarship for playing baseball. That plan was out the window when I ended up receiving an offer from the Titans halfway through my senior year of high school.

The offer meant leaving the only town I had ever known to move eighteen hours away to play the sport I revolved my entire life around.

I was living the dream. The dream I had always wanted… but that was only until the first time I injured my shoulder.

Movement from the stall to my left catches my attention and a dapple-grey horse lifts its head over the stall door, extending its neck as it blows out a breath. A smile drifts across my face and I step closer, recognition swelling in my chest. This stall was Diesel's when I left and I'm happy to see he's still the one who's occupying the space.

"Hey, old bud," I murmur, rubbing my palm against the front of his head. He nuzzles his nose against the center of my stomach, pushing against me as I scratch at the whorl in the center of his face. "Why aren't you out with the others?"

"Because someone figured out how to unlock the damn gate."

A grin tugs on the corners of my lips and I whip my head to the side, finding my brother Cash walking into the barn. My hand falls away from Diesel's head and I turn my body to face him. "Hey little brother," I say, my grin widening.

"Aren't you a sight for sore eyes?" Cash steps over to me, pulling me in for a hug. "What the hell are you doing here?"

We break apart and I take a step back, shoving my hands into the front pockets of my jeans. "I did it. I retired."

"You did?" Cash lifts his eyebrows. "Shit." He lets out a low whistle, his eyebrows sinking. "I thought you were gonna try for another season?"

I slowly nod, pausing to chew on the inside of my cheek. "I don't want to do anymore damage," I admit, feeling the tightness in my shoulder as I shrug. "I had six good years in the league. I'm more than grateful for that."

"Yeah, that's true," Cash says slowly, nodding his head in understanding before he turns to the tack room door across from Diesel's stall. He walks over to it and I follow him inside. It looks like I remember, the walls lined with saddle racks and various bridles hanging. The far wall is lined with cabinets and a sink. "Hand me one of those bridles," he says as he grabs a bucket and begins to fill it with water.

I reach over, grabbing the one he motioned to, noting the grime on the leather as my brother moves to sit down at the table in the center of the room with his bucket and rag. He squirts some leather cleaner into the bucket and takes the bridle from me as I hand it to him.

"Anything else that needs to be cleaned?"

Cash points to one of the western saddles on the far side of the room. "I used that one this week."

I walk over, pulling it from the rack and transferring it to one of the free standing saddle racks. Heading over to the counter, I find another rag and share the bucket with Cash as we both work the cleaner into the leather. The equipment typically gets wiped down after every use, then normally cleaned and deep conditioned once a week.

"I know it sucks that you had to retire earlier than you planned, but I'm glad you're back," he says softly, his blue green eyes shining at me. His gaze drops to my bad shoulder, his eyebrows pinching together before his gaze meets mine once more. "We missed having you home."

Growing up, Cade, Cash and I always talked about running the family ranch together. We each had two years between us, Cade being the oldest, then me, and Cash being the baby of the family.

"I'm glad to be home," I admit, tipping my chin as I work the conditioner into the saddle, sliding the rag around the sides, avoiding the suede seat. "I planned on comin' back eventually and being in pain for two years has a way of making you wish you had the comforts of home."

"How is your shoulder feeling?" Cash asks me, his eyes trailing to my joint.

Instinctively, I roll it, feeling the familiar stiffness inside, although after a few seconds, it moves with ease. "It's okay."

I would be lying if I said it didn't bother me at all, but without the repetitive moments of pitching, it's been feeling much better than it did while I was still playing baseball.

Cash slowly nods. "Well, just don't overdo it here on the ranch," he says softly, immediately shrugging off the emotion. "We can use your help, but you're no good without a working shoulder."

I snort, shaking my head and rolling my eyes. "You sound like Cade now."

Although the three of us are close, we couldn't be more different than one another.

"He didn't know you were comin' back, did he?"

I shake my head at my younger brother. "No. I got everything squared away three days ago and flew in this morning and figured I would surprise y'all. I shipped most of my stuff and left all the furniture in my house while I rent it out, so there wasn't much to come now."

Cash's face lights up. "Does that mean you're back for good?"

I swallow, a slow smile creeping across my lips. There's a twinge of sadness lingering in my chest, knowing that my career in baseball is officially over. But there's also a sense of relief. Contentment. This is where I belong now, with my family.

"It does."

"Hell yeah," Cash says, grinning back at me. "Cade and I were planning on goin' to the Silverspur Tavern for dinner and drinks tonight. Let's celebrate you being home."

"I dunno if I really feel like goin' out tonight," I admit as I finish cleaning the saddle and put it back on the rack on the wall. Cash is done with the bridle and he gets up to hang that up too. "I don't think we really need to celebrate."

"Alright, fine," Cash agrees, nodding his chin. "At least come get dinner with your brothers. Cade will want you to come."

"What about me?"

I glance over my shoulder to the door at the sound of his voice. "Hey!"

Cade steps into the tack room, his broody face cracking into a smile as he walks across the room and pulls me in for a hug. "Cole, what the hell are you doin' here?"

"He's back for good," Cash says to him as he walks over to the sink to clean out the bucket we used.

"No way," Cade draws as we break apart. "You aren't gonna try and get another season out of your shoulder?"

"Nope," I shake my head at him. "I had a good run, but this is where I'm supposed to be now."

"Well, this is your home," he reminds me, dipping his chin. "Where did Cash say I'd want you to come?"

"To get dinner tonight," Cash cuts in, stepping up to the two of us.

Cade looks at Cash and back at me. "Oh yeah," he agrees, nodding eagerly. "We're all back together again."

"Just like old times," Cash says.

I look back and forth between my two brothers, warmth settling in my chest. "Just like old times," I repeat. The three of us were so close growing up. When I moved away, that connection wasn't severed, but it was strained.

Being back here with them, where I can physically help, it feels a hell of a lot better than the separation or the guilt of being away.

"So, does this mean you're gonna come with us?" Cash questions me.

Cade raises an eyebrow, waiting for a response.

I let out an exaggerated sigh, but a smile cracks my face. "Yes, I'll come."

Cash lets out a whistle, wrapping both arms around the tops of Cade and my shoulders, pulling us in with him. "The Wild brothers are back together, baby."

My head tips back, laughter escaping me as my younger brother starts hootin' and hollerin' as he finally releases the two of us. This is exactly what I've been needing.

Home.

CHAPTER FIVE

ELLA

Standing along the railing, I close my eyes and inhale the scent of the air drifting across the lake. It carries wisps of my hair across my face. I reach up to brush them away before looking back out at the water. The serenity of it wraps itself around me. The sun is beginning to set from behind, casting its orange glow across the shimmering surface of the water.

It looks like the painting I worked on last week, except the hues are much more vibrant in real life. Contentment rolls through me, my soul soothed as a soft smile crests my lips. This is everything I've worked so hard to achieve. A slow and peaceful life where my cup is filled.

"Hey," Remi says softly as she walks up beside me, bumping her shoulder into mine. "There's everyone's favorite bartender."

"I was finishing up my break and getting ready to come back in." I tilt my head to the side, raising an eyebrow at her. "What brings you out here? Need a break from the madness inside?"

"Pfft," Remi blows out the sound, rolling her eyes.

"There's barely any room for anyone to walk around." She glances back at the door. "I told Rose I needed a minute of quiet."

"Is she okay in there?"

Remi nods. "Yeah. Maisie just got here a little bit ago, so I think everything is good for now." She pauses, a smirk dancing across her lips. "When I was walking out, I saw all three of the Wild brothers walking in."

My heart picks up the pace as my eyes widen at Remi. "All three of them?"

Cole Wild, the middle Wild brother with tousled dirty blonde hair and the softest of ocean blue eyes.

"I know, I was just as surprised to see him." She purses her lips. "Did you know he was going to be back in town?"

My forehead creases and I shake my head at her. "No. I haven't talked to him in years."

"Do you remember how you had the biggest crush on him when we were in high school?"

I snort, shaking my head at her. "We were children then, Remi," I laugh softly. I may have had a crush on him back then, but so did every other girl who went to Silverspur High.

"You're not children anymore though," she informs me, wagging her eyebrows. "You're single and maybe he is too."

"You're crazy," I chuckle, rolling my eyes. "Who knows what his dating life is like? He's probably married with kids of his own."

Remi purses her lips and raises her eyebrow at me. "So, you are curious about his dating status."

I stare at her, the laughter vanishing and I swallow hard around the lump lodged in my throat. "No, Remi. Just because you're a hopeless romantic, doesn't mean the rest of us are. Some of us are realistic and have no plans of being with anyone. Ever."

Remi's expression softens and she reaches for my hand, giving me a gentle squeeze. "I'm sorry, babe," she says quietly. "One day, you might change your mind."

I force a smile onto my lips and shrug. "I wouldn't hold my breath, but I suppose you never know."

"You're right." She releases my hand, bumping her shoulder into mine. "Maybe the boy you had a crush on years ago ends up changing your mind."

Laughter escapes me and I playfully push her shoulder with the palm of my hand. "You're impossible," I giggle, my head moving from side to side. "I don't know what the future will hold, but I do know for now that I'm perfectly happy by myself."

Remi stares at me for a moment, her expression unreadable before she nods. "We should probably head back inside," she says softly, a smile lifting her lips. "We shouldn't leave the ladies alone in there with the madness for too long."

"After you," I say, moving my arm in a sweeping motion toward the door. Remi heads in through the back of the bar and I follow. The sound of country music playing through the speakers wraps around us as it mixes with the various conversations happening throughout the restaurant.

Remi strides through the kitchen, heading straight through the doors that lead to the bar. There's no hesitation from her. She thrives in this kind of environment. I prefer the quiet, calmer parts of life, although here at the bar, I've been trying to make the best of it. I've been trying to find what fun I can have in it and I've found that putting on a smiling, friendly face who offers warm conversation brings happiness to the customers.

I pause by the door, sucking in a deep breath before letting it out. I push on the doors, stepping back into the familiar space behind the bar and I dive right back into my work. I relieve Rose of the customers she was taking care of in my absence and I make my way through, making sure they're all content and served.

I finish with the second to last group and that's when I see the Wild brothers sitting at the end of the bar. Cash and Cade sit side by side and there, seated to the right of Cade, is none other than Cole Wild.

My heart skips a beat in my chest and I wipe my hands on my apron before heading in their direction. I shove down the embarrassment that creeps up, hoping and praying that maybe Cole forgot the time I tried to kiss him. Cash leans on his elbows, talking to Cade while Cole stares down at the laminated menu in his hands.

"Well, good evenin' boys."

My eyes scan the three of them, Cash sitting back in his seat with a goofy grin on his lips. "Hey, Ella."

Cade tips his head. "Howdy."

Cole slowly sets down the menu, lifting his head as his gaze collides with mine. "Hey El."

His voice is a little deeper than I remember it being, but then again, it's been a long time since I last saw him. He looks good, like time has been on his side. He's only twenty-six—three years older than me.

Stark, sharp bright blue eyes. His nose straight and jaw line perfectly chiseled with a dusting of stubble along the sides of his face. There's a small scar above his left eyebrow, but I remember that he got that when he was thrown off a horse in high school. His dirty blonde hair is tousled and wavy, falling above his eyebrows.

"What can I get y'all tonight?" I ask the three of them, my eyes bouncing between them all. Cole's gaze travels across my face, down to my mouth before landing back on my eyes again.

"We'll each take a bourbon on the rocks, whatever you have that isn't bottom of the barrel," Cade tells me, the smallest smile on his lips. "I'll take a burger, medium well."

Cash chimes in. "Yeah, I'll do the same."

I don't bother writing any of it down, since the order is simple enough. I look back to Cole and find him watching me once again.

"What would you recommend?" He questions me, tilting his head to the side as amusement passes through his irises. "I haven't eaten here in a long time."

I swallow roughly, smiling at him, dipping my chin. "I mean, I'm a little biased, but anything on that menu is good."

"Hmm," he murmurs, his eyebrows shifting slightly before relaxing once more. "I'll have what they're having."

"Sounds good," I tell the three of them, the smile still on my face. "I'll get your order in and be back with your drinks."

The three of them thank me simultaneously before Cash ropes the two of them into a conversation. My heart pounds as I walk over to the screen to put in their orders. My fingers shake as I enter in their order.

I pause, sucking in a deep breath, closing my eyes while I focus on my breathing for a few seconds. When I open them, the shaking is gone, but my heart still has a mind of its own, pounding away.

Something about Cole makes me feel like I'm off kilter.

It must be the remembrance of the crush I had on him and those old feelings speaking. It was never mutual. Cole was best friends with Wyatt, so he never once made a move on me. I wouldn't have expected him to, but there was a part of me that had hoped he would.

I was just a delusional teen, obsessed with her older brother's best friend.

We're adults now and there are no crushes to be had.

Only drinks to make and burgers to serve.

Ignoring the burning curiosity and urge to look back at Cole, I busy myself with all three of their bourbons before carrying them back over to their spot at the bar. I walk over, finding two empty barstools and one Wild brother sitting by himself.

My heart pitter patters again as I set two of them down and the last in front of Cole. "Did your brothers abandon you?"

Cole lifts the glass, a smirk on his lips as he shakes his head. "Nah, they're back there," he motions behind himself to the pool table. "They're both still trying to learn how to have patience."

I laugh softly, looking back at Cade and Cash before directing my attention to Cole. "It seems like you do, though."

His cheeks lift a little higher, his eyes narrowing in the slightest bit as he nods. "Oh, I am. I learned to be patient long ago."

He doesn't elaborate and I don't ask what he means by that. "I'm surprised to see you back in town."

"It's been a while." His throat bobs as he swallows hard. "I figured it was time I got back here to help out on the ranch."

"Did something happen?" I question him, even though I know what happened.

He half shrugs. "Just bullshit injuries," he tells me. "Healing properly becomes an issue when you rush it. I never healed properly from my shoulder injury two seasons ago. Last season was rough and after MRIs showed the amount of scar tissue inside, I realized it was time to hang up my hat."

"It was that simple?"

Cole chuckles, shaking his head at me. "No, El. Nothin' is ever that simple." He lets out a soft breath. "It was the hardest decision I've ever had to make, but I know it was for the best."

"I'm sorry that happened," I say, my voice soft and quiet against the noise inside the bar.

"It's not uncommon and it is what it is, ya know?" Cole pauses, chewing on the inside of his cheek.

"So, are you back for good then?"

Cole lifts his drink, taking a sip as his gaze pins mine. "I think so." His tongue darts out to wet his lips. "Coming home was always my plan, it just happened a little sooner than I expected."

He tilts his head to the side. "What about you? What's new with Ella Dani—"

"Well, shit Cole," Cash calls out, cutting off Cole as he comes striding over toward the bar with Cade behind him. "Why didn't you tell us Ella brought our drinks?"

Cole runs his tongue over his top teeth, turning in his seat to look at his brothers. "Y'all were busy."

"Thanks, Ella," Cade says, smiling as he takes his drink. I nod at the three of them as Cash and Cade slide back onto their barstools. I glance over my shoulder, seeing that one of my other customers' drink is empty. She sees me looking at her and smiles. I use the opportunity to excuse myself from my conversation with Cole. I don't know what he was going to ask, but I have an idea it might be about my life now.

"I'll be back with your food in a bit. If y'all need anything, just let me know."

My life is good. It's better than it was before, but that doesn't mean I feel like spilling all the details to a man I haven't seen in years.

I end up getting Miss Nancy another drink and check on the rest of my customers to stay busy on the opposite side of the bar. One of the cooks rings the small bell to alert me and I head back, grabbing two plates to take out before returning for the third.

All three Wild brothers are sitting and waiting with smiles as I set their plates in front of them. Cole's eyes meet mine.

"I'll be right back with yours."

"Take your time," he says softly, mischief dancing in his eyes. "I'm a patient man."

My breath catches in my throat and heat immediately creeps up my neck. Spinning on my heel, I control my movements, forcing myself to walk—not run—back to the kitchen as my heart pounds erratically in my chest.

My hands are shaky as I grab Cole's plate and I force myself to pause and take a few deep breaths. He doesn't make me uneasy, not in a bad way. Just in a way like I'm standing face to face with an old crush who's a grown ass man now.

I have a daughter to worry about and I swore I would never put myself in a vulnerable position to get hurt again. Cole can be nice to look at and that's it. Nothing more. Ever.

"Here you are," I tell Cole, setting his plate down in front of him.

"Thanks, El," he murmurs, his blue eyes slowly searching mine.

I shove my hands awkwardly into the pockets of my apron. "You guys enjoy."

The three of them dig in and I leave them to it. A few customers pay their tabs and head home for the night, right as we end up getting another late evening rush. Ignoring Cole's gaze that follows me around, I throw myself into my work, making sure that everyone is taken care of.

By the time I'm done, I see that the Wild brothers finished their meals and left more than enough money lying on the bar next to their empty glasses. My eyebrows pull together. Certainly, this was a mistake.

I lift my eyes, doing a quick survey of the building when I see Cole coming out of the bathroom. Excusing myself past Rose and Remi, I slip out from behind the bar and half jog across the room, holding out the two-hundred-dollar bills.

"Hey, Wild!" I call out to him when I see him reaching for the door to walk out of the bar.

He slowly turns around, tilting his head to the side as the corners of his lips twitch. "Hey, El."

I hold out the money to him, along with the bill. "Here, you left way more than what your bill was. Do you have less than this or I can get you change."

His brows furrow. "No, that wasn't a mistake."

"But—but this is way more than what your bill was." It's like a ninety-dollar tip.

"Well, the service was great and I tip accordingly."

A frown immediately tugs my lips downward. "Cole—"

"Ella." He shakes his head at me. "Just keep it, okay?"

"I can't."

"Yes, you can." He scratches the back of his head. "I gotta go, but I'll see you around, alright?"

I take a step closer, attempting to hand him the money again. "Cole, no."

He quickly sidesteps, a deep chuckle rumbling in his chest. "Goodnight, El," he laughs before ducking out through the doors, leaving me standing with his bill and cash.

Frustration boils inside, but instead, I find myself unable to conceal the grin that pulls across my face. I laugh quietly to myself, mentally cursing him as I head back to the bar to pay his tab. Instead of pocketing the cash, I slip it into the shared tip jar for everyone working.

Cole Wild has always been impossible to ignore.

And clearly, that's something that hasn't changed a bit.

CHAPTER SIX

COLE

My mind is still reeling as I climb into Cade's truck. He gets in, shutting his own door behind him. Cash climbs into the backseat as Cade starts the engine and begins to back out of his parking space.

Turning in my seat, I glance back at the bar, half hoping to see Ella still standing there, but she isn't.

"What did Ella want?"

"Huh?" I say, turning back around to glance at Cade.

"Ella," he says, his brow furrowing. "She followed you out of the restaurant."

I swallow roughly. "Oh, yeah. She thought the tip I left was a mistake." I crane my neck, glancing at Cash in the back. He's holding his phone and the light illuminates his face as he types something out. "You didn't tell me she worked there."

Cash lifts his eyes to mine, raising an eyebrow. "Are you sure? I thought I mentioned that."

"No, you didn't."

"Oh," he says, his lips forming the shape of an O.

"Well, she works at the bar. I know she's Wy's little sister, but I didn't know if you'd remember who she is."

Of course I remember her. How the hell could I ever forget her?

She was impossible to forget, with those bright blue eyes and her unruly, curly blonde hair. She's three years younger than me and was always deemed as off-limits. Her brother would have killed me if he would have caught the way my gaze lingered a bit longer than it should have.

He never once questioned the way I always sided with her, the way I always picked her to be on my team. If Ella was tagging along, I was the one who ended up keeping an eye on her.

Wyatt Daniels never knew that his best friend was secretly pining after his younger sister.

Cade lets out a low chuckle. "Did you forget he had a thing for her when we were younger?" He asks Cash as he glances at him through the rearview mirror.

Mischief dances in Cash's eyes as he looks back at me. "That's right. I don't know how I forgot that."

My heart stutters in my chest and I press my lips into a straight line. "I didn't have a thing for her," I retort, lying straight through my teeth as my heart pounds harder in my chest.

"Come on, Cole," Cade interjects, a chuckle rumbling in his throat as he shakes his head. "We all knew it, 'cept for Wy. That fool was as blind as a damn bat."

I shake my head at the two of them. "It was nothin'. We were teenage boys; I think we all had a thing for any girl who was pretty."

Cash snorts, a smirk breaking out across his face. "Yeah, we did, but it was different with you and her."

Different in the sense that I never would have acted on

it. I only ever wanted to protect Ella and back then, I knew I was no good for her.

"She's Wyatt's sister. I never would have tried to pursue anything with her."

"I know," Cash says, nodding, although he doesn't look fully convinced. "That was then, though. Things are a lot different than they used to be."

"How so?" I question him, raising an eyebrow before I look back at our older brother. Cade doesn't look at me, keeping his attention on the road as he drives us closer to the ranch. "She's still Wy's little sister."

"She's not a kid anymore, Cole. She has a little girl of her own now."

My breath catches in my throat.

Her daughter.

Wyatt told me about her, but with how sporadic our conversations have become over the years, we never really got the chance to talk about her. He mentioned when Ella moved back to Silverspur.

My heart picks up its pace inside my chest. "Wyatt told me she has a kid," I admit. "How does she seem like she's doin'?"

Cash lifts his shoulders. "Good."

"Yeah," Cade chimes in. "We see her around town sometimes and she always seems to be in a good mood. She lives on Iris' property, in that guest house she has."

"Oh yeah?"

I knew her and Wyatt sold their family home to pay off some debts that were left behind after their parents' accident.

"Yep," Cash confirms, popping the *P* sound. "You know, I think she's single. I haven't seen her with any other guy."

Heat creeps up my neck and I slowly turn in my seat, directing my gaze back out the window. My stomach quickens and a lightness flutters inside my chest. "Hmm."

"Welcome home, brother," Cade says with a soft laugh.

Keeping my gaze out the window, I blow a breath through my nostrils and slowly shake my head back and forth. My brothers aren't always the most reliable source of information and I'm sure neither of them talk to Ella enough to know what's actually going on in her life.

She could be seeing someone and keeping it private. Neither of them would ever know, so I can't put a lot of weight on the things they say.

Cade pulls his truck onto our lane and we drive between two massive fields on either side of the driveway. As we reach the ends of the fences, the lane splits into three different routes. The one to the right is the main house where Cash and Cade live, the one in front of us leads to the barns, and to the left is the secondary house that I've moved into.

Cade starts to turn the truck left, but I hold my hand up to stop him.

"Just go to the main house. I'll walk to mine."

Cade glances at me, raises an eyebrow, and then simply lifts both shoulders before they relax. Whipping the truck to the right, he heads over to the main house, parking his truck right out front of the detached garage, next to Cash's.

The three of us say goodnight and I don't bother hanging around as my brothers head into the house. Dust kicks up from beneath my feet as I walk along the gravel driveway, following along the fence line. I make my way back to the end of the main lane, to where the intersection is.

The cool mountain air drifts around me and my eyes adjust to the darkness of the night. We don't have many lights out here and the only ones that shine are the ones near the entrances to the barns. All the other lights we have on the buildings are either controlled by switches or motion-sensor.

Absentmindedly, I kick at a few rocks, my eyes traveling along the planes of our property. My shoulders relax, my breathing evening as a lightness engulfs me. This is everything I've been missing and exactly where I need to be. Texas was not for me, not in the slightest bit.

I pause in the center of the intersection, tilting my head back to stare up at the night sky. You can see so many stars out here—so many more than you see within any city limits. I let my eyes wander, drifting over the infinite number of stars twinkling in the darkness. The moon is only a small sliver, poking out from a stray, wispy cloud that drifts through the sky.

I know there's nowhere else that calls to me like home and I can't help but wonder if it's the same for Ella.

She left Silverspur Springs long before her and Wyatt lost their parents. She moved away, got married and started an entirely new life. Something happened that made her come back home after the accident, but I don't know why. Wyatt never told me the specifics, other than her ex was an asshole and that Ella left him.

Did she come back here because she had nowhere else to go?

Did she find herself feeling the same way I did?

Like she just needed to come home to the one place where her soul can rest...

CHAPTER SEVEN

ELLA

"Hey little sis."

I smile as my brother's voice comes through the speaker of the car. I glance at Chloe in the backseat as her eyes widen. "Hey big brother."

Chloe's eyes light up. "Wy-Wy!"

"Hey little lady. What are you guys up to?"

"We pulled up in front of the grocery store. We need to do some food shopping." I pause, looking at the time on the dashboard. My gaze drops down to my hands and I pick away some of the paint that didn't wash off my fingertips earlier. "What are you doin'?"

"I just finished with rounds. I was looking at my calendar and can get off on their anniversary." He falls silent for a moment. "I thought we could go to the cemetery together."

The anniversary of our parent's death. It's coming up soon and I've been avoiding thinking about it. That day is always a rough one and Wyatt hasn't been home for it since we lost them. He comes back to visit when he can, but always avoids that specific date.

I'll never forget the day we lost them. Wyatt was home from college for the summer break before he was leaving again for med school. They went out one evening for dinner, but neither of them made it home.

Wyatt and I both struggled with our grief and handled things differently. Wyatt started drinking but I was frozen in place, unable to move forward. One night, Wyatt got so drunk, he ended up in the hospital and that's when he knew he needed to turn his life around. He knew he needed to finish what he set out to do, which was going to school to become a doctor. He knew they would have wanted him to finish and get that degree.

So, he left.

I didn't blame him for it. We both needed space from here, from the memories of them, but this was the only place that ever felt like home. Eventually, I returned, although Wyatt still kept his distance.

"I would really like that."

"Okay. I have to get back to work, but I'll see you soon, okay?"

"Okay," I say quietly, the heaviness weighing on my chest. We're still a few weeks away from the day, but it has a way of suffocating me. "Love you."

"Love you too. Love you little lady!"

"Love you, Wy!" Chloe calls from the backseat. I stare back at her as I end the call with my brother, wishing my parents were here more than ever. They would have loved her so much.

My heart cracks but I immediately shove the feelings away. I have to keep moving forward. *Always moving forward.*

I get out of the car and get Chloe out, setting her down on the ground before locking the car.

"Come on, Clo," I say softly, tugging on her hand as

we walk through the parking lot. I fight the urge to scoop her up and carry her inside. She's going through the toddler stage of finding some type of independence. She hates to be carried unless she is tired. Other than that, she wants to be on her feet leading the way.

Her soft curls bounce as her little feet scurry along. A giggle escapes her as she hops up onto the curb with two feet as we reach the front of the grocery store. We step inside the building and I lead her over to where the little carts are lined up. They are bright red with little white flags on them that read *Shoppers in Training*. Chloe loves to push them around and pack the basket full of the things we need.

I grab a bigger cart and she follows behind me as we head to the produce section. Chloe stays with me, and I keep an eye on her as I begin to work through the list I brought along. She helps me as I hand her different things to put inside her cart. As we move around the store, she tries to be sneaky, grabbing little things to slip into her cart when she thinks I'm not paying attention.

She simply smiles at me and giggles when I frown at her and pull the things we don't need from her cart to return to the shelf.

Her smile is infectious and I can't help but return it and wink back at her. It's so hard to try to be stern with her sometimes. She isn't disobedient, she just has a little bit of a fiery streak to her. I can't fault her for that. I want her to grow up to be strong and fierce. I want her to know what independence is, but to know that she can always count on me. I will always be here for her, for whatever she needs, at whatever stage of life.

I fought through my own struggles to be the best example I can be for her. That doesn't mean there aren't nights when I go to bed thinking that I am the worst mother in the world. That also doesn't mean there aren't times that I wish I wasn't doing this alone. She doesn't have a father figure and that's okay. Chloe has never asked about hers–not yet at least. I have no idea how I am going to approach that topic when it finally comes up.

She's going to have questions. It would only be natural. I don't want to lie to her, but I'm afraid to one day tell her the truth. Jacob made it clear that he wanted nothing to do with her.

I called him three days after I left. He was mad that I walked away from our marriage and had the audacity to accuse me of cheating. He refused to believe that I left because I no longer wanted to be with him. He convinced himself that I left him for another man. That I ran back to my hometown to be with someone else.

When I told him I was pregnant, he called me a whore and said that he'd never believe me that the baby was his. I filed for divorce and he signed the papers without any dispute.

I still put him on the birth certificate and when I filed with a lawyer for child support, he ended up signing over his rights completely.

He didn't even fight for her, for the possibility of her being his child. I told him he could get a paternity test and instead, he wanted to wash his hands of us completely.

He doesn't deserve to have Chloe in his life now and I don't want to make her feel bad if I tell her the truth about him.

I push the thoughts away from my mind. She's almost three, so I have a few years before I really need to worry about her asking questions. I will deal with it when the issue comes to fruition.

Chloe walks beside me as we move to pass one of the aisles. I see the front of another cart, so I stop mine to let them go first. Chloe doesn't realize what's happening and keeps walking as she pushes her cart directly into the one that was moving in front of us. The metal clatters into one another and Chloe stumbles a bit, but catches herself before she topples over.

"Oh my goodness," I say, crouching down to make sure that Chloe is steady. "I am so sorry."

A deep chuckle rumbles from above and I lift my chin, looking up. My eyes collide with familiar blue irises that stare back at me. A look of amusement fills Cole's gaze and the corners of his lips lifts. "It's quite alright. Is she okay?"

I bob my head while rising to my feet and lift Chloe into my arms. "She's fine, just wasn't paying attention."

Cole smiles as he looks from Chloe to me. "She looks like you," he says quietly.

I swallow roughly over the emotion lodged in my throat and force a smile onto my lips while ignoring the way my chest constricts. Her features favor mine more than her father's. "This is my daughter, Chloe," I say, my voice remaining calm, unlike my insides right now. "Chloe, this is Mr. Cole. Can you say hi to him?"

Chloe looks up at him, her blue eyes bright as her curls shift against the base of her neck. "Hi!" She grins as she waves at him.

"Look at all of this stuff you have in your cart," he says as he crouches down to check out her cart. Chloe wriggles in my arms, fighting to get down as she kicks her feet. I set her down and she quickly shuffles over to him to peer at the groceries alongside him. "You must be the best helper ever."

"I is," Chloe giggles as she quickly nods. "The best."

Cole laughs and the sound slides across my eardrums. My breath catches in my throat and the muscle in my jaw tightens as I watch the two of them. Chloe begins to riffle through the different boxes as she proudly holds each one up to show him. Something silver catches my eye at the bottom of the cart and my eyebrows pull together and I reach past her to pull it out.

It's a small toy truck inside the plastic packaging. I look at Chloe and purse my lips. "Clo, I told you we were only here to get food, not toys."

"I sorry, Momma," she says sweetly with a frown. "It's pink!"

"I know, baby, but we can't get it."

Cole's gaze meets mine and his expression is unreadable as he watches me. I set the truck on top of some cans on the shelf beside us. Chloe pouts for a moment but Cole looks back at her and whispers to her.

"I used to sneak stuff into the cart when I was little too."

Chloe giggles and gives him a toothy grin as he stands back upright.

"Well, we should probably keep movin'," I say apologetically, guiding Chloe back to the side of her cart to push. "I'm sorry again for runnin' into you like that."

Cole shakes his head. "You don't have to apologize, darlin'. You can run into me any day."

My breath catches again in my throat and I quickly force myself to exhale. "Say bye to Mr. Cole, Chloe."

"Bye-bye, Mist-uh Co," she says with a wave.

"Just Cole," he tells her with a chuckle. "Bye Chloe."

I give him a small smile and a nod, but I keep my lips closed, not allowing another word to betray me. I start walking in the direction we were heading in, with Chloe in tow. We continue on with our shopping trip, hastily loading up the rest of the cart. Seeing Cole here caught me off guard, mainly because he's been gone for so long, I got used to not seeing him around town.

But now he's here… and it doesn't seem like he'll be going anywhere anytime soon.

CHAPTER EIGHT
COLE

Looking back at the toy truck sitting on the shelf that Ella discarded there, I can't help myself as I pick it up. A smile pulls on my lips. What a mischievous little girl, trying to sneak the pink truck into her shopping cart.

She reminds me so much of Ella when she was a kid. Bright blue eyes, unruly curls, and a wild spirit.

The smile doesn't leave my face and I continue on through the grocery store, collecting the items I need. It doesn't take me long before I pay for my things and head out into the parking lot in search of my truck. I catch sight of them again when I turn down the row. My heart crawls into my throat and I pause, watching for a moment.

The little cart is gone and Chloe stands in the trunk of Ella's car, giggling as she moves out of the way as Ella begins to load her bags into the back. The corners of my lips twitch and I don't bother to hide the fact that I'm blatantly staring.

Chloe's eyes meet mine from across the parking lot and she begins to wave. Ella glances over her shoulder and her gaze crashes into mine. I lift my hand to wave and Ella gives me a smile as her eyes soften. I'm not sure if it's an open invitation but it seems like my feet have already made the decision to approach her without my permission.

Ella turns to face me when I stop by her cart. "You again."

The corners of my mouth twitch. "Me again."

"Hi Mist-uh Cole!" Chloe says with excitement.

"Hi Chloe," I smile at the exuberant little blonde-haired girl. "You know, when I was gettin' ready to leave the store, someone came up to me and said that they thought you forgot somethin'."

Chloe looks at me with her eyebrows scrunched. "I fuh-get?"

Reaching into one of the bags in my cart, I pull out the small pink truck that Chloe had her sights set on earlier. It may not be the right thing to do and I don't want to piss Ella off, but I couldn't resist it. After seeing the disappointment on Chloe's face when Ella told her she couldn't get it... I knew I had to get it for her. Just to be able to put a smile on that little girl's face.

Chloe squeals as I hand it to her and she shows it to Ella. "Look, Momma. Da twuck!"

Ella smiles at her and I don't miss the touch of sadness that crinkles around her eyes. "I see it, baby. What do you say to him?"

"Tank you!" She says with a sweetness that has my heart melting inside my chest.

"You are so welcome." I turn to look at Ella as Chloe starts to take the truck from the packaging. "I hope it's okay that I got it for her."

Ella's gaze shifts from her daughter to mine. She chews on the inside of her lip as she nods. "It is. I've been trying to teach her that we don't have to buy a toy every single time we come to the store."

"Well, let's call it a loophole then," I say with a wink. "Technically you didn't buy it."

Mischief dances in her eyes as she watches me. "A loophole," she says softly as she tilts her head to the side. "I guess you're right."

"Let me help you put the rest of your bags in your car," I offer, stepping around her and reaching for one of the handles.

"You don't have to do that; I can get it."

I glance over my shoulder at her, placing the groceries inside the trunk. "I know I don't, but I want to. Let me help you."

There's a conflicted look that washes over her eyes and I can see it right then. She has trouble accepting help. I don't want to make any assumptions about her life, but it's clear to see. Ella's a fierce, independent woman. She doesn't need anyone, and she certainly doesn't want any help.

That doesn't mean I didn't want to offer it anyway.

Ella reaches into the trunk of her SUV and pulls Chloe out while I pack the rest of her groceries into the back for her. It doesn't take me long and I close the door before turning to look at the two of them. Ella holds onto the packaging from the pink truck as Chloe makes noises driving it up and down Ella's bare arm. She shifts to the side of the car and I reach past her, opening the door for her as she puts Chloe in her car seat and straps her in.

I take a step back and Ella closes the door before turning back to face me. "Thank you, Cole," she says softly, with appreciation glimmering in her eyes as she stares back at me. Her lips part like she's going to say something else but she quickly closes them before smiling at me.

She's absolutely breathtaking. The gentle breeze is laced with the smell of hay fields and sunshine and it carries wisps of her curls that break free from the messy bun on top of her head. Her bright blue eyes shimmer from the rays of sunlight shining from above and I resist the urge to reach out and touch her tanned skin. I find myself staring, completely captivated by her.

I clear my throat, breaking free from the trance I was caught in. "It was my pleasure."

"I'm sure I will see you around?" She murmurs with a questioning tone as she steps to the front door and pulls it open.

I look at her for a moment. "Yeah." A smile spreads across my lips. "I think you will."

"Good." She bites back her grin, dipping her chin at me. "Bye Cole."

She climbs into the driver's seat and turns back to look at me once more.

"Bye El."

CHAPTER NINE

COLE

The weekend passed by in typical fashion. I took yesterday to catch up on cleaning the barn and ended up saddling my blue roan gelding, Rocky, and headed out onto the range for a much needed escape from the monotony of ranch work.

"Hey, Cole," says Amber, one of our summer stable hands. She smiles at me when I walk into the barn. "With the heat wave today, your brother said we can take the day off from working the horses."

My chin dips and I walk over to the closest stall, rubbing my hand against the dappled gray who pokes his head out over the stall door. "I was thinking the same thing. No one wants to be outside on a day like today."

"Isn't that the truth?" She chuckles, shaking her head. "I was going to finish up with cleaning the stalls and then I have an appointment this afternoon I need to get to."

"No worries," I say, offering her a smile. "There's not much we can do about the weather, so take the rest of the day."

"Are you going to take the day off too?" She asks,

tilting her head to the side. "Cade isn't here to crack the whip on anyone today."

I snort, blowing a breath through my nose and rolling my eyes. Cade is always on someone's ass to make sure things are getting done.

"You know what, I think I will find something to do to stay out of the heat too," I say, smiling deeply. I leave Amber to her work and give everything a once over, making sure there isn't something I absolutely need to be doing before heading back out to my truck.

The air is thick with heat as I roll up the sleeves of my shirt and climb into the front seat. Cade and Cash left earlier this morning to look at a new trailer with living quarters.

With neither of my brothers here, I feel free in a way. My stomach grumbles and I laugh softly to myself, knowing exactly where I can go to take care of my hunger pains. I start the engine of my truck and put it in gear, driving through the property in the opposite direction of my house.

I keep driving until I get to the other side of the lake and find myself pulling into a familiar parking lot. The bar is fairly empty in the middle of the day on a Monday. I park my truck and head inside, finding an empty barstool. Remi walks over to take my order when she sees me and disappointment settles on my chest as I order a water and sandwich.

My eyes survey the space, not seeing Ella anywhere. I pull out my phone, deciding to text my friend, Austin. Growing up, it was Wyatt, Austin, and me who were the inseparable trio. The three of us all left Silverspur at the same time, headed in different directions, although Austin was the first to come back.

After he finished college and got his masters in Psychology, he opened his own practice here.

Wyatt settled into a life in Cheyenne after he graduated and started his emergency medicine residency program last month.

My fingers move across the screen, typing out a message to Austin. I want to see if he wants to go out on his boat to fish later this afternoon, hopefully after the heat dies off a bit.

"You again."

Pressing send, I lift my head from my phone, my heart skipping a beat at the sound of her voice. My breath catches in my throat as my eyes meet hers. Ella stands before me, as she adjusts her black shirt that hugs her curves, with a smile drifting across her lips.

Her curly blonde hair is pulled away from her face, revealing her delicate features and icy blue eyes. I watch her for a moment, my heart hammering in my chest as she tilts her head to the side.

"Me again."

She points to my water. "I see you've already been taken care of."

I'd rather if you took care of me.

My head nods. I'm not sure if she just got here or if she has been here the entire time. My chest expands and a warmth washes over me. I'm happy to see her.

"I'll be around if you need anything," she informs me with a bright smile and a wink before she disappears to the other side of the bar.

Glancing at my phone, I see Austin texted me back and I respond to his message. He's busy this afternoon with appointments so it doesn't work for him. Ella being at the bar changes things. Suddenly, I don't feel like going out on the boat anyways.

The crowd at the bar is relatively low key and there aren't many people here today. I wait patiently for my food, checking my emails while watching the sports highlights that play on the TV screen hanging above the bar. Ella makes her way back to me with a bright smile on her face. She tends to gravitate toward me when I'm here but I can't quite read her. I can't figure out why. Does she enjoy the conversation as much as I do or is she only being friendly because of our history?

"You didn't come in the other night," she says softly as she gets herself a water and takes a sip of it.

Her words catch my attention and I stare at her for a moment. She noticed I wasn't here. "Yeah. I ended up getting caught up helping my brother with something."

She nods, still smiling. "That's right. You mentioned you were going to be helping him with one of the yearlings he bought, right?"

My head tilts to the side. Most times we've spoken, I wasn't sure if she was making conversation as a nicety. I didn't realize she was actually paying attention and listening to the things I was saying. She remembered a small, miniscule detail from a conversation we had a week ago. "Right. You remembered."

"You seem surprised."

"Because I am," I admit as a soft laugh escapes me. "You work at a bar, Ella. You know how to talk to your customers and be friendly with them. I'm surprised because I never expected you to remember the things that I've told you."

Her icy blue eyes pierce mine as she studies me for a

moment. "You're right. I have a lot of conversations with a lot of people. Sometimes certain ones stick out more than others."

She leaves without another word and confusion encapsulates me. Ella is a closed book and I want to peer inside her mind. I want to dissect her thoughts. I want to know everything I can possibly know about her.

She stays over on her side of the bar for a while and she's gone long enough for me to finish my entire meal. Cade texts me, asking when I'll be back at the ranch. They ended up buying the trailer and came home early.

I respond, telling him I'll be there in a little bit. Remi comes back over to me and I hand her my card to pay my tab as Ella starts walking back over.

"Are you leaving already?" She questions me with a touch of sadness in her tone. "I'm so sorry, I got caught up when that rush of people came in."

"You don't have to apologize, El," I say. "Cade needs me back at the ranch. Him and Cash are both home early and we need to move the cattle to a different pasture."

"No, no, I get it," she says with an unreadable expression on her face. A touch of emotion washes over her irises but it passes too quickly that I don't get a chance to see what it was.

"I don't have to leave just yet," I say with a shrug. I can't help but feel like I should stay. Her lips part, as if she's going to say something but she quickly closes them. It's like watching a door close right in front of your face. There's a part of me that thought she was opening that door to further our conversation but then I watched her close it again, like she made a mistake.

"Oh, no," she waves her hand dismissively. "I don't

want to keep you. I'm sure I'll see you another time." She forces a smile onto her lips that almost looks genuine. "Bye Cole."

She turns her back to me and I can't let her walk away. "El, wait."

She quickly turns back to look at me, her eyes shining brightly. Her lips part once more and I watch her chest deflate as she exhales. "Yeah?"

"Can I take you out sometime?" I pause, letting out a breath. "Just to dinner or somethin'."

Her eyes widen and I feel the same feeling inside my chest. I don't know where the hell the question came from but my brain and mouth didn't make the proper connection and the words slipped out before I had the chance to stop them.

She nervously shifts her weight on her feet. "I'm sorry, but I can't do that."

My stomach sinks. Of course she can't. "I apologize. That was rude of me and I shouldn't have asked. I didn't even think about you not being single."

Her eyebrows pull together and she shakes her head. "No, I am. It's not that–" She pauses and lets out a ragged breath. "I just don't think that it's a good idea."

"Why not?"

She pulls her plump bottom lip between her teeth and bites down before releasing it. "It's complicated." She blows out a breath. "You're friends with my brother, Cole. And I have Chloe."

My head cocks sideways. It's an excuse and a bullshit reason. Hell, it's not even a real explanation. Her brother isn't here anymore, so I refuse to accept that as a complication. He's been in Cheyenne since he left medical school and has his own life away from Silverspur.

The Chloe part—I can see how she might think of that as a complication, but really, it's not. Not in my mind, at least.

She stares back at me as if she's contemplating running in the opposite direction. I'm beginning to wonder if maybe I've overstepped.

"I'm sorry. Forget that I said anything."

A conflicted look passes through her eyes. "Please don't apologize. I'm not in a place in my life to be dating or seeing anyone."

Regret strikes my chest. Ella doesn't say it, but I imagine she means because of her daughter.

"It's only dinner, Ella. Nothin' more. I just want a chance to talk to you away from here." I pause, letting out a soft breath. "We used to know each other, remember?"

She shakes her head. "Things are different now, Cole. Our lives look nothing like they did when we were kids."

I'm not sure how to proceed. For the first time in my life, I'm at a loss for words. "Okay," I say with simplicity as I rise to my feet. "I understand."

"I'm sorry," she says again, softly, with a frown pulling down the corners of her lips. "I just don't think it–."

"El, stop. It's fine, I understand." I force a smile onto my lips. "Thank you for being honest with me. I promise this changes nothin' and we can pretend like this never happened."

She stares at me for a moment, like she doesn't believe a single word I said. Her forced smile matches mine and she bobs her head. "I would like that."

"I'll see ya again soon," I say before turning my back to her and walking away. I hate myself for saying anything, but it was only a matter of time before I did. I know now that she's much more guarded than I realized.

We can pretend like this didn't happen, but we both know it did.

And she isn't going to scare me away that easily.

CHAPTER TEN

COLE

"What's goin' on with you?" Cash questions me as he walks into the tack room, hanging up the bridle he was using.

We went out for a ride this morning to condition the two blue roan mares he's taking to the rodeo this weekend. Not much conversation was had between the two of us while we were in the arena.

"You've been weirdly quiet all damn morning."

"Nothin's up," I lie with a shrug. I slide my saddle onto the rack, turning back to him. "I'm good."

"Come on," he presses as he walks over to me. He clasps his hand on my shoulder. "You're my brother. I know you better than anyone else, except maybe Cade. You haven't been acting like yourself."

Dammit.

Cash has always been an easy going, go with the flow type of person with everyone but me. If he wants an answer, he's going to be persistent as hell until I give him an explanation of some sort. I suppose we aren't much different from one another, considering that we're only separated by eighteen months in age.

I sigh, my shoulders immediately sagging in defeat. "I asked Ella to get dinner and she turned me down."

Cash's eyes widen. "Hold on. You asked her to go on a date? I mean, I know you've had a little thing for her forever, but I didn't think you'd ever act on it."

My forehead creases. "No, I haven't and not on a date. Just dinner."

Cash snorts, shaking his head as he releases my shoulder. "Yeah, okay. You were always on her side when we were kids. Always stickin' up for her and takin' her side."

I purse my lips. "Because you guys were always pickin' on her. She needed someone on her side." I shake my head at him. "It doesn't matter anyways. We're adults now, things are different."

Cash's face cracks and laughter spills from his lips. My fingers twitch with the urge to slap him upside the head, but I resist the temptation. "I'm sorry," he chuckles. "I shouldn't laugh. I just don't know how you didn't see that rejection coming. She's Wyatt's little sister, for god's sake. She knows better than to get involved with a Wild."

"What's that have to do with anything?"

"She knows that the legacy we're building here is more important than anything else." He shakes his head again. "I think everyone knows that." He tilts his head to the side. "There's three of us and none of us have settled down yet."

He's not wrong about the legacy we've been building. Running a ranch comes with more responsibilities than I realized I would have. When the three of us took over the ranch to relieve our parents from managing it, I wasn't here, so I was more of a voice in the decisions rather than being hands on at the time.

Our parents gave their lives to this ranch and it was only right for us to take that burden away from them. Neither of them traveled much outside of where the professional rodeo circuit took the two of them years ago. They decided to leave Wyoming and do some traveling in South America. After finding an equine sanctuary in Argentina that needed volunteers, they chose to settle there temporarily.

I narrow my eyes on him. "Maybe because none of us have found someone to settle down with yet."

"Speak for yourself," he says with a shrug. "I have no plans of ever doin' that."

"I'm not sayin' I do either," I say defensively. "I just–I don't know. It was stupid. I thought it would be nice to get dinner and talk to her outside of only seein' her at work."

Cash raises an eyebrow. "Are you actually interested in her?"

"I don't know, Cash." I let out an exasperated sigh. "It's Ella."

He smirks. "Right. Dumb question." He reaches past me, grabbing the small bucket with leather cleaner and a rag. "Give her some time and ask her again."

I stare at him. "Isn't that a little pushy?"

"I prefer to call it persistent, but whatever," he says, shrugging his shoulders. "Stay away from the bar for a while. Let her miss you."

"I can't believe I'm actually takin' advice from you," I laugh, the sound vibrating in my chest. "This is really coming from the guy who is so allergic to relationships that he broke out in hives when–."

"We're not talkin' about me," he cuts me off, a scowl

sitting on his face. "That was one time and I never want to talk about it again."

"Fine," I say, holding my hands up. "We'll never talk about that again."

"Thank you," he gives me a curt nod, turning his attention back to his bridle and saddle as he finishes cleaning them. I do the same, cleaning off mine before we go back out to check on the horses.

They're both rinsed off and washed, tucked away in their stalls with a flake of hay.

"I didn't mean to ask her out, you know?" I admit after a few moments pass as we stare at the horses. "It just kinda happened."

Cash lifts his shoulders again. "I don't think you were wrong for doin' it and you can't take it back now. I think it would be best to put a little distance there before you try anythin' else."

"How are you even qualified to give advice?"

His eyebrows pull together and he presses his lips into a flat line. "I'm sure I'm not, but you need someone's help here." He pauses, a softness entering his gaze. "Which, by the way–thanks for helpin' me this mornin'."

"That's what I'm here for," I remind him with a smile, swinging my arm around the tops of his shoulders. "I'll always have your back in life."

"I know." He returns the smile before pushing me away. "Let's go get food somewhere or somethin'... and not at the bar."

I can't help but laugh as I nod in agreement and wink. "Deal."

CHAPTER ELEVEN

ELLA

y car does a weird little stutter thing as I pull onto one of the back roads that lead towards the petting zoo. Chloe is unsuspecting in the backseat as she plays with the small truck that Cole gave her and a few of her other toys. I glance down at the gas gauge that reads empty. The thing is messed up and I knew it when I bought the car. I have to keep track of how many miles I drive and I know the amount of miles a full tank will get me.

So far, I haven't had any issues. I keep track of my miles so I know when I need to fill it up. I stare at the gauge and pull the car off to the side of the road. I can't remember what the mileage was on my car the last time I got gas. I haven't been keeping track like normally and I have no idea when I was supposed to fill the tank again.

Dammit.

I ran out of gas.

After pulling safely off the road, I get the car in park just as it stops running. This has never happened before and my heart races inside my chest, my stomach churning with panic. Chloe pays me no mind as she continues to play with the small toys on her lap. I grab my phone and quickly find Remi's number. I hold it up to my ear, I listen to it ringing until it goes to her voicemail. I curse under my breath and end the call before trying Iris. The same thing happens.

What the heck am I going to do?

I open the web browser on my phone and look up the nearest gas station. It's only a little over a mile away. I glance at Chloe through my rearview mirror, feeling guilty that we couldn't have at least made it to the miniature animal farm before this happened. Her bright yellow sunglasses hide her eyes and she still isn't looking at me. I promised her we would go to see the animals on my day off, but it looks like the universe has other plans for me. We can walk to the gas station and I can get a can of gas, then bring it back to my car and we will be able to continue on with our day.

Even though Remi and Iris didn't answer doesn't mean I can't figure it out on my own.

I get out of my car and walk over to Chloe's side. She looks up at me as I pull open the door. "Did you want to go for a walk?"

Chloe looks up at me, her eyes shining brightly behind her sunglasses. "Are we dare?"

I shake my head, my lips lifting in a forced smile as I unbuckle her. "We have to make a quick little stop and I thought we could take a fun walk before we get to the farm."

Her face lights up and she nods eagerly. I grab her toys and set them down on her seat only to have her grab that damn pink truck before coming to stand in the grass with me. She clutches the little thing in her tiny hand and I can't help but smile and grab her other hand instead. We start our journey, walking along the side of the road, heading in the direction that my phone says to go.

Chloe doesn't have a care in the world and she rambles on about the grass tickling her legs before bouncing to another subject. Her little mind works in mysterious ways and I follow along with it, talking about whatever it is that catches her eye. A few cars drive past as we walk along the road, but no one bothers to stop. Why would they? My car is a few minutes away from us at this point and we are simply a mother and daughter walking down the back road.

No one knows. I guess no one ever truly knows what is going on inside someone else's world unless they dare to take a peek.

We keep walking and Chloe's small strides begin to shorten, her legs growing tired as she tries to keep up with me. About ten minutes into our walk, I bend down, scoping her up to carry her instead. I don't want to tire her out because of my negligence with keeping track of how full my gas tank was. As we turn the corner, a white pick-up truck pulls up to the stop sign at the intersection. I lift my gaze, looking up through the windows and my heart skips a beat in my chest.

Cole Wild.

I haven't seen him in over a week, when he came into the bar for lunch. He slides his window down, his eyebrows pulling together as he looks at the two of us. "Hey darlin'." He wastes no time and jumps right to the chase. "What are the two of you doin' out here?"

I stare at him for a moment, trying to wrack my brain for some type of a believable lie but nothing comes to mind. If I tell him that we are out for a walk, he will undoubtedly question that. There is no sense in telling him anything other than the truth. A sigh escapes me. "I ran out of gas, so we are taking a walk to the gas station to get some."

"How did you run outta gas? Where's your car?"

I point back to the way we came from. "About ten minutes that way on foot. My gauge doesn't work and I forgot to keep track of my miles so I would know when I needed to refill my tank."

"Get in."

I tilt my head to the side. "What?"

"I'll take you to the gas station. I'm not lettin' the two of you walk there and then walk back with a tank of gas." He pauses for a moment, rolling his lips between his teeth. "El, please get in and let me drive you guys there."

Conflict laces itself through my body. I hate asking for help, but I hate accepting it even more. Chloe shifts in my arms. She is beginning to feel heavier the farther we walk. Going with Cole is convenient and as much as I don't want to agree, I have to. It makes the most sense.

"I'm not some kind of damsel in distress," I say, opening the back door and plopping Chloe on the seat. She's too small to not have a car seat, but we have no choice. I strap her in and climb in with her, securing my arms around her. Cole watches me through the rearview mirror with a soft smile on his face. I narrow my eyes on him.

"No one said you were," he reminds me with a pointed look. His white t-shirt is smudged with dirt and he grabs the brim of his baseball cap, lifting it from his head before spinning it around backwards.

"That's what it feels like. I don't need your help, Wild."

He tilts his head to the side and the muscle in his jaw twitches. "No, you most certainly do not. That doesn't mean I don't wanna help you. And that sure as hell doesn't mean you can't accept it."

"Sorry," I say in a hushed voice, regret lingering in my tone. He just so happens to be at the right place at the right time. I can't fault him for that and it's only natural for him to want to extend a helping hand. I'm being a bitch to him for no reason. "I'm a little stressed out and this was unexpected. I shouldn't have projected. I apologize for acting that way."

"Stop apologizing for everything, Ella," he says softly with a warmth swirling in his gaze that continues to penetrate mine. "Most people would say thank you, but it's okay. I get it."

I swallow back my emotion. "Thank you."

"See, that wasn't so hard, was it?" The corners of his lips lift upwards. "Seatbelt," he adds with a wink as he points over my shoulder.

Following his command, I grab the belt and pull it across my chest before clicking it in place. He waits with a patient smile on his face until I'm ready before he whips his truck around and heads in the direction of the gas station.

"What were the two of you doin' before you got stranded?"

I glance out the window to avoid studying the side of his perfectly sculpted face. "I have off today so I promised Chloe we would go to that miniature animal farm."

"It's a beautiful day for it."

"It is," I agree, finally looking at him. "What were you doing? I hope we're not interrupting your day at all."

Cole shakes his head. "Not at all. I was actually on my way home from the store. I had to get some medicine for a few of the horses."

"Well, thank god for that. If you hadn't shown up, it would have proved to be quite the challenge getting back with a gas can." I pause and let the smile break out across my lips instead of fighting against it. "I didn't really think about having to lug it the whole way back to my car with a toddler whose legs are already tired."

He glances at me from the corner of his eye. "It worked out perfectly." He turns his truck into the station parking lot and pulls up to one of the pumps. "Didn't you have anyone to call or were you too stubborn to ask anyone for help?"

His words aren't meant to be malicious, but my body immediately tenses. "I called Remi and Iris, but neither of them answered."

I'm not going to argue with him about my stubbornness. There's no sense. What he doesn't understand is that I'm not coming from a place of being stubborn. It's coming from a place of not wanting to be a burden. The last thing I want to do is trouble anyone else with my problems. They are mine to deal with and mine alone.

Cole turns his truck off and climbs out. I also get out, leaving my door open since Chloe is still in the backseat. "Be back in a few."

"Hold on, cowboy," I call out after him, seeing the smirk and arch of his brow. "I can get it. If you don't mind staying here with her, I'll run in and grab it."

"No can do," he says with simplicity, turning his back to me and promptly walking into the gas station without another word or glance in my direction. My nostrils flare in frustration and I drop back down in the truck. I glance at Chloe, who quietly inspects her little pink truck.

Cole reappears and marches straight over to the pump. I quickly climb back out of the back, my footsteps purposeful as I stride to where he is. He already has his card out, about to insert it into the card reader.

"I don't need you to pay for it. You drove us here, which was more than enough."

He tilts his head to the side, pushing the card in the slot. "I know you don't need me to, El. Can you stop fightin' me on doin' the things I wanna do? You're allowed to accept people's kindness. It won't kill you."

Emotion washes over me but I quickly push it away. I know he's right, it's just hard for me to do when I thrive on my independence. It's something I've worked so damn hard for, it's difficult to put it to the side.

"Can I at least pay you back?"

A ghost of a smile dances across his lips and he shakes his head. "I don't want your money."

"And you call me stubborn," I mumble under my breath which earns a soft laugh from him. "I owe you."

"I'll be sure to remember that when I'm ready to collect," he replies with a look of mischief in his eyes.

I stand with him, the comfortable silence settling between us as he finishes filling the can and loading it into the back of his truck. We both head to our opposite sides and climb back into the cab. I pull my seatbelt back across my body when I notice Cole glancing at Chloe in the back-seat. His gaze shifts from her to the pink truck in her hands and his expression softens.

"She refuses to go anywhere without it," I say quietly.

His gaze flashes to mine and my chest warms. "I like that."

So do I.

"Thank you for everything, Cole."

He shakes his head and a wave of emotion washes over his irises. "You don't have to thank me, El. I don't do things I don't wanna do."

I can't argue with that.

"Okay," I whisper, not fully trusting my own voice.

His lips part slightly and a soft breath escapes him before he directs his attention to the dashboard. He starts the engine, putting it in drive, and begins to head back to where my car is. The silence encapsulates us, but it isn't awkward. It is warm and comfortable. Familiar, even. I feel at ease around him, even if it does feel like he throws me off balance.

Cole parks behind my car and gets the gas tank from the bed of his truck while I get Chloe out. I let him go ahead and fill my tank and I settle her back into her car seat. She's quiet and her lips part as she lets out a yawn.

She nestles in her seat and I watch as her eyelids fall shut. It's a bit earlier than when she normally naps, but after all the walking we did, I'm not surprised she's falling asleep.

"You're all set," Cole says from behind me. I turn around to face him as he peers through the door, a smile dancing across his face as he sees Chloe drifting asleep. "Looks like someone's tuckered out."

"I'm hopeful that a quick little nap isn't going to leave her grumpy when I wake her up to see the animals," I laugh softly and shake my head.

Cole chuckles, the sound vibrating against my

eardrums. "Well, I guess you won't know 'til you wake her up."

I gently close the door and Cole walks over to the driver's side with me. I pull open my door, turning to face him, immediately meeting his gaze. His expression is unreadable and a nervousness washes over me under his watchful eyes. "Thank you again for coming to our rescue."

"Anytime." His eyes shimmer. "Can I give you my number? I'm sure you won't use it, but I'd like you to have it just in case." He pauses his half rambling sentence and the corners of his lips twitch. "You don't have to give me yours. I just want you to have mine."

I can't tell him no with the hopeful look in his eyes. I pull my phone from the back pocket of my jean shorts and open up a new contact before handing it to him. His fingertips brush mine and the touch burns against my skin as he takes the device from me.

I suck in a sharp breath, heat creeping across my cheeks as his mouth twitches but he doesn't look up at me as he types his number. His eyes flash to mine as he lifts his head and hands me back my phone. "There you go," he says, his voice husky. "Have fun at the miniature farm. You should bring her to the ranch sometime."

"I'm sure she would love that."

His gaze is fixed on mine. "We'll talk about it. I'm sure I'll see you soon."

"You know where to find me."

I feel the heat creeping up my neck and instantly want to take the words back. Cole raises an eyebrow at me, a smirk lifting his lips as he begins to back away. "Bye El."

"Bye, cowboy," I murmur as he turns around on the heel of his boot and heads back to his truck. I quickly tear my gaze from him and the way those jeans hug his ass. I force myself into my car, pulling the door shut in a rush before turning on the engine. My phone is still in my hand with his contact information shining back at me.

I swallow roughly, tapping on the message button. I shouldn't text him this soon, but I want him to have my number. You know, just in case.

My heart pounds erratically in my chest as I type out my message, acting purely on impulse and press send.

ELLA

I owe you...

COLE

You do owe me.

But don't worry. I won't be collectin' that debt 'til you're ready.

I stare at my phone, the unfamiliar feeling of butterfly wings wildly flapping in the pit of my stomach. I want to hold on to the sensation, even if it seems too good to be true.

ELLA

I hope you do.

COLE

I'm a man of my word, El. I always follow through.

A giggle escapes me and I can't help myself as I cover my mouth. A smile breaks out across my lips and I'm grinning like a damned fool as I glance in my side mirror. Cole is still sitting in his truck behind me and I don't miss the smirk on his face as he stares back at me. He waits until I pull my car onto the road before he whips his truck around and disappears in the opposite direction. Deciding against going to visit the animals, I head back home with Chloe sleeping in the back. My thoughts keep swirling around Cole Wild and the way he looked at me with those bright blue eyes of his.

It's been a long time since I've felt any of these feelings.

And I'm not sure whether I should embrace them or run in the opposite direction.

CHAPTER TWELVE

ELLA

"Ella honey, can you please grab some extra napkins on your way in?" Iris calls from the dining room as she arranges the food on the table.

Reaching into the cabinet where she keeps them, I pull out a small stack of napkins and hand them to Chloe. "Take those into Grammy Iris, please," I say with a gentle smile. Chloe quickly takes them from me and goes running into the other room.

We have a tradition of doing Sunday dinners at Iris' house. We aren't always able to do it every week, so we try to make sure it happens at least twice a month. It's just Chloe and I here with Remi and Iris. We usually come over early in the afternoon and the three of us cook together while we sip some wine.

We all head into the dining room after we finish cooking and settle into our seats around the table. No one hesitates as we all start to pile food onto our plates.

"Who wants to start?" Iris says cheerfully after swallowing a mouthful of food. She looks around between Remi and I.

We always go around the table, taking turns telling everyone how their week was. After that, we each pick one bad thing that happened during our week, followed by a good thing.

"I'll go," Remi offers and sets down her glass of wine. "My week was pretty good. Everything at the bar has been great and I was able to go paddleboarding a few mornings on the lake."

"That's so good to hear, honey," Iris smiles, her eyes softening as she stares at her daughter and then glances at Chloe. "What about you, Clo? How was your week?"

"Good!" She exclaims in a bright and cheery tone. She reaches into her lap and lifts up the pink truck she's been taking everywhere with her. "Got new twuck! From Co!."

"Oh, would you look at that!" Iris says with excitement as Chloe holds the little truck up for everyone to see with a proud smile on her face. "It's pink!"

"Co? Cole?" Remi asks her with a smirk as she flashes her eyes to mine. "As in one of the Wild brothers?"

"Momma friend," she tells her matter-of-factly.

Remi looks at me and tilts her head to the side with her eyebrows raised. "Momma has a friend?"

I give her a look. "He's an old friend, you already know that. We ran into him at the grocery store and he saw that Chloe had snuck that truck into the cart, so he surprised her with it."

"He drived big twuck."

"What?" Iris gives me a questioning gaze.

Dammit. I haven't told either of them about the incident because I knew Remi would demand every detail possible in private later.

"That's why I called you both. I forgot to tell you about it afterwards, but I forgot how many miles I had until my car ran out of gas," I explain with a soft laugh. "We were on our way to that little farm with all the miniature animals the other day and my tank was empty. Thankfully, he happened to drive past when we were walking to the gas station and he gave us a ride there and put the gas in my car."

Iris stares at me for a second with her expression unreadable. Remi, on the other hand, isn't hiding anything. She's completely intrigued and invested.

"Cole motherfuckin' Wild," Remi murmurs, a soft breath blowing out of her nose. She shakes her head.

"Remi, language," her mother scolds, narrowing her eyes. They both have a habit of wearing the same expressions, with their matching brown eyes and dark auburn hair.

"Sorry," Remi apologizes, rolling her eyes before pining them on me. "I didn't know the two of you talked outside of him always showing up at the bar to occupy an empty stool."

"We don't," I say dismissively and direct my attention to Iris. "How was your week?"

A slow smile creeps onto her lips. "Let's hear about your week first. It sounds like it might be far more interesting than mine."

Heat blooms across my face. "My week was good. Nothing out of the ordinary."

Remi snorts. "Bullshit," she coughs out.

"Okay," Iris says with a devious grin. "My week was good, as well. Nothing happened that was exciting or exhilarating like running out of gas or getting new toy trucks."

"Mhm," I mumble before shoveling a forkful of food into my mouth. Thankfully, Iris lets it go at that, but I know Remi is chomping at the bit, impatiently waiting for the chance to corner me after dinner to get all the details. The conversation shifts into the good and the bad that happened over the past week. It's no surprise when Chloe has no complaints and only wants to talk about how special her little truck is.

Damn Cole for getting it for her.

I can't forget the way he looked when he saw her playing with it. The emotion was palpable and I wanted to know what he was thinking at that moment, but I was too scared to hear what he would have actually said. There's a lot about him I don't know anymore and it's better if I leave it that way.

When we finish up dinner, Remi and I clear off the table while Chloe helps Iris wash the dishes. It's one of her favorite things to do and even though it ends up being messier than it needs to be, Iris is always quick to let her assist. There are bubbles all over the place and the sound of her laughter fills the house. The warmth spreads through my soul and happiness settles in my chest. I'm truly happy, without a single thing in life I find myself needing.

Although, my mind can't stop drifting back to those bright blue eyes…

"Okay, spill." Remi follows me out of the dining room. "I need the real details about Cole Wild."

I shrug with indifference and wander into the living room, sitting down on the couch. "There's not much to tell. You heard everything that happened at dinner."

"Come on, El. I know you're not blind. Everyone can see the way that man looks at you." She pauses as she laughs and drops down next to me. She throws her arm over the back of the couch and pulls her legs underneath herself. "He only comes to the bar when you're working and he barely even drinks. We all know what he's actually doing there."

"I don't know what you're talking about," I retort in denial, refusing to actually acknowledge it.

"Fine," she sighs, but I know she isn't done yet. "You know, just because things with you and Jacob didn't end well, doesn't mean you can't take a chance with someone else. Not all men suck. Just most of them."

"I know that, Remi," I say with an exasperated sigh. I know that much is true, yet I can't seem to get my brain to be okay with the prospect of letting someone else into my life like that again. I am terrified of what might happen.

The last time I let someone in, I ended up betrayed, pregnant, and alone.

I refuse to put myself in a position like that again.

"I'm not saying I think you should go get married to Cole or anything like that, but I think you should at least let him take you out to dinner." She pauses and adjusts on the couch. "Worst case, you discover he actually sucks and you never see him again."

I stare at my best friend for a moment as my thoughts run wild. She doesn't know he already asked me to dinner and I declined. It's not exactly something I want to talk about, considering it's a bit embarrassing on my part.

She doesn't understand because she has never been in my position before. I am happy for her because I never want her to ever experience that. Remi doesn't know how daunting the thought of getting to know someone is, especially when you are constantly questioning who they really are.

It's so easy for a person to pretend to be someone they aren't.

Cole Wild has never struck me as that type of person,

but I truly don't know. He has never been anything but kind to me and I've never witnessed him being cruel or rude to anyone.

He has always had a big heart, but the Cole I knew growing up could be a different version than the man he is today.

"I suppose it wouldn't hurt to let him buy me some food," I admit quietly, dropping my gaze to my hands and picking at the cuticles around my thumb. "Like you said, if it doesn't go well, I never have to intentionally see him again."

Remi smiles at me. "Exactly." She reaches over and grabs my hand, giving it a gentle squeeze. "You're stronger than you give yourself credit for, El. You've already done the hard things in life. You can get through anything after you were able to leave Jacob. Look at the life you've built with Chloe."

"I know," I say, giving her a small, yet sad smile. "Sometimes it doesn't feel like it though. Sometimes I feel like I'm moving through life with so much strength and then I'm reminded of reality. Of the fact that I'm doing it all alone. And those moments are when I feel overwhelmed and small. Like I have the weight of the world constantly on my shoulders. It's terrifying and paralyzing at times."

Remi's eyes soften, the subtle creases in her skin forming around the corners of her eyes. "I can't pretend to know how you're feeling. I cannot imagine and it breaks my heart to know you feel that way." A tear springs from her eye and she laughs it away as she wipes it from her cheek. "You have an entire tribe surrounding you, Ella. You're not alone anymore and you don't have to do it by yourself. If you can't lift yourself up, let us do it for you.

"When you think of the woman from your past, think

of how you would never want any of that for her again. You know what you will and won't accept. Everything is okay now, Ella."

I can't help myself as my tears begin to fall. I don't mean to get emotional like I am, but since we opened the doors on this conversation, I'm struggling to get a hold of myself. "I never want Chloe to think behavior or treatment like that is okay."

"And she never will," Remi reminds me as she squeezes my hand tighter. "Look at who she has as a mother. That little girl is going to be a force to reckon with. She's going to be so strong, all because of you and the way you raise her."

My thoughts drift to Chloe as a young woman, straightening her spine and refusing to let a man walk all over her. I can see it now. Laughter escapes me and I shake my head, wiping away the lingering tears. "Okay, I didn't plan on crying tonight," I say with a soft laugh.

Remi smiles at me, her face warm and familiar. Welcoming and safe. "Should we get back to talking about Cole then?"

"You're impossible," I laugh again and shake my head. "But, yes. Would it be weird if I texted him?"

"Absolutely not," she tells me with her eyes wide like she doesn't believe the words I just spoke. "I can guarantee that man has been waiting to hear from you."

Remi releases my hands and I slide one into the back pocket of my jean shorts for my phone. I slowly pull it out, my heart knocking against my ribcage at a rapid pace. My palms begin to feel damp and I look up at Remi as I hold the device in my hand. "I'm nervous, Remi."

"Do you want me to leave the room?"

My eyebrows pull together. "I'm not calling, just texting him."

"True. I didn't know if me being here was making it worse."

"I don't know if I can do this," I admit, my voice quiet and I unlock the screen to open my messages. I type in the first three letters of his name, watching his contact show up.

"You can," she assures me. "You've already proved you can do anything."

My chest expands as I suck in a deep breath and slowly exhale. I swallow roughly, urging my heart to calm down. I nod to myself and begin to type out a message. It's short and sweet. I press the send button before I get the chance to second guess myself and back out.

ELLA

Hey.

"I did it."

Remi claps excitedly as she drops her feet off the couch and scootches closer to me. "Let me see. What did you say?" Her eyebrows cinch closer as she reads the message. "That's it?"

I spin in my place to look at her. "What was I supposed to say?"

Remi rolls her lips between her teeth and shrugs. "I don't know, actually. That was good enough."

"Auntie Remi!" Chloe comes bounding into the room and jumps into Remi's lap. "Kitties?"

Iris walks into the doorway as she dries her hands with a hand towel. "I told her about the kittens you found behind the shed."

Remi smiles down at my daughter and slides her hands

under Chloe's armpits to lift her into the air as she rises to her feet. Chloe squeals and wraps her arms around the back of Remi's neck. "Of course, Clo. Let's go check them out!"

My phone vibrates and my heart halts. Iris disappears back into the kitchen and my eyes widen as I stare at Remi.

"We'll be back in a few," she winks. "You've got this."

I watch the two of them head out the door that leads to the garage. My confidence is weak and I wish I had an ounce of Remi's. My gaze drops down to my phone. Cole's name is on the screen with a message from him. Panic erupts inside me, my stomach fluttering wildly. I abruptly rise to my feet, staring at my phone like it's a bomb about to detonate. The room begins to shrink, like the walls are closing in on me.

My feet immediately move and I make a beeline straight for the back door, letting myself out onto Iris' back porch. You can't see the rolling fields from here, but it's close enough that you can smell the growing alfalfa and dust. The smell of lake water mixes with it, drifting through the night sky. I walk over to one of the chairs on the deck and sit down.

COLE

Hey.

I stare at my phone for a second and let out a nervous laugh. What the hell? He couldn't give me a little more than that to make this easier on me? I guess I did text him, but now I am supposed to lead the conversation too? This was a stupid idea.

ELLA

How are you?

He responds immediately and my heart betrays me, skipping a beat as I read his messages.

COLE

I'm good, better now that I've heard from you.

How are you, Ella?

I read over both texts twice before typing out my own response. My heart thumps harder and faster, thrumming to its own beat that I have zero control over. I refuse to acknowledge the butterflies that are trying to flutter to life in my stomach.

ELLA

I'm doing well.

COLE

Good.

Is everything okay?

There was a point to me texting him and I suppose I should get to it sooner rather than later. I don't know the last time I felt this frazzled from talking to someone. It's just Cole and it is *not* a date. I'm allowed to get a meal with someone and make no commitment. He is a friend and nothing more. We can eat together and leave it at that.

ELLA

Everything's good.

I wanted to change the answer I gave when you asked if you could take me out to dinner.

Three little bubbles appear and disappear four separate times. I'm frozen. Paralyzed. My fingers move, but I can't get them to cooperate. I can't continue where I was going with this thought and now I'm wondering if I should have even entertained the idea.

COLE

My obituary is going to read: Cole Wild
quietly passed away from the suspense of
waiting to hear Ella Daniel's new answer.

A soft laugh escapes me and I smile down at my screen as tears burn my eyes. Damn him and having to make something that feels so heavy, light.

COLE

Do you want me to ask the question again?

I swallow hard over the lump lodged in my throat as my fingers move across the screen.

ELLA

Yes please.

COLE

Can I take you out for dinner sometime?

ELLA

I would love that.

COLE

I like the new answer a lot better.

When would be a good time for you?

It feels strange, feeling giddy like this while talking to a man. Like I should be kicking my feet from excitement. I resist the urge to, even if the butterflies are fluttering away inside my stomach.

He remembers that I don't have the flexibility to go out

whenever. I have a job. I have a daughter. I have responsibilities that must be taken care of first.

ELLA

I need to check with my sitter first, to see if there's a night that works best for her, if that's okay.

I don't know what your schedule looks like.

COLE

I will clear my entire schedule for you, El.

Figure out a day that works best for you and I will make it work.

My eyes widen as I reread his message again. And again. And again.

Holy shit.

ELLA

I will let you know.

COLE

There's no rush. I'll be here whenever you're ready.

ELLA

I'll let you know then.

I lock my screen and hold my phone to my chest as I stare out into the darkness, listening to the sound of horses whinnying in the distance. There isn't a single similarity between Cole and my ex.

Cole Wild scares the hell out of me because he is nothing like Jacob Evans...

And I know he could potentially be a real threat to my heart.

CHAPTER THIRTEEN

ELLA

I walk through the restaurant to the bar, my eyes doing their typical surveillance of the crowd, making sure there isn't a familiar face I've been running from for years. It's a habit I developed after I left Jacob and one I've been struggling to break.

I don't think he would come looking for me, considering the way we ended things, but there's always that fear lingering in the back of my mind.

What if one day he wakes up and decides to change his mind about Chloe?

I don't think that Jacob would be a bad father, but at the same time, I don't know who he is anymore. I didn't feel like I even truly knew him when I left our marriage.

I walk over to Remi as she's typing something into the computer screen for an order. "Hey." I let out a breath while pulling my hair back into a bun. "It's busy here tonight."

Remi glances at me from the corner of her eye as a grin dances across her lips. "It is. One of your favorite customers is here this evening, too."

My heart skips a beat in my chest at the possibility. "Cole is here?"

She turns her entire body to face me after logging out of the computer. "Yep," she confirms, nodding her head to the right behind me. "He got here maybe five minutes ago. I told him I'd be with him shortly, but since you're here, perhaps you can cover that side of the bar instead."

"Sometimes you're really a pain in the ass," I mutter, sneaking a glance over my shoulder. Cole is sitting there on one of the barstools with his friend, Austin next to him. I haven't spoken to him since I texted him and told him I wanted to go out some time.

Something inside still has its grip on me, holding me back from going through with my desires. My fears prove to be much greater and I want him to chase them away. I want him to wash away the thoughts that plague my brain. The thoughts that tell me I can't possibly trust anyone.

It's unfair to view Cole that way, especially when he hasn't given me a reason not to trust or believe him.

The prospect of it all still scares the daylights out of me.

"You love me," Remi argues as she flashes her perfect white teeth at me and winks. "Consider this like a personal favor. You like him, don't you?"

My eyes widen slightly and my breath gets caught in my throat for a moment before I collect myself. "I don't know about that."

"Let me rephrase. You're interested in him, no?" She shrugs, noncommittal. "You don't have to commit to any feelings, but there's a part of you that wants to explore the excitement he makes you feel, right?"

I mull over her words, playing them back to myself in my mind, letting them sink in a little deeper. She's right. I can admit I have an attraction to him without declaring I have feelings for him. I'm allowed to appreciate the way he makes me feel and the way he looks without committing to anything deeper than that.

"Right."

"This is Cole Wild, we're talking about. Walking, talking green flag. The man who would give you the shirt off his back." She looks over at him and back to me. "You're safe with him. And if he does anything wrong, I'll make sure he never walks again."

I can't help myself as the laughter bubbles up my throat and I shake my head at my best friend before looking her up and down. "Says the woman who is barely over five feet tall."

Remi huffs, pushing her shoulders back as she crosses her arms over her chest. "Don't underestimate the short people in the world. We have a lot more to prove and what we don't have in height, we make up for in fierceness."

She's not lying. Remi may be the most take no crap person I've ever met. There isn't a single fear in her body. She'd jump in front of a bullet for those she loves without a second thought.

My brain circles back to Cole and his friend, who are caught up in a conversation together. They're patiently waiting for one of us to come over and take their order, never mind the rest of the patrons at the bar who most likely aren't being as patient.

"What do I even say to him?"

"You could start by takin' their order," she offers with a laugh and starts to walk to the center of the bar. "Just go with whatever feels right, but don't you dare let that man leave without making plans to see him again."

"Why do I have to be the one to make plans with him?"

Remi gives me a stern look. "Because you're a bad bitch who is doing what she wants without owing anyone a single apology. You're taking your life back, one dick at a time."

I choke on air and heat instantly breaks out across my face. "I don't know about all that."

"You know what I mean," she says, shrugging while she spins on her heel and heads to her side of the bar. I watch her for a brief moment and attempt to slow my heart rate. My eyes travel across the bar and my gaze collides with Cole's, instantly stealing my breath.

There's an intensity in his stare and electricity sparks on the molecules dancing within the distance between us. The corners of his mouth lift, transforming into the subtlest of smiles, yet one that brightens his irises.

So much for my heart rate calming down. Instead, it kicks into overdrive, pounding erratically and uncontrollably in my chest. The terrified part of me is urging my body to turn around and run in the opposite direction. Forget about my job and head out of Silverspur Springs without looking back.

Remi was incredibly wrong. This man is going to become a threat if he keeps looking at me like that.

Inhaling deeply, I force myself to take a chance and to do my damn job. I move across the bar, walking until I'm standing directly in front of Cole and his friend. His lips stretch, smiling at me as I adjust my weight on my feet.

"Good evenin'." My tone hitches higher and it sounds foreign to my ears. I fight the urge to shake my head at myself for sounding like an idiot. I duck my head momentarily, grabbing two drink napkins and set them on the wooden surface in front of them. "What are we drinking tonight?"

Austin speaks first. "I'll take a bourbon."

"Make that two," Cole adds, his voice a deep vibration against my eardrums. I didn't realize how much I was missing that sound until now. It's like a hit of dopamine my body has been craving.

I smile my brightest smile at them in an attempt to push away the lightening feeling that enters my chest. Turning my back on the two of them, I begin to busy myself with their drinks before taking the glasses over to them.

Glancing down the row of people, I tell Cole I'll be right back and collect the other orders before returning back to them. They break their conversation to turn their attention to me.

"Will either of you be ordering any food?"

Cole nods. "Yes, ma'am. What about you, Austin?"

His friend nods as well. "If you have other people you need to take care of, you can just come back to us then. I'm in the process of trying to convince Cole to buy a boat."

"It's okay, I think everyone is okay right now," I say after doing a quick scan of the other patrons. No one appears restless or like they need me at this moment.

Cole rolls his eyes and chuckles. "I already told you, I don't see a point in buying a boat when I can use yours."

"Well, what if I want to use it at the same time you want to?"

They both look at me, like they're looking for some help. I shrug and laugh softly, looking at Austin and then rest my eyes on Cole's. "He does have a point."

He narrows his eyes, although there's mischief dancing

in his blue irises. "You're not helping my case here, darlin'."

"I like her," Austin declares with a smile. "I mean, I might be saying that because of one sentence, but you're helping me get what I want so…"

"Hey, I'll take it."

Cole glances between the two of us. "I guess I should probably introduce the insufferable asshole whom I call my friend. Ella, you remember, Austin, right?"

Austin rises to his feet and holds his hand out to me. "I do," I say, shaking his hand. "It's been quite a few years."

"It has," he agrees as he releases his grip on my hand and returns to his seat. "I've heard so much about you recently, though."

Those eight words feel like a shock to my heart, causing the organ to come to a complete standstill. My breath catches in my throat, my eyes widening slightly as my mouth goes bone dry. I look at Cole and back to Austin, forcing my brain to say something, anything that isn't stupid.

"I hope good things," I manage to get the words out without sounding as nervous as I feel inside.

"Oh, yes," he assures me with a gentle smile that twinkles in his gray eyes. "Nothin' but good things."

"Okay, she gets it," Cole interjects and I silently thank him for saving me. His eyes are soft and kind as he watches me for a moment as Austin rises to his feet and excuses himself to use the restroom. Cole waits until he's gone before speaking again. "You'll have to excuse him. His parents taught him manners, but I'm afraid he forgets them at times."

I laugh softly, appreciating the way he effortlessly changes the subject and directs it away from the fact that he's clearly talked about me to his close friend. "You don't have to apologize for him," I tell Cole, tasting the risky words dancing on my tongue. They drift into my brain and instead of ignoring them, I decide to take a chance and speak boldly. "If I'm being honest, I like that you've talked to him about me."

Surprise dances across Cole's expression. His perfectly rounded lips part slightly and he tilts his head to the side. "Good," he says quietly, almost like he can't form a coherent thought. The thought of that sends a surge of power through my body. It makes me feel like I'm on top of the world, knowing I'm the one who threw his brain off kilter now.

"I'll be back in a few to get y'alls order for food," I say with a sweet smile, leaving the conversation at that and heading back to my other customers. Cole looks at me like he wants to say something else, but instead he clamps his lips together and nods at me with a smile.

My footsteps are light and it feels like I'm floating on a cloud when I walk over to the other people, taking their orders and getting their food and drinks. Whatever that was with Cole induced a lightness in my chest, like I can conquer anything. My confidence is palpable—like a drug induced high—and I busy myself with my work, spending the rest of the evening tending to the customers.

Cole leaves me alone, but his gaze never wavers. It never wanders as he watches me. And that alone feels like another hit of ecstasy.

I don't realize the time and two hours pass before the bar starts to slow down a bit. Cole and Austin already paid their tab and the two of them are saying their goodbyes as they rise from the bar. I meet Austin's gaze and he throws his hand up to wave at me. I look at Cole and he simply smiles and nods before the two of them turn around and head toward the exit.

"When's the wedding?"

Remi bumps her shoulder into mine and I duck my head, laughing softly. "I am never doing that again."

"Touche," Remi laughs as she stands next to me. "But when's the first date?"

I'm silent and don't bother looking at her as I grab a glass and begin to fill it with ice. The silence stretches between us and I know it's only a matter of seconds before Remi disrupts it.

"Ella."

"Remi."

"You didn't do it, did you?"

I lift my head, turning to look at her. "I'll ask him next time."

She abruptly grabs the glass from my hand and clicks her tongue at me. "Nope. You go out there right now and don't come back until you have plans with him."

"Excuse me?"

Remi sets the glass down, grabs my shoulders and spins me around to face the exit before giving me a gentle push. "You heard me. You had one thing you were supposed to do tonight, now go be a bad bitch and do it."

I grumble under my breath, cutting my eyes at her over my shoulder before heading out of the bar. Stepping out on the pier, I move to the side for a couple coming in when I see Cole halfway toward the parking lot.

Dammit.

My steps momentarily falter and I start to second guess myself. Remi is right. It's time for me to be a bad bitch and do the things I want to do without letting my fear control me. I'm not able to push the nervousness away, but I'm able to swallow enough of it that I break out into a light jog down the dock.

"Hey, cowboy!" I call out to him, hoping the sound doesn't get carried away by the valley air.

He turns around, looking a little surprised as he sees me jogging in his direction. His lips move as he glances at Austin and looks back to me. Austin says something back and smiles before he continues his walk toward the boat.

"Hey, El," Cole says gently as I come to a stop in front of him. "Is everything okay?"

I'm a little breathless, both from the physical activity and the way he's looking at me right now. "Yes. Well, no."

His eyebrows pull together. "What's wrong?"

"I wanted to ask you something before you left and I didn't get the chance to. Not because I didn't want to but because it got really busy and it's been a long time since I've done this. Actually, I don't know if I've ever done this before."

I instantly want to cringe at the word vomit that just spewed from my mouth in rapid succession.

Cole reaches out and grabs my hand, giving it a gentle squeeze as his eyes search mine. His expression relaxes and there's a tenderness in his gaze, in the way his lips lift. "You don't have to be nervous, El. You can always ask me anything."

I let out a ragged breath and mentally collect myself. I have to get the words out or I'm sure I'll never work up the courage to do it again. "I've been meanin' to text you about goin' out sometime and well–would you like to go out with me?"

The smile on his lips is slow as it blisters across his face. "Are you askin' *me* on a date, Ella Daniels?"

"What?" The shock is apparent on my face and a blush

quickly blossoms across my cheeks. "No, not a date. Just dinner."

His expression is unreadable and his eyes shimmer under the moonlight. "Did you talk to your sitter?"

"I'm off Monday night and she's able to watch Chloe then."

It's half a lie. Remi and I are both off Monday and since she practically forced me out here, I'm making the executive decision that she's babysitting.

The corners of his eyes crinkle. "Then it's not a date," he says with a wink as he squeezes my hand again before releasing it. "I'll pick you up at six."

I watch him as he slowly backs away and turns around before walking down the dock towards Austin's boat. My eyes follow him for a few seconds and then I begin to head back to the bar. A smile breaks out across my face and I don't bother trying to hide it as my heart beats to a new melody.

A song I haven't felt in my soul in far too long.

Hope.

CHAPTER FOURTEEN
COLE

Sitting in my truck, I pull out my phone, my heart ticking faster in my chest as I type in Wyatt's name. He's probably working, so I send him a text, cutting straight to the chase.

> Hey man. I hope all is well with you. I wanted to let you know that I'm takin' your sister out to dinner tonight. It's not a date or anything, but I didn't want to piss you off.

I stare at the message after I send it, wishing I would have written something a little better worded. Wyatt and I were best friends growing up. We may not see each other often and only talk sporadically now, but that doesn't change our friendship.

My phone vibrates and I look down, surprised to see Wyatt answered me almost immediately.

> WYATT
>
> Cool. Thanks for letting me know.

COLE

That's it? Cool?

WYATT

Yep. El could use some fun and I trust you.

I stare at my phone, tilting my head to the side. In a way, this feels like it could be a trap, although I know it isn't. That's not Wyatt's character at all. If he's feeling a certain kind of way about a situation, he'll be the first to tell you about it.

Thanks, man.

After he likes my message, I tuck my phone back into my pocket and climb out of my truck. My footsteps are light as I walk up to her front door. My heart pounds a little harder and I shift my weight on my feet, lifting my hand and curl it into a fist. I almost texted her after Wyatt, but then I decided against it. She doesn't want this to seem like a date, which is fine. I will never push her to do something she doesn't want to do. That doesn't mean I can't be a gentleman.

Ella has skeletons in her closet. She has a past that I know nothing about. With the way she responds to men, I think it's safe to assume that someone left her feeling jaded.

I push the thought away from my mind and knock on the door. From the corner of my eye, I see the curtains along the front window shift. Taking a step back, I tuck my hands in the front pockets of my jeans while I wait for her to come to the door.

Ella's face appears on the other side of the glass that takes up half of the door. I can't help but wish she had a more protective door. Someone could easily break in just by breaking through the glass.

A smile spreads across her perfect lips and she unlocks the deadbolt before pulling it open. "Hey," she says a bit breathlessly as her eyes meet mine. "Sorry. I was trying to clean up the kitchen before you got here. It's easier to do when Chloe isn't here," she adds with a soft laugh.

I smile at her, as I take the door in my hand and hold it open so she doesn't have to keep her arm stretched out. A soft yellow sundress falls right above her knees and I allow myself a moment to appreciate how goddamn good she looks in that color. Her blonde hair is pulled back, half of it up with the other half falling in big loose curls around her shoulders.

"I'm sure she's probably a great helper when she is around though," I say with a wink.

Ella laughs again and shakes her head. "She's not here so we don't have to pretend for her sake." She leans closer to me, her voice dropping to a whisper. "She has a habit of making a mess while trying to help."

I match her, leaning close to her ear. "Why are you whispering if she isn't here?"

Ella quickly straightens her spine as hues of pink drift across her cheeks. She ducks her gaze, dropping it to the floor as she shifts away from me. "Good point," she chuckles, shaking her head dismissively. "If you give me two minutes, I'll be ready to go." She lifts her gaze back to mine as she takes a step back through the threshold. "You can come in if you'd like."

I don't miss the nervousness in her tone and the way her body language significantly changes. I'm not sure that I make her uncomfortable, but it's evident that this situation does. "I appreciate that," I assure her with a warm smile, nodding my head over toward my truck. "I need to make a quick call to the farrier, so I can wait in the truck."

She rolls her lips between her teeth, clamping them together for a fraction of a second as she nods. "I'll be right out."

"Take your time."

Ella disappears back into the house and I let the door fall shut behind her. I don't move for a moment. Instead, I stand there staring at the front of her house, resisting the urge to follow after her.

I have every intention of learning everything I can about this version of Ella, even if it means I have to do it on her time.

Spinning on my heel, I walk down the four steps that lead to the paver walkway. I head over to the small driveway and slip back into the driver's side of my truck. I don't have a phone call to make, but I don't want her to feel any pressure.

Ella finally comes out a few minutes later. I lift my gaze from my phone and lock the screen. She pulls the front door shut behind her, turning around to make sure that it's locked before she begins to walk toward my car. I use the opportunity to drink her in without her seeing me.

She pulls her black sunglasses over her eyes, shielding them from the sun that's beginning its descent towards the horizon. Her hair dances in the breeze behind her, the bottom hem of her dress swishing around her legs. She's wearing a pair of black cowboy boots with a jean jacket draped over her arm and a small black purse hanging over her shoulder.

Before she reaches me, I climb out of the vehicle and walk over to the passenger's side to open the door. Ella lifts her gaze to mine as she meets me along the side of the truck.

"You didn't have to do that," she says softly, with a warmth lingering in her tone.

I smile at her, shaking my head. "Like I told you before, I don't do things I don't wanna do, Ella."

She studies me for a moment, chewing on her bottom lip before she nods. "Thank you," she finally says as she brushes past me. The scent of vanilla and honey invades my senses and I savor the scent as she climbs into the truck.

"My pleasure," I respond, waiting until she's situated in her seat before closing the door. I make my way around the back of the truck until I reach my side. Pausing for a breath, I try to collect myself before getting behind the wheel with her next to me.

She drives me wild and has absolutely no clue.

Ella's quiet as she straps her seatbelt and I begin to pull out of her driveway. I let her sit in her thoughts for a few minutes as we ease into the drive. The restaurant I picked isn't that far away. It's situated on the outskirts of town, on the side opposite of the lake. It's still considered part of the hollow, but there's a restaurant called Harvest at the base of Silverspur Mountain.

"I should have asked before makin' the reservation, but you're okay with Harvest right?"

Ella glances at me, a soft smile touching her lips as she shakes her head. "I am. I've actually never been there before."

"Thank god," I let out a nervous breath that I didn't realize I was holding. "I was hopin' to be able to take you somewhere different."

A soft laugh escapes her. "Well, you're in luck today." She pauses for a moment as she looks out the window and then looks back at me. It's like she's contemplating whether or not to say something and the fact that she holds back kills me inside.

"What is it?" I ask, glancing over at her before looking back at the road. "I would give anything to hear your thoughts right now."

She chews on the inside of her lip as she turns her head to me. "I've been trying to figure you out. Trying to find something bad, something that looks like a red flag."

Her words are so brutally honest and so unexpected, I'm completely caught off guard. "And what have you found out?"

"Nothing," she says with a frustrated sigh. "I can't find a single thing and I feel like that should be a red flag."

My eyebrows pull together, flipping on my turn signal and pulling into the parking lot of the restaurant. It's relatively busy and takes a moment to find a spot. I don't turn to look at her until I kill the engine and undo my seatbelt.

"Why do you say that like it's a problem?"

She undoes her seatbelt and pushes open her door, immediately taking away the opportunity for me to do it for her. I've never seen Ella with her guard down, but this feels like she's building another wall to her fortress.

"Because it is," she says quietly as she turns away from me and glances out at the meadow. "No one is perfect, Wild. You have to have some kind of a flaw."

"I promise you I'm not perfect," I admit with a soft chuckle. I push open my own door and lower myself out of the truck. Ella doesn't make a move to get out, so I walk around to her side and hold my hand out to her. "Come have dinner with me and I'll tell you all about my flaws."

Her gaze drops down to my hand and she stares at it before placing her own in mine. Her palm is warm against my skin and I revel in the feeling of her as I wrap my fingers around the back of her hand. Ella steps onto the running board before lowering her boots onto the hardtop.

She's still holding onto my hand as she stands in front of me.

"Just so you know, a flaw doesn't have to be a red flag."

Releasing her hand, I push her door shut and begin to head in the direction of the restaurant. I wait for her to fall in step beside me and we walk to the front together.

We're both silent as we walk up to the hostess' desk and I give her my last name. She smiles, collecting the menus and asks us to follow after her. I step to the side, my hand finding the small of Ella's back instinctively. She doesn't move away from my touch and a pink tint creeps across her cheeks as she walks in front of me as the woman guides us out onto the back deck.

When I called, I requested a private table out here. I love the view, with the way it looks out across the plains with the mountain right behind you. She takes us to a table that is tucked away from everyone else. I move in front of Ella, pulling out her chair for her before she sits down.

"Here are the food and drink menus," the woman tells us with a bright smile as we both sit across from one another. "Your server will be with you in a few minutes."

Ella and I both thank her at the same time and I don't miss the way the blush creeps across Ella's cheeks as she drops her eyes to the menu. She lifts it up in an attempt to hide from me. I give her a few moments of that before I reach over and push it down, just enough that her gaze can meet mine above the laminated pages.

"I'm surprised you've never been here before," I admit, looking over my own menu.

"I haven't had anyone to bring me," she says quietly as

she reaches for the drink menu. "Is there anything you'd recommend?"

My gaze lifts to hers. "I've only been here once before with my family. I can tell you what everyone liked, though."

I go through the things I would recommend, along with the drinks. When our server appears and Ella orders one of the bourbon drinks I suggested, I can't help but smile and tell the woman I'll have the same. We fall into a comfortable conversation, one that's relatively mundane as we both discuss what we'd like to eat. Ella settles for a fish entree and I end up choosing the same again.

Ella lifts an eyebrow at me after our server leaves. "Are you copying me?"

I take a sip of my drink and smirk as I set it down. "What can I say? You have good taste."

"Tell me your flaws, Cole Wild."

Tilting my head to the side, I lean back in my seat and let my hands fall into my lap. "Are you lookin' for a reason not to like me?"

"Answer my question first."

Technically, she didn't ask me a question, but I keep that thought to myself. Even though she's still guarded, something has changed about her. She appears to be comfortable with me right now and I have no intention of sabotaging that.

"Flaws... okay." I pause and look past her, sifting through my brain for things that might fit her criteria. "I have a habit of forgettin' about the clothes in the washer, I mismatch my socks frequently, and I am a poor sport when it comes to playin' board games."

Ella doesn't say anything for two heartbeats. "Those aren't flaws, Cole."

"I may or may not have flipped a few Monopoly boards in my life."

Conflict and relief mix together in her expression, warring with one another. "Tell me the worst thing you've ever done."

The worst thing I've done. What the hell? I want to strangle the person who gave her the reason to have these questions about people.

"I don't know that I have an answer for that, Ella," I admit, disappointed I can't give her what she wants. She's looking for a reason to run in the opposite direction and that's not something I can offer her. "When my brother and I were kids, Cash and I were tryin' to trip the other and I ended up fallin' and scraped my knee, so I pushed him and he fell face first into a pile of cow manure."

She stares at me for what feels like an eternity. "That's the worst?" It's almost as if she's having a difficult time trying to understand or believe me.

"That's the only memory that sticks out in my mind." I lean forward, resting my forearms on the table. "I won't pretend like I know what happened in your past, but I just want you to know that not everyone is bad. Not everyone has ill intentions."

Ella's lips part and the conflict laces in her expression again. "Maybe not," she breathes, her voice barely above a whisper. Her gaze locks on mine. "I have difficulties trusting people."

I nod in understanding. "I get that. I'm not askin' you to trust me," I explain to her in an attempt to remove any pressure or expectations. "All I'm askin' for is a chance to show you that you can trust me."

"That's it?"

A smile lifts the corners of my lips. "That's it," I repeat.

She's silent again as if she's at war with herself. I don't miss the tortured look in her eyes that is washed away by resilience. A confidence she's still trying to get a grasp on. As she pulls her bottom lip between her teeth, she blinks, releases her lip, and lets out a soft breath.

"Okay," she says with a gentleness in her tone. She doesn't elaborate, doesn't say anything else. She simply sits there and stares at me with a small spark of hope shimmering in her eyes.

And in this moment, I make a promise to myself and silently to her.

I will never let that spark diminish from her eyes.

I will help her feed and cultivate it until the only thing she sees is the good this world has to offer.

CHAPTER FIFTEEN

ELLA

Cole steps to the side, holding the door open for me as I step across the threshold. There's another couple waiting to get through and I give the woman a small smile and move aside to wait for Cole. He stops next to me, his arm brushing against my own. A gasp escapes me and I quickly look up at him, my lips parting involuntarily.

"Can I be honest?" He asks me, his voice soft and gentle as he turns to face me. I shift my body, so we're standing toe to toe. He lifts his hand, his fingertips brushing against the side of my face as he pushes a stray tendril of hair from my cheek.

"Yes," I whisper, silently begging for nothing but his honesty.

The ball in his throat rolls as he swallows roughly. "I'm not ready for the night to be over. I'm not ready to take you home yet."

A wave of excitement washes over me, my heart picking up the pace in my chest as it begins to thrum harder. "Neither am I."

The softest smile breaks out across his lips. Cole folds his arm, offering me the crook of his elbow as he holds his palm against his abdomen. "Would you like to go for a walk with me?"

I can't decipher whether I'm nervous or excited; maybe a mixture of the two. My heart beats harder. Fast. This is a chance moment, one I'm not quite sure I want to slip away. Pulling my lips between my teeth, I roll them together before releasing them. I exhale, rolling the dice, and thread my arm through his, linking us together.

"Lead the way."

Cole's smile doesn't falter. His scent—leather and bourbon—infiltrates my senses. My eyelids flutter shut, only for a fraction of a second as my mind catalogs the way he smells. We fall into step together while Cole guides me away from the restaurant and through the parking lot. It's a short walk to the water and he leads me toward a path through the trees.

As we reach the edge of the clearing, Cole comes to a standstill, kicking off his boots and releases my arm. I watch him for a second, studying the way his shirt tightens around his muscles as he bends over, takes off his socks and grabs his boots. I slip my own feet from my boots and collect them before we're both standing upright again.

"Shall we?" he questions me as the moonlight dances across his face, illuminating his bright blue eyes. Cole moves his hand in a sweeping motion, gesturing toward the path that leads into the sandy area along the bend.

My eyes trace his facial features, memorizing the arches of his eyebrows and the way the smallest dimples form in his cheeks when he smiles. "We shall," I say quietly with a nod, holding my boots by my side and walking past him.

Granules of sand tickle the spaces between my toes as

they sink beneath the surface with every step. My footsteps are light as I pad across the powder, following along the path until it leads to the deserted beach along the river-bend. A few pieces of driftwood are sticking out of the ground and I move around them as we head down to the water.

The waves are gentle, caressing the shore as it dances across the tan sand. A soft breeze drifts past my face, swirling stray wisps of hair that broke free from my hair tie. Dropping my sandals onto the ground, I grab a handful of my dress, lifting it higher up my calves before stepping into the river. The water is crystal clear and cool, shifting around my ankles as I wade in a little farther.

A sense of peace and calm settles over me, soothing my soul. My eyes fall shut and I inhale deeply, tipping my head back. Since I moved back to Silverspur Springs, I've been waiting for the other shoe to drop. For Jacob to change his mind and show up. For everything to go up in flames.

Moments like these are few and far between. They are fleeting and I grasp at them like sand running through the cracks between my fingers. If I can get one second of peace, one heartbeat where everything is calm, I hold onto it as tightly as I can, holding my breath until the moment passes.

And then I exhale, feeling reality awakening around me.

Slowly opening my eyes, I turn back to look at Cole, expecting him to be standing with me, but he isn't. He's at the edge of the water, the breeze tousling the waves on top of his head, brushing strands of hair across his forehead. His hands hang loosely by his sides and his gaze penetrates mine.

Vehement emotions swirl within the depths of his irises as he watches me with his lips parted.

"What are you doing?" I question him, my voice breaking into jagged shards over my words.

The slightest creases form around the corners of his eyes as his cheeks lift. "Savoring the view."

I tilt my head to the side with butterflies fluttering to life in my stomach. "Of the river?"

Cole chuckles with a tenderness as he shakes his head once. His feet begin to move, his strides long as he closes the distance between us. He steps into the crystal clear water only coming to a stop as his toes brush mine beneath the surface.

"The view of you."

My throat constricts, my breath catching within the confines as he plucks the oxygen from my lungs with his words. I swallow roughly, forcing my emotions back down into my chest, tucking them away in the neat little box I keep them in. I'm conflicted—so goddamn torn.

"Cole," I start, my voice trailing off as his name dissolves on my tongue.

He smiles at me, shaking his head again as a touch of sadness creeps into his expression. "Compliments are allowed to be accepted, El." He pauses, letting out a ragged breath. "Please, just let me speak my truth."

The fact that he reads me like an open book has me instinctively wanting to take a step away. It's like he reaches inside my brain and plucks my thoughts out with his fingertips. My facade is threatened by him. My mask has cracks in it and if he stares too intently, too closely, he'll see the broken pieces inside.

What happened with Jacob and I destroyed my self

image and confidence. Only within the past year have I grown more confident in myself and in my own skin.

I struggle accepting compliments from Remi and Iris. My mind can't even begin to fathom accepting them from someone like Cole.

Someone who might mean it.

"Tell me about yourself," I chance, breaking through the silence, attempting to shift the conversation. It's an easy question, almost like an icebreaker. I'm not asking him to tell me his deepest, darkest secrets. Just the simple things.

"You already know me." Cole tips his head to the side as he tucks his hands into the front pockets of his shorts. "What do you want to know, El?"

"Pretend this is your first time meeting me. What would you tell me if I were a complete stranger?"

Amusement dances in his eyes and he laughs quietly as he ducks his head. I watch him walk a slow circle around me, gently kicking the water with the tips of his toes. Droplets scatter along the surface of the river. He's silent with his own thoughts and I desperately want to know what he's thinking.

I want to know what keeps making him look at me from the corner of his eye with a coy smile, like he's cradling a secret only he knows.

"What if we play a game?"

My lips form a flat line and I snort with annoyance, although I'm not annoyed at all. I'm entertained by this man. Enchanted, if you will. "We're not children anymore, Cole."

He chuckles softly, shaking his head. "No, I know that, Ella. Trust me." His eyes darken slightly before softening. "Let's do two truths and a lie. That's easy enough, right?"

I swallow back the hesitation. "Right. You go first."

Cole blinks, a smirk lifting his lips. "Okay. I never planned on staying in Silverspur Springs, but after I left, I found myself wanting to be back here." He pauses as a thoughtful look passes through his eyes.

His voice dissipates, getting carried away by the breeze. I don't care what words he speaks, I only want to hear more. I want to hear everything.

"That's only one thing."

He titters, glancing at me from the corner of his eye. "Greedy," he mumbles as he shifts his weight on his feet and moves beside me.

My heart skips a beat as his arm brushes against mine and he doesn't move away. We both stare out at the river, the stars speckled in the night sky above us.

"My favorite color is green. I wanted to ride bulls instead of playing baseball, but I chose baseball instead." He lets out a breath and turns to look at me. "And I enjoy long walks along the river at night."

"We're not even walking," I say pointedly as a smile creeps across my lips. I look at him and meet his eyes.

He shrugs with a mischievous grin. "Tomato, tomato. Standin' or walkin'—I just like the water."

"Fair enough, but that was four different things."

"Damn," he chuckles, wrapping his hand around the back of his neck. "It was, wasn't it?"

"Yep," I laugh softly. "The lie was riding bulls. You never wanted to do that."

His eyes narrow, not in a negative way, but like he's assessing me. "How do you know that?"

"Because I remember you talking about it when we were younger. You were only ever interested in baseball, not rodeoin'"

"Hm," he blows out a breath. "Alright. It's your turn now."

Well, darn. I didn't think about me having to do the same thing. I shift my weight from foot to foot, anxiety dancing in the pit of my stomach.

"Are we keeping things superficial?"

"You're in control, Ella" he tells me in a hushed tone, his eyes burrowing through mine. "We can go as deep as you want."

Heat creeps up my neck, quickly spreading across my cheeks and I break the stare, looking back out at the river, clearing my throat. I give myself a moment, trying not to focus on the two different meanings his words could hold. The surface of the water shifts, shimmering beneath the moonlight.

"Yellow is my favorite color. My favorite food is home-made apple pie. I also like to paint."

Cole doesn't say anything at first and I reach up to push a chunk of my hair behind my ear. A nervousness washes over me and I quickly push the uncomfortable feeling away. My spine straightens and I stand firm in the things I told him, feeling confident, even though the self doubt creeps around the edges. I chose the safest, most superficial option of telling him the same kind of things he said to me.

He turns to face me and I mimic his actions. "You hate apple pie," he finally says. "You still paint?"

"Um," I start, my eyebrows momentarily pinching together. It wasn't the question I was expecting. "I do, but just for fun."

"I'd like to see them sometime."

Absolutely not. My paintings are private. Chloe and Remi are the only ones who see them and I've been turning down Remi's stupid suggestions of doing something with my art for a while now.

"They're not all done. I ran out of supplies and haven't had a chance to get more yet." The words tumble from my lips in a nervous rush. I shouldn't have even brought up painting, but I didn't think that was the one piece of information he'd hold on to. "I don't think they're ready for anyone else to see."

He stares at me for a second, his gaze holding onto mine before he nods. "That's okay," he assures me with a tender smile. "You can always tell me no, but if you ever decide to change your mind, I'd very much like to see them."

My lips part and I shut them before responding. "Okay."

Why can't my brain form any coherent thoughts tonight?

A droplet of rain randomly falls from the sky, landing on my cheek. Lifting my chin, I tilt my head back, watching the clouds as they begin to hide the stars. There's a low rumble of thunder off in the distance and I feel another drop of rain on my skin.

"Well, this is disappointin'," Cole says quietly as he lets out a sigh. "I suppose we should probably go."

I'm not ready to return to reality. It's like we are encapsulated in our own little bubble, tucked away from the rest of the world. Chloe is safe with Remi and this is the first time in many years that things have been quiet in my soul. I haven't once looked over my shoulder, haven't second guessed a single second on this beach with Cole Wild.

"Just a little bit longer?"

Cole smiles and nods, a look of contentment settling across his expression. "As long as you want."

Silence settles around us, enveloping us in its warmth.

It isn't long before there's another rumble of thunder, followed by a flash of lightning, illuminating the night sky.

"Wyatt's comin' back to town next week," I say, lifting my eyes up to look at the sky.

"Oh yeah? How long will he be here?"

"Only for the day," I say, my voice quiet. "It's the anniversary of our parents' accident, so he said he'd come visit their graves with me."

Cole is quiet for a beat. "I'm sorry, El."

"It's okay," I offer, shrugging my shoulders, turning back to look at him. "It will be three years, which is crazy." I let out a breath, shaking my head. "I miss them, but it's gotten easier, ya know?" Guilt pricks my heart when I admit the words out loud.

Cole nods, his expression thoughtful. "They'd be proud of both of you."

My chest constricts and emotion wells in my throat. "Thanks," I say, my voice barely above a whisper. I roll my lips, tears stinging my eyes as a crack of lightning sounds around us, streaking across the sky as it illuminates the darkness.

Cole immediately steps closer. "Let's get out of this storm before we get struck by lightning."

The droplets of rain are progressively getting larger as they begin to fall faster. "I think that might be a good idea," I agree with a soft laugh.

It's as if the sky decides to open up at that moment, bringing on a downpour. Cole grabs my hand, making a run for it as we race across the beach, back toward the path that cuts through the dunes. My feet pound against the ground and laughter bubbles out of me as my hair whips behind me.

We're out of breath when we reach Cole's truck and he

fumbles with the key and ends up dropping it on the ground. "Dammit," he groans, laughing as he bends down to pick it up.

"Shoot, I forgot my shoes," I half laugh, half mumble, bumping into the side of him accidentally.

Cole stops, turning to look at me as the rain falls harder. Concern washes over his expression and he shifts his weight like he's about to move in the direction we came from. "I can go get them."

I shake my head dismissively, reaching out to grab his arm to stop him. "It's okay, I have other pairs." Cole falls silent, his eyes scanning my face like he's memorizing the placement of every freckle before his gaze meets mine again. "What?"

His eyebrows pinch before releasing. "God, you're beautiful," he breathes, like the admission is a weight off his chest. Something unreadable passes through his eyes and I find myself drawn to him.

My feet move without my direction, inching closer to him until I have to tilt my head back to look up at him. He looks conflicted as torment weaves itself through his expression and the fire burning in his eyes. He lifts his hands, his movements soft and slow as he cradles the side of my face.

He slowly lowers his head, his lips a fraction of an inch away from mine. My breath gets caught in my throat, my heart threatening to break free from my rib cage as Cole's breath fans across my face.

"I really wanna kiss you right now, but I'm not goin' to."

Rejection hits me like a freight train. "Why?"

"Because once I start, I'm afraid I won't be able to stop." He pauses, pulling back enough that his gaze collides with mine. "When this does happen, I want you to be ready for it. I don't want you to second guess anythin' between us."

My heart lodges in my throat. "What if I'm never ready?"

"One day, El," he says gently as he lifts his head and presses his lips against my forehead. "One day, you will be. And I'll be here waitin'."

CHAPTER SIXTEEN

ELLA

Chloe releases my hand and breaks out into a skipping movement as she heads down the path through the cemetery. The sun shines in the sky above without a single cloud in sight. It warms my skin and I watch Chloe, falling in step beside my brother as we both carry our own bouquets of flowers.

"I wish I had half the energy she has," Wyatt says quietly, a soft laugh following his words as we trail behind her. Chloe pauses at the end of the row, glancing over her shoulder at the two of us.

I point to the right and she smiles, heading in that direction. "I know. I've had no choice but to become a morning person with her."

"Well, she's a happy little girl, El. And that's all that matters."

I let out a soft breath, both of our steps slowing as we reach their headstone. "I know," I breathe, smiling at Chloe as I wave her over. She went past the gravesite, but didn't wander too far.

She comes skipping over to us as Wyatt and I both

stand in front of the piece of granite with both of our parents' names etched into it. The manicured grass is deep green and trimmed along the bottom. A soft breeze blows across us, carrying the air from the mountain through my hair. Reaching up, I brush a stray tendril, kneeling down to hand the flowers to Chloe.

Her smile grows wider across her lips as she plops down onto her butt, holding the flowers in front of her. I crouch down, helping her slide them into the vase that's built into the headstone.

Emotion wells in my throat, my chest constricting and I place my hand against the stone. It's cold against my palm and I know neither of them are truly here, but it helps me to connect. My eyelids fall shut, my lungs expanding as I suck in a ragged breath.

I miss them so much it hurts sometimes. Time has helped to ease the pain, but there are moments where it just feels like there's an emptiness lingering inside of my ribcage. The corners of my eyes begin to burn and I squeeze my lids tighter, attempting to keep the tears from breaking free.

The lump lodged in my throat aches and I swallow over it, my nostrils flaring. I suck in another shallow breath. God, I wish they were both here. I miss the sound of her voice and the tightness of his hugs. The first tear falls, followed by a string of others, trailing down my cheeks.

"Mama," Chloe says softly, her tone an octave higher with a twinge of worry. "Mama hurt?"

My eyelids lift and I find Chloe standing directly in my face, her features blurred by my tears. A smile lifts the corners of my lips and I remove my hand from the stone, hastily wiping the moisture away from my cheeks.

"Yes, baby," I murmur, wrapping my arms around her,

pulling her flush against my torso. "Mama just misses your grandma and grandpa."

Chloe wraps her arms around my neck, pushing her weight against me as she silently holds on for a moment. "To-tay, Mama," she murmurs, patting my back. "No sad."

A soft chuckle escapes me and I smile through the tears. "Thank you, Clo. Mama isn't sad anymore."

She pulls away, bringing her hand to my cheek as she gives me a soft pat and kisses the tip of my nose. She releases me, spinning around to face the headstone, just as a butterfly flutters past. I watch it as it dips through the breeze, landing on top of the granite stone.

Chloe lets out a low 'ooo' sound, her lips round as she watches it in amazement. Movement from the corner of my eye has me turning to look at my brother, his eyes damp as he leans down to slide his bouquet into the other attached vase.

Rocking back on my heels, I push upward, standing beside him as we watch Chloe inch closer to the butterfly. She reaches out her tiny fingers and the butterfly lifts back into the air. It slips past me and Chloe runs behind me, watching as it floats away.

"They both would have loved her," Wyatt says quietly as we turn around to watch her as she steps into the pathway that winds around the cemetery. She walks over to the other edge of the grass, plucking a dandelion from the ground below.

"She would have loved them too," I say, my voice barely above a whisper. "I wish they were here."

"So do I, sis," Wyatt admits as he slides his arm over the tops of my shoulders, pulling my side against his. "I miss both of them every single day."

I turn to look up at my brother, his dark blue eyes meeting mine. "They'd be proud of you, you know." A tender smile drifts across my lips. "You're making a difference in the world. You're saving lives."

His smile is sad as he looks down at me. "It won't bring them back," he says softly, his voice filled with sorrow. "I hope I can save someone from suffering the same fate as them."

"And even if you can't, it's because it was beyond your control," I remind him. My brother has always been his biggest critic. Living with the guilt of patients dying has to weigh heavily on him, even if he doesn't show it. "You always do the best you can."

He lets out a soft breath. "I know." He tears his gaze from mine, turning to look at Chloe as she sits down on the ground, picking the petals from the stem. "They'd be proud of you too."

"You think so?" I question him, watching Chloe as she stands back up and turns to face up.

"I know so," he says, giving my shoulder a squeeze before releasing me. "You've done well, little sis."

Chloe comes sprinting towards us, half tripping over her own feet as her giggling drifts through the breeze. She recovers without falling, stopping in front of Wyatt and I.

"You wanna go get ice cream, little one?" My brother asks her, bending down to scoop her up.

"It's not even lunchtime yet," I half scold him, a smile tugging at my lips as we turn back to the gravestone. My eyes trail over the lettering, over our parent's names.

Until we meet again.

"You know there's an international ice cream for breakfast day, right?"

"Is it today?" I question him, lifting an eyebrow.

"No, but we can pretend it is."

Chloe twirls her stem between her fingers before looking at me eagerly. "Eye cweem?"

I bite back my grin, rolling my eyes at my brother before tapping Chloe on the nose. "Only because you asked."

Wyatt chuckles, glancing back at the headstone before he starts to walk away. I pause for a beat, staring back at the granite stone.

"Love you mom and dad," I tell it quietly, the words catching on the lump in my throat. I linger for a moment or two, my heart beating steadily in my chest before I turn away and follow after my brother and my daughter.

Wyatt holds her close to his chest and I watch her as she points out into the distance, the two of them having a quiet conversation as we head through the cemetery and make our way through the gates. Dust kicks up from Wyatt's shoes as he walks through the gravel, heading to his truck parked in the small lot along the road.

"I'm glad you were able to come today," I tell my brother as we fall in step walking up to the passenger's side of his truck. I pull open the back door for him, moving out of his way as he sets Chloe down in her carseat. "It was nice to do this together."

"I'm sorry I'm not around more," he tells me, stepping back after securing her buckles. He grabs the door, gently closing it. "I just—it's hard, being in Cheyenne."

I reach for his hand, giving him a gentle squeeze. "I know, Wy. We're just glad you're here right now."

He squeezes mine back, his smile not reaching his eyes before he lets go. There's sadness in his gaze before he turns away and walks around to his side. I glance back at the cemetery one last time before climbing into the truck.

Wyatt has made a life for him outside of Silverspur and I can never be anything but proud of him. *Just like our parents would be.*

The three of us find an empty table out front of the creamery and sit down with our ice cream. Chloe lifts her spoon, a few rainbow sprinkles rolling off the scoop as she pushes it past her lips. Chocolate coats them, making a mess around her mouth, but it doesn't bother her at all.

"Darn, girl, you're messy!" Wyatt laughs, handing her a napkin. "I think we're going to need more of these than what we grabbed."

I laugh softly, looking at the small pile that we had collected at the counter. "Yeah, you're probably right," I agree, sticking my spoon back into my bowl. "I'll be right back."

I get up, watching Chloe shoving another spoonful into her mouth. Wyatt laughs at her, taking a bite of his and I leave them both at the table. I head back into the ice cream shop, walking over to the counter to grab more napkins. After collecting more than enough, I hold them in my hand, making my way back out onto the sidewalk. A couple passes by me and I sidestep to avoid walking into them, right as I collide with a hard, warm body.

"Oh my gosh, I'm so sorry," I say in a rush, my eyes widening as a few napkins break free from my grip. I reach to grab them as they float through the air, but a hand grabs them first.

"Well, hey there, darlin'." His voice vibrates through my body, immediately capturing my attention. My eyes bounce to his, my heart skipping a beat inside my chest.

"Cole." I let out a breath, heat creeping up my neck as it threatens to spread across my face. "Hi. I'm sorry, I didn't see you."

"No worries," he says, waving his hand before handing me the napkins. "I told you before, you can run into me anytime." He pauses, his head tilting slightly to the side as he looks at the creamery and back at me. "Are you eating ice cream for breakfast?"

A sheepish grin breaks out across my face and I nod before motioning over to the table. "We were at the cemetery and it was Wyatt's idea."

Cole's expression softens, his eyes warm and tender as he stares at me for a moment. My breath catches in my throat, my heart jerking. His feet move, inching closer to me as he extends his arm. His fingertips brush against mine and my stomach flutters, just as I think he's going to pull me to him.

"Oh thank god, there you are," Wyatt's voice sounds behind me, immediately pulling me from the moment. Cole's hand drops away and my fingertips itch to feel his again. "Your daughter is about to be covered in chocolate." I turn around to look at him and he looks past me. "Well, aren't you a sight for sore eyes?" He laughs, walking past me to Cole.

I leave the two of them to reunite, hearing the sound of their voices behind me. I walk back to the table where Chloe's waiting. The bottom half of her face is covered in chocolate and she smiles at me, licking her lips as she puts her spoon back in the ice cream.

Laughter bubbles out of me and I slide onto the seat with her, turning her to face me and I start to wipe the chocolate away. "Uncle Wy was right. It looks like you took a bath in chocolate."

Chloe giggles, wiggling in her seat as she half fights me, reaching for one of the napkins to try to help clean her own face. My own ice cream is melting, Chloe's is three quarters of the way gone, and Wyatt's bowl is empty.

I clean Chloe's face as best as I can as Wyatt and Cole walk over to the table. Wyatt slides back into his seat, but Cole doesn't move to sit beside him. He stands at the table, sliding his hands into the front pockets of his jeans.

He dips his chin at Chloe, smiling at her. "Hey Miss Chloe."

"Hi!" She says brightly, lifting her hand to wave at him. Cole chuckles, staring at her for a moment before looking back at me. His lips part slightly, his blue eyes lingering on mine.

"Did you want to sit?" I ask him, my voice soft and I motion toward the bench. My heart pounds a little harder inside my chest.

Cole shakes his head. "Thank you, but I oughta get goin'. Cash's waitin' for me to get back." He glances at Wyatt. "What time are you headin' out?"

"Later this evening," my brother tells him, rolling his wrist to check his watch. "Probably after dinner."

Cole's head bobs up and down in understanding. "We'll plan on gettin' together next time you're in town." He looks at me, mischief dancing in his eyes before he looks at my brother again. "Is it okay with you if I take Ella out to dinner again sometime?"

My eyes widen, my stomach doing a somersault as I'm caught off guard by his question. What the heck is he doing?

Wyatt raises an eyebrow at Cole, glancing at me before looking at him again. His eyebrows slowly lower and he narrows his eyes at Cole for a moment. "You like spending time with my sister?"

"She keeps me out of trouble," Cole tells him, winking at me before looking at my brother. He gives him a simple shrug. "I like company that isn't either of my brothers, sometimes," he tells him with a chuckle.

"I don't mind," Wyatt says after another moment of silence.

"You don't?" I blurt out, before I get the chance to swallow back the words.

Wyatt looks at me. "You deserve to have some fun, Ella. I trust Cole and he knows I'll—" he pauses, curling his fingers into a fist as he sticks out his thumb and runs it across his neck, "if he does anything," he adds.

Cole chuckles. "I like being alive very much, thank you," he tells both of us. "So, what do you say, El? You wanna get dinner later this week?"

My heart crawls into my throat and I look at my brother and back at Cole. "I'm off on Thursday."

"Perfect," Cole smiles, showing his white teeth. "I'll pick you up at six." Cole puts his hand out to my brother. "We'll catch up soon, bud."

"Sounds good," Wyatt stands, shaking Cole's hand as they pull each other in for a half hug. "Thanks for watching after these two."

Cole releases him, taking a step back. "Always," he promises my brother, grabbing the brim of his hat as he dips his chin. "Y'all have a good day."

I watch Cole as he turns around, heading past the creamery and down the street. My gaze lingers, following after him as he makes his way to his truck.

"Is there somethin' goin' on with you and Cole?" Wyatt questions me, his voice breaking through the moment.

I swallow roughly, tearing my eyes from Cole as I glance at my brother. "No, we're just friends," I say in a rush, clearing my throat. I push my spoon through the melted ice cream. Chloe laughs, reaching over to dip her spoon in with mine. "I'm perfectly content with it only being Chloe and I."

"Okay," Wyatt says, almost with hesitation. His eyes slowly search mine, his chest rising and falling. "He's one of my best friends." He pauses, blowing out a breath. "The thought of there bein' anything between the two of you is weird and I'm not sure I wanna think about it, but if there's one person I would trust to keep you safe, it's him."

I laugh softly, shaking my head at him. "It's not like that, Wy."

He raises an eyebrow. "Maybe for you, but I'm not so sure about him anymore."

My heart stutters inside my chest. "I doubt that," I chuckle, the sound foreign and I try to ignore the nervousness that flips my stomach. "We've only been spending time together as friends."

Chloe flicks her wrist, splashing the melted ice cream from the bowl. It flies across the table, almost hitting Wyatt as he moves out of the way.

"Okay, I think we're done," I chuckle, pulling the bowl away from Chloe. Wyatt is already on his feet, collecting all the trash and takes the melted ice cream from me.

"Good idea," Wyatt laughs, as he throws the trash away and comes back over as I'm lifting Chloe into my arms. "Let's go find something else to do to keep that little monster busy."

"Rawrrr!" Chloe bellows at him, her voice too high to be frightening, but he cowers anyway, earning a belly laugh from her. I fall in step with my brother and Chloe reaches for him. I hand her over to him as we head down the sidewalk to his truck.

Wyatt and Chloe are both making monster noises at each other when I hear a soft beep from the street. Whipping my head to the side, I glance over, catching a quick glimpse of Cole as he drives past us. He holds his hand out the window, waving as he passes.

Wyatt stops beside his truck, waving back at him before putting Chloe into her seat. I step out onto the street, walking to my door when I catch Cole's gaze in the rearview mirror.

He stares back at me, his mouth curving as he shuts his right eye, winking at me. He gives the truck more gas, the rumble of the engine echoing down the street as he zips away. My breath catches in my throat, my heart hammering against my ribcage and I watch his taillights fade into the distance.

CHAPTER SEVENTEEN

COLE

ELLA

I hate to do this, but unfortunately I'm
having some babysitting issues so I have to
cancel tonight.

I reread her message again, wishing that the words on the screen would change. Standing in the bathroom, I reposition my towel around my waist before typing out a response. I was supposed to be leaving in thirty-five minutes to go pick her up for dinner. I would be lying if I said I wasn't disappointed.

It's okay. I hope that everything is okay.

ELLA

It is. Remi is working and Iris had
something come up with a vendor for the
bar, so she has to go out of town for the
evening. Would we be able to reschedule?

A sigh escapes me and I set my phone down to finish drying off and get dressed. I understand with Ella's life there are a lot of moving parts, so I'm not upset with her that this happened. I only wish there was something I could do about it.

And then I realize there is something I can do about it.

Maybe I can't take her out to dinner, but I can certainly bring dinner to her.

What if we don't have to reschedule?

I watch the three small dots show up and disappear three separate times and it feels like my heart may spontaneously combust in my chest. Her response finally appears in the message thread.

ELLA

What do you mean?

Even though I've already met Chloe, I don't want to impose on her life. I don't want to insert myself somewhere I may not be welcome, out of respect for Ella and her daughter. Meeting her was a chance encounter at the grocery store that one day. I don't intend on seeing her again until Ella wants me to or would be comfortable with it.

What time does Chloe go to bed?

ELLA

Usually around seven thirty.

Why?

I smile to myself, walking through my house until I reach the kitchen. I love these little interactions with her. I love the way she questions everything, as long as she isn't questioning herself. Ella surprised me the other night with her admitting she liked knowing I told Austin about her.

She had a renewed sense of confidence I hadn't seen in her before. It looks good on her, even if it's something she isn't comfortable with yet.

> I have an idea, but if you don't like it, we
> can always reschedule.

She doesn't respond immediately and when she does, the corners of my lips stretch farther.

ELLA

Don't keep me waiting here.

> Since you can't go to dinner, I was thinkin'
> what about if I were to bring dinner to you.
>
> We can get takeout from wherever you'd
> like and I'll bring it over after Chloe is
> asleep.

It feels like an eternity as I wait for her response. My phone vibrates and I quickly check it, expecting it to be her, but it's only my brother telling me about the hay shipment coming in. I type out a message to him and Ella texts me back. I abandon the conversation with Cade entirely.

ELLA

That actually sounds really nice. Could we
get tacos or something like that?

A weight lifts from my chest and I let out the breath I didn't realize I was holding in.

> Absolutely. Let me know when Chloe is in
> bed and I'll come over.

ELLA

It's not a date.

Goddamn her and the things she's doing to my heart.

Just dinner.

Ella texted me a little after seven thirty and I already had an order placed with takeout to pick up on my way to her house. I saved her address from the last time and timed my route accordingly so I would be pulling into her driveway a little after eight.

And I'm right on time as I park my truck behind her car.

All of the lights look like they're off inside, but the light on her front porch shines brightly above me as I walk up the steps towards her door. Ella opens it when I reach the top step and I swear my heart skips three beats in a row.

Her hair is pulled back in a French braid and she's wearing a pair of soft black shorts and a simple white t-shirt. There's the smallest amount of makeup on her face, enough to illuminate her already strikingly beautiful features.

"Hey cowboy."

I stop in front of her, holding out a small bouquet of flowers. "Hey darlin'."

"What are these?" she questions me as she hesitantly takes the bundle of daisy's from my hand. "We agreed this wasn't a date, Wild."

I tilt my head to the side, feigning a look of innocence. "It's not a date."

"So, why the flowers?"

I shrug with a whole hearted attempt at appearing

indifferent. The acrobatic routine my stomach is doing says otherwise. "Because it's not a date."

A smile blooms across her face and I don't miss the pink tint that deepens on her cheeks. She steps out of the way, holding the door open. "Come in. I need to put these in a vase and we can eat out back."

I walk into her home and she pushes the door shut behind me. I do a quick survey of the space. It smells warm and welcoming like sugar cookies. *Like her.* There are a few toys scattered on the coffee table in the living room to the right of the foyer. I follow her into the kitchen and watch as she moves over to the sink along the back end of the house. Ella reaches into one of the cabinets, her body elongated as she lifts up onto her tiptoes. As she reaches above her head, the bottom hem of her shirt moves farther up her torso, revealing part of her midsection.

My mouth is dry, my heart pounding erratically in my chest as I study her movements, my eyes trailing along the sliver of skin. Her fingertips graze the outside of the glass vase and she's unable to grab it. Closing the distance between us, I stop when I'm beside her and I reach up for the vase she's trying to get.

"Let me get that for you," I say softly as my arm brushes against hers.

Ella sucks in a sharp breath and my fingers lightly brush hers as I wrap my hand around the vase and bring it down. It's not a far reach for me, seeing as I'm over a foot taller than her. Ella falls back onto flat feet, her head tilting back to look at me as I turn to face her.

"Thank you," she says with a shy smile as our fingers touch again when she takes the vase from me. The electrical current ripples between us and I want to reach out and wrap my hand around it. I want to savor the feeling.

Jesus christ, I want to savor every fucking moment with this woman.

We both fall into a moment of silence as she fills the vase with water. I take the opportunity to help, unwrapping the flowers before handing them to her. Ella quickly snips the bottoms of the stems, cutting them at an angle while I pour the powdered flower food into the water. Standing side by side, she slides the flowers into the water and arranges them until they're sitting in the vase perfectly.

"I love them," she says in the most gentle tone as she looks back at me with another smile. She takes a few steps to the island in the center of the kitchen and sets them down so they are the new centerpiece. "I love flowers," she tells me as she turns back around. A soft pink tint blossoms across her cheeks, like she's embarrassed she shared the small piece of information with me. "Come," she motions for me to follow her. "We should eat before the food gets cold. Do you want anything to drink?"

I don't tell her I don't care about the food.

I like these moments with her, away from the hustle and bustle of the bar. The soft, quiet moments where she shows me parts of herself I'm almost positive she doesn't share with anyone else.

"Sure."

"There's some water and beers in the fridge," she says and points toward it. "Do you mind grabbing them and I'll have whatever you decide on too?"

"Of course." I walk to the fridge, grabbing two waters and two beers before meeting her by the door. I don't want her to feel pressured to drink, so I'll let her choose and base my choice after hers.

Ella leads the way, heading out onto her back patio. There's a sectional set along the side of the house with a small fire pit in the center. Over to the right, there is a table with a set of chairs and a large umbrella overhead. My eyes scan the back yard, noticing the toys from Chloe scattered in the yard and a trampoline with netting around it in the back left corner.

"You have a beautiful home," I say, taking a seat across from her at the table. Ella's eyes meet mine and I see a mixture of emotion welling in the depths of her irises.

"Thank you," she says with a hoarseness in her voice. She opens the bag of food I brought, reaching inside before pulling out the separate containers. "It took me a while to get to where I am now and I wouldn't be here without Remi and her mother. They've done so much for me, helped me get on my feet so I can have a place like this for Chloe to grow up in."

I watch her for a moment as she pops open both containers. Each one has two tacos and a side of rice and beans. She looks over them, realizing the tacos are both the same kind, and hands me one.

"I'm sure you already know this, but you're doin' a great job, Ella." I take the plastic fork from her as she hands it to me. Setting it inside the styrofoam container, I look at her. "You are an amazing mother and it's clear to see that Chloe is loved and well taken care of."

She doesn't say a word. I swear, she doesn't breathe. Her gaze is glued to mine and emotion washes over her expression in one fluid motion before it pools in her irises. "I don't–I–Thank you," she stumbles over the words, again struggling with a compliment. "Sometimes it doesn't feel like I am, so it's nice to hear that."

Her words sink in as she turns her attention to her food. I watch her as she lifts a taco and takes a bite of it as I do the same with my own. I mentally make note that Ella enjoys words of affirmation. She may not realize it right now, and may struggle to accept compliments, but the emotion in her eyes is palpable. She's a single mom working to support her daughter, just out here trying her best and hoping she's doing everything right.

I know she has important people in her life, but it's clear that Ella needs to hear it more often.

She needs someone to remind her that she is doing her best and what she's doing isn't going unnoticed.

"How was your day?" I ask her, deciding to pull the conversation to a safer territory, away from a subject that is clearly packed full of emotion.

Ella looks back at me and dives into her day, telling me what she and Chloe did. I hang on to every goddamn word that falls from her perfect lips, fixated on the way they move and the shapes they take around the words she speaks. Ella turns the conversation to me, asking about my day, and it pales in comparison to the fun day she and Chloe had.

I tell her about the horses I worked with today and the calf that ended up getting into the wrong pasture. My brothers and I went on a wild goose chase for the little guy. I follow up by showing her pictures my mother sent from the work they're doing in Argentina.

Her face lights up. "That's so cool what they're doing there." She pauses for a moment. "South America is so beautiful."

"Have you been before?"

She nods. "My ex took me to Belize before I got pregnant with Chloe." Her words trail off, the silence enveloping us as her eyes grow distant and she looks past me into the darkness of her backyard. "That was a different lifetime."

My heart drops into my stomach. This is the first time she's ever spoken of her past. Part of me wants to keep the conversation going, for her to elaborate. Yet, I find myself not wanting to pour salt in her wounds. I don't want her to talk about her pain unless she absolutely wants to.

I decide to take a chance, to see if she'll continue or shut down.

"Did you travel often before Chloe was born?"

Ella nods as she sets down her taco and cracks open the beer. "Not often, but I've been to a few places."

My spine straightens and I drop my eyes down to my container to refrain from her seeing the way my blood is beginning to boil. She hasn't given me much, but it makes a little more sense why she responds the way she does. "Where is your favorite place you've been?"

"I loved France," she tells me and I find myself looking back at her as I hear the smile in her voice. "It was beautiful there and we were surrounded by art. Honestly, I didn't want to leave. I wanted to stay there for the rest of my life, spending my days drawing and painting."

She's so wistful in the way she speaks about her passion—another thing she hasn't really told me much about.

"What is your favorite medium?"

She tilts her head to the side, settling into the conversation with more comfort than she did the last time we spoke of her painting. "I love oil paints," she admits with a bashful smile. "They're my favorite to work with."

I don't put the pressure on her again about wanting to see her work. Instead, we transition the conversation through a multitude of safe topics, never once touching back over her past or painting again. The two of us finish our food and drain our beers until there's nothing left in the cans.

"Did you want another one?" Ella asks me as she rises to her feet and begins to clean up the empty containers.

Standing up with her, I help put the trash into the bag. "That would be great," I say as she rounds the table, taking the bag with her. "May I use your restroom?"

"Absolutely." I follow Ella into the house and she directs me down the small hallway. "It's the room at the end of the hall," she instructs as she pushes the trash into the can and walks over to the fridge.

Leaving her in the kitchen, I wander to the bathroom to relieve my bladder. After flushing and washing my hands, I pull the door back open and step out into the hall. There's a door that is cracked open to my right and I catch sight of an easel with a large canvas sitting upon it. Glancing down the hall, I look for her before I peek through the small crack, looking at the painting. It's a land-scape of the mountains with cotton candy colored clouds dancing across the horizon.

"Cole?" Ella questions me as she steps into the hall, holding two beers, and catches me red handed. "What are you doing?"

Shit.

I slowly stand up straight, meeting her head on with my gaze with no apology for snooping. "When I was comin' out of the bathroom, your paintings caught my eye and I couldn't help myself."

She stares at me, unwavering before she lets out a sigh and walks over to me. Her scent invades my nostrils as she leans past me and pushes the door open. Her body brushes against mine. "I don't usually show these to anyone, but since you've already seen it, come on."

There's almost a twinge of defeat in her voice and I instantly feel regret. It's chased away as I follow her into the room and I see various paintings laid around the room and a stack on the floor. "Ella," I breathe her name, walking over to the wall, inspecting the paintings she has hanging. "These are breathtaking." She doesn't respond as I walk around the perimeter, taking in every piece of art she has created. "These belong in a museum."

Ella lets out a laugh as I turn around to face her. She stands in the center of the room, shaking her head at me. "That's a little generous."

My feet move on their own accord, my footsteps soft and I walk directly to her, stopping when my toes are a few inches from her own. "Who told you you weren't enough, El?" I question her, my voice barely audible as she tips her chin up to look at me. "Your paintings are incomparable to how beautiful you are, but goddamn, it's a close second."

"Cole," she breathes, her lips parting as she blinks. Her nostrils flare and she lets out a breath as I reach for her, cupping the side of her face with my left hand. Using my right, I trail my fingers across her cheek, pushing her hair behind her ear as her eyelids flutter shut. "Kiss me."

My heart stops in my chest. For a second, I'm afraid I'm hallucinating. "Are you sure?"

"Yes," she says as her eyes open and her gaze burns against mine. "I want nothing more than for you to kiss me right now."

My chest constricts and I cradle her face in both of my hands, my thumb sweeping across her bottom lip. "I feel like I've waited an eternity to do this," I admit, my voice hoarse, my thumb trailing along her cheek. My movements are slow and I bring my face down to hers, her eyelids fluttering shut again.

I close my own, breathing in the scent of her as our mouths touch. It's a soft brush at first, my lips grazing hers gently. Ella lets out a breath, sighing as I pull back a fraction of a centimeter, the electrical current rippling across my flesh. I inhale, dropping my mouth back to hers. My lips claim hers, kissing her with a tenderness that has my insides melting. Ella's hands grab my biceps as my tongue slides along the seam of her lips. She parts them, allowing me access as our tongues touch. She holds onto me, kissing me deeply as I steal the air from her lungs.

I breathe her in, memorizing the softness of her lips, savoring the moment, letting it consume me before I pull away from her. It takes every ounce of my self control. I have to stop it here before things go any farther. I have every intention of taking it as slow as she needs. She looks at me, her eyes glazed over as she lifts her fingertips to her swollen lips.

"I don't know the last time I was kissed like that," she admits breathlessly.

A smile dances across my face. "I'd like to make a habit out of it."

"Of what?"

My face dips back down to hers, my lips brushing against hers in the softest caress. "Kissin' you."

CHAPTER EIGHTEEN

ELLA

COLE

When do I get to see you again?

Outside of the bar, I mean.

I t's been three days since Cole brought me dinner.
Three days since I saw him.
And three days since he kissed me.

A little eager, aren't we?

I'm not in the habit of wastin' precious
time, El.

"Where the hell does she get all her energy from?" Remi questions me from where she's sitting on the bench next to me. We're tucked under a tree, shaded from the hot summer sun as Chloe runs around in the grass. She picks a flower and spins around, her dress twirling around her small body.

I smile, setting my phone down, watching my daughter explore the world with wonderment. "I ask myself the same question daily. I swear, sometimes it's her bedtime and I'm the one falling asleep during story time."

Remi laughs softly and I wave Chloe over, calling her name. "I feel safe telling you that has definitely happened to me when she has slept over."

Shaking my head, I laugh with her and hold my hands out as Chloe comes running. I lift her up, swinging her onto my lap. She holds out a flower, handing it to Remi.

"It's so pretty, Clo," Remi tells her as she tucks the flower behind her ear. "Where did you find it?"

"Ova dare," she says, pointing to a patch of wild flowers. She wiggles on my lap and looks up at me with her bright blue eyes. "Can I get moe, momma?"

I help her onto the ground and I swear her legs are moving before her feet touch the grass. "Of course, baby. We'll be here watching."

Remi and I are silent for a breath or two as we watch Chloe sprinting back towards the flowers. "You never did tell me how the other night went with Cole."

My heart skips a beat as I think back to that night. Instinctively, I raise my hand, my fingertips lightly touching my lips. I inhale sharply at the memory, the thought of his mouth claiming mine. No one has ever kissed me with a reverent passion like he did. I suppose that's what it feels like to be properly kissed.

Pulling my hand away from my mouth, I sit up a little straighter and clear my throat. "It was nice. He brought tacos over and we sat out back and ate."

There's a pregnant pause.

"That's it?" Remi probes, clearly unsatisfied with the minimal information I've given her.

I shrug with indifference, glancing at her before I look

back to Chloe. "I mean, I don't know what you want to hear, Remi. We're just friends."

Apparently friends that kiss now.

"Girl, have you been to the eye doctor?" She squints her eyes at me, leaning closer like she's inspecting my vision. "You have to be blind if you don't see the way that man looks at you."

"I am not blind. My vision is perfectly fine, thank you."

"So, you see it then?" She leans back against the bench.

I let out a sigh and shake my head as Chloe skips around. "I can assure you that we are only friends. We may have kissed, but that doesn't change anything between us. I'm not looking for a relationship right now… or ever."

Remi doesn't say a word. I wait almost half a minute before I turn my head to look at her. She's staring at me with her eyes wide, her jaw slightly agape. "What?" I ask her with my eyebrows tugging together. "I am perfectly fine with being single."

"Um, I'm already up to date on your relationship status, but hold on. Back up." She stands up and sits back down so she's now facing me. "He kissed you?"

My eyes widen and I quickly try to remember what I just said to her. I was thinking about the kiss, but surely I didn't speak it out loud. Unless I did and didn't realize it while I was rambling.

"No."

"Don't you dare lie to me, Ella May Daniels." Remi gives me an incredulous look, narrowing her eyes at me. "You literally just said you kissed."

"Did I?" I've always been a terrible liar. Considering the fact that I just spoke the truth before lying isn't helping my case at the moment. "I didn't mean to say that."

"Well, you definitely said it." Remi lets out a laugh as she shakes her head at me. "Okay, spill. How and when did this happen? He looks like he would be a good kisser. Please tell me he is because that would be so heartbreaking that your first kiss–after all the things you've been through–was terrible."

I stare at her for a beat before I let out a laugh. "You are by far the most annoying person I've ever met."

She clicks her tongue at me and taps on her wrist with her forefinger. "You're wasting precious time here."

"Fine," I agree with a long, exasperated sigh. "He was not a bad kisser. It was actually quite enjoyable. It happened at my house, after dinner. He went to the bathroom and I found him looking in my art room and it kind of happened…"

Remi smiles the biggest damn smile I've ever seen. "El, this is huge. This is such a big step for you and I want you to know I am insanely proud of you."

"It's not that big of a deal," I argue, trying to downplay the entire situation, but she is right. It is a big deal, considering the fact that I didn't think I was ready for this again. "Okay, I guess it is a little bit of a deal."

"Screw that!" She practically yells at me. I watch her face as she winces and glances at the elderly woman walking past us who is now giving her a disapproving frown. "Sorry," she apologizes with a small smile to the lady before she looks at me again. "This is a big deal. You went from being afraid of asking him to get dinner to letting him kiss you."

"I know," I admit, nodding my head even though heat is creeping across my cheeks. Something flutters in my stomach and my heart is currently operating in overdrive.

"Honestly, my mind is still reeling over the fact that it happened."

"Did he kiss you and then leave?"

I shake my head, rolling my lips between my teeth to fight back my grin. "We didn't make out, make out, but we kind of made out, you know?"

"Yeah, sure," she says with a shrug. "You guys made out."

"Not really. We kissed for a couple minutes and then stopped. It was getting late, so I walked him out to his car. He kissed me again and then he left."

"That was it?" She questions me with a burning curiosity. "He left with nothing else? The two of you didn't even make plans to see each other again?"

I'm giving her way more information than I intended, but I can't stop now. If I'm being honest, it's nice having her to talk to. Before Jacob, I was more open than I am now, but Remi is my best friend. She's the closest thing I have to a sister. She's a safe place for me to confide in. She has rightfully earned the opportunity to hear all the juicy details.

"He said he wants to make a habit out of kissing me."

Remi's jaw falls open and she smiles at me with her eyes shining brightly under the sunlight. "Holy shit, he's good."

"He is," I agree with a soft laugh. These feelings are foreign to me. Feelings I can't even put into words at this point. My mind is a jumbled mess from this man and I need a moment to straighten out my thoughts. "We've texted on and off the past few days."

"Okay, okay," Remi nods eagerly in agreement. "I like this plan." A devious grin pulls on her lips. "I'd be willing to bet it won't be long before he's asking when he can see you again."

I mull over her words, weighing them with my feelings. My heart knocks against my ribcage and there's a lightness in my chest. Those damn butterflies flutter their wings again.

"Is it bad that I want to see him?"

"Not at all." Remi's smile doesn't falter as Chloe comes running back to us. Remi rises to her feet and lifts Chloe into the air as she turns back to me. "It's a good thing, El. A real good thing."

"What's good?" Chloe asks the two of us in her sweet little voice. She pushes her hand into her pocket and pulls out her small pink truck and holds it out to me. It's the pink truck Cole gave her.

I take it from her, smiling as I spin the wheels with the tip of my index finger.

"Everything is good, baby."

Everything is good.

CHAPTER NINETEEN

COLE

Walking out of the barn, I pull the doors shut behind me, giving a once over to make sure everything is cleaned up. Cash is back on the road heading to another rodeo and Cade had to go into Cheyenne to meet with our accountant.

I walk along the gravel drive heading towards my truck, glancing up at the ever-changing colors of the sky as the sun begins to set off to the west. It's decorated in varying shades of orange and pink, along with wispy clouds scattered within the colors. It's something I missed when I was away. Coming home and being able to see the sunsets like this again truly is a gift.

I glance at the time on the dashboard as I climb into my truck. It's eight o'clock at night and I know tonight is one Ella typically works. It's been four days since I kissed her in her art room. For four days, I've been living as a starved man. The text messages between us aren't cutting it anymore.

I need to see her before I end up losing my mind.

Without a second thought, I turn on my truck and

head off the ranch, driving in the direction of the lake. I don't stop until I'm pulling into a spot outside of the bar.

My footsteps are light, yet purposeful as I stride down the dock, not stopping until I'm walking deep inside the building, heading straight to the counter. There's a man getting up from his stool and I use the opportunity to sit down when I see he paid his tab and is leaving for the night.

The place is unbelievably packed and so busy. It tends to calm down a bit after the dinner rush is over, but right now, it's hard to see an end in sight.

My eyes scan the bar and I catch a glimpse of Ella working on the other side. Her hair is pulled back in a high ponytail and she's looking down as she finishes garnishing a drink. I watch her body as she moves along the counter, smiling at a woman while she hands her a drink.

"Cole, what a surprise to see you here," Remi greets me with a wink as she clears the plate and empty glass away from me. She grabs a bottle of spray and a rag and quickly wipes down the spot in front of me.

"I thought I'd stop by for a drink after work."

She sets a square napkin in front of me. "I bet you did," she says, like she has a little inside joke I don't know about. I chuckle, winking at her. Jokes on her because I know all about it.

"What can I get you?"

I smile at her. "Ella would be nice."

Remi snorts, rolling her eyes as she shakes her head with a smirk. "I'll get her."

She walks over to Ella and her gaze collides with mine as she turns around. Her eyes are momentarily wide, almost as if she's shocked to see me here. She nods at Remi and I see her lips move as she says something to her. A shy smile drifts across her mouth as she quickly walks over to me.

"Hey cowboy," she says in greeting, her voice soft and a little breathless. "I'm getting ready to go on break. Did you want to meet me out back?"

"Absolutely," I nod, rising to my feet. She looks around for a moment, almost as if she's in a panic before looking at the clock and back to me. I can see the conflict in her expression and take the opportunity to ease her worried mind. "Take your time, El. I'm not goin' anywhere."

She gives me a small smile and bobs her head. "Thank you."

I watch her head over to the other side of the bar before I walk to the front door and slip outside. Walking through a few groups, I round the side of the restaurant and head to the back of the building. There's no one out here, so I lean against the railing, watching the water splashing against the poles buried deep beneath the surface.

A few minutes pass before I hear the door behind me open and close. Pushing away from the railing, I turn around and see Ella as she walks closer to me.

"It is insane in there tonight," she says with a sigh as she adjusts her ponytail. She walks past me and leans her back against the trailing as we both turn to face one another.

"Has it been this busy all day?"

Ella shakes her head. "It's been like this lately in the evenings." She tilts her head back, looking up at the night sky. "Don't get me wrong, I love working here. I am so grateful for the opportunities Iris and Remi have given me, but I do not want to do this forever."

I walk over to the railing and link my fingers together

as I lean against it again, looking out to the lake. "What do you wanna do?"

"I don't know," she says softly as she lifts her head upright. "I haven't really given it much thought."

"What about your art?"

Ella half snorts and half laughs. "That's only a hobby, Cole. It's not something I could ever plan on making a career out of."

My head moves sideways and I study her profile, counting the freckles on the right side of her nose. "Says who?"

"Do you hear how ridiculous that sounds?" She laughs to cover up the pain as she looks at me. I don't miss the way it swirls within the depths of her irises. "I have no formal training or experience. I didn't go to college and study art. It's something I do for myself."

"Don't do that, Ella," I say as I stand upright, my hands gripping the railing.

She turns her body as I do the same. "Do what?"

"Don't discredit yourself like that. Art can't be taught, it can only be felt. There are plenty of people who try to learn it and lack natural ability." I pause for a second, calculating my moves before following through on the thought. "You are incredibly talented, El. It's not something you should let go to waste."

Emotion washes over her expression as she stares at me for a breath. She blinks, as if she's pulling herself from the moment and drops her gaze to the wooden floorboards beneath us. "It's a nice thought, but I don't even know how I would go about trying to get my art out there."

I watch her as she lifts her head back up and gives me a sad smile. I've witnessed a multitude of emotions on Ella's face since I've met her and I think I've just encountered the one I dislike the most. The one I never want to see dancing in her irises again.

"Austin's cousin owns a gallery in the city." My mind drifts to Vera. I've met her before at Austin's house. "She's an art dealer and has a lot of big spending, high profile clientele."

Her eyes widen and her lips momentarily part as if my words surprise her. She clamps her mouth shut and swallows roughly before shaking her head. "I can't ask you to say anything to Austin." She looks down at her hands, picking at her nail bed. "If his cousin has clients like that, I'm sure they have specific tastes or are looking for specific pieces."

Irritation pricks my skin—not because of her, but because of whoever ruined her confidence. I can't help myself and I don't bother to control my actions and abruptly close the distance between us. Sliding my finger beneath her chin, I tilt her head backwards until she's looking up at me.

"I swear to God, El. If I ever meet the man who made you feel this fucking small, it will not end well." I pause, letting out a ragged breath as she stares back at me with doe eyes. "You are talented. You are smart. You are insanely beautiful. There isn't a single doubt in my mind that your dreams are attainable." I slip my fingers beneath her jaw, trailing them across her flesh. "Tell me, darlin'. What *are* your dreams?"

Her throat bobs as she swallows hard. "For Chloe and I to both be happy and healthy."

"What else?"

She blinks twice. "For us to be safe."

The muscle in my jaw ticks at the thought of her feeling unsafe, but I don't visit that topic... not now. "What else?" I press. "You don't want to work in a restaurant and bar forever. What is your dream career?"

A soft breath escapes her. "I want to own a gallery. I want my paintings all over the world, hanging on the walls inside people's homes."

Relief floods me as she finally speaks her true dreams out loud. I want her to reach past the stars. To wrap her delicate fingers around them and pluck them from the sky. Every single star belongs to Ella Daniels.

"Can you do something for me, El?"

"Maybe," she says gently as the corners of her mouth twitch. The moonlight above shimmers within the depths of her eyes.

My hand cups the side of her face, my thumb softly stroking her cheek. "Finish the paintings you haven't finished. Start new ones. Just paint until your fingers stop working."

"And then what?"

I smile at her, my mouth inching closer to hers. "Then you watch as the stars align and your dreams come true."

"The stars aren't aligning if you're playing God with my dreams," she breathes against my lips as they drift across hers.

"Maybe I point a telescope at the stars that deserve to be seen," I murmur against her mouth. "What happens after that is beyond my control. Your art will speak for itself and I won't need to play God."

Ella surprises me as she steps closer, pressing her body flush against mine as she lifts her arms and encircles the back of my neck with her hands. Her mouth crashes into mine, her lips soft and plump as she kisses me with tenderness. There's a part of her that is hesitant, like she doesn't fully trust herself in this moment.

With one hand caressing the side of her neck, I drop my other to her waist and hold her tightly against my body. I ignore the way blood rushes to my cock, knowing damn well she can feel the hardness pressing against her. The movement alone supports the confidence Ella was struggling to wrap her mind around.

The tips of her fingers dig into my skin as her tongue sweeps along the seam of my lips. Without a second thought, I part them, letting her in. Gone is the hesitancy she was once feeling. Instead, Ella takes what she wants. Her tongue dances with mine, both of us caught up in the moment as she breathes me in.

Our surroundings fade away and it's the two of us. Nothing else matters. The water laps against the pillars under the pier. The moon casts its glow across us and bounces off the surface of the lake. Ella has me completely captivated. She's stolen my heart—her and that blue eyed little girl of hers—and she doesn't even know it.

And I won't be the one to tell her until the timing is right.

There's a vibration that sounds as if it's off in the distance. As my mind is pulled away from the moment between us, I realize it's coming from her pocket. Ella breaks from my lips, but she doesn't move away. Her lips are red and swollen and she looks up at me with a dazed stare.

"Sorry," she mumbles, blush creeping across her cheeks. I smile to myself, knowing I'm the one who put it there. "It might be Iris."

"You don't have to apologize, Ella," I assure her, taking a step away to give her space. Chloe is her top priority, as she should be. I am more than okay with being second place to that little girl.

She pulls her phone out of her pocket, her eyebrows pulling together as she looks at the screen. "Maybe it decided to block her information," Ella wonders out loud as she answers the call.

I watch her for a moment, confusion washing over her face as her eyebrows pull together and she says hello again. She pulls her phone away from her ear, looks at the screen, and repeats herself once again.

A frown tugs her lips downwards as she ends the call and stares at the device for a lingering moment. "That was strange."

"Who was it?" I question her out of curiosity and concern.

Ella looks back to me and shrugs as she tucks her phone back into her pocket. "It must have been a wrong number." She lets out a breath and shakes her head. "As much as I don't want to go back inside, I'm afraid I need to get back in there."

Disappointment weighs down my shoulders, but I brush the feeling away, giving her a smile. "I'm sure Remi is wondering if I stole you away for the night." I let out a soft chuckle. "I should have."

"That sounds very enticing," she laughs as her smile reaches her eyes. I'm addicted to the sound of her laughter. It's delicate, like the finest silk against my eardrums.

"How about a rain check?" I ask, taking a step closer to her. "Are you able to get away for an evening soon? I have somethin' I'd like to show you."

She tilts her head to the side, her face lighting up with curiosity. "I might be able to later this week. Can I see if Remi or Iris can watch Chloe and let you know?"

"That sounds perfect," I murmur, bringing my face down to hers. I sweep my mouth across her soft lips, kissing her gently before I pull away. "I have no intention of pushin' you to do somethin' you don't feel comfortable doin', but I want you to know that Chloe is welcome to come along if you can't find a sitter."

Her throat bobs as she swallows roughly. "I appreciate that," she says quietly with a nod. Her lips part like she's about to say something else, but the conflict is evident in her gaze. She gives me a small smile before she continues. "I will let you know."

"I'll be waiting to hear from you."

Ella's smile grows as the blush creeps across her face. "Goodnight, cowboy."

"Goodnight, darlin'."

CHAPTER TWENTY

ELLA

"Come, momma, come!" Chloe calls from the front of the house as she taps on the door. With the childproof lock on the knob, she's not able to turn it, but that doesn't mean she doesn't try anyways.

It's become part of our morning routine and I swear the little girl is in love with the outdoors. Most days in Silverspur Springs are flooded with sunshine and warmer temperatures this time of year. After breakfast, we go outside to look at the birds and the flowers while I finish my morning coffee. The tender moments with my daughter tug at my heartstrings.

A chuckle escapes me and I shake my head. I walk over to her, finding her trying her hardest to unlock the door. "Let me get it, Clo," I laugh quietly and gently remove her hands from the knob. She falls back onto her flat feet and clasps her hands in front of her chest as she waits.

I unlock the door, turn the knob, and pull it open. She doesn't hesitate to push the screen door and she takes off running across the front porch to the stairs. She takes the steps, two feet at a time, holding on tightly to the railing as she safely makes her descent. Watching her do it makes me nervous every time, but she's been adamant on having her independence.

She wants to do everything by herself and as much as I love seeing my daughter grow, I would love for time to slow down a bit.

The wood floorboards creak beneath my feet and I let the door close behind me. I'm about to step down onto the first step when something catches my eye off to the right. On top of the small table by two wooden chairs is a brown paper bag with handles.

My eyebrows pull together and I eye it suspiciously. There's no branding or label on the outside. My heart picks up the pace in my chest, anxiety licking my veins. I swallow hard and glance back out to Chloe. She's crouched down in the front yard looking at a small patch of weeds that are disguised as flowers.

I look back at the bag and hesitantly walk over to investigate. I'm not sure what it could possibly be but the paranoid instincts in my brain always have a way of circling back to Jacob.

Gently grasping the sides of the bag, I pull them open, leaning over to see what's inside. The air leaves my lungs in a rush, the same moment confusion and excitement washes over me. It's nothing threatening, nothing that could be a danger to Chloe or I.

It's a bag full of art supplies.

My throat constricts. *Who left these here?* I lift the various paints from inside, my eyes widening as I inspect the bottles. There's at least a dozen oil paints, a new set of brushes and a sleeve of chocolates from France. Emotion washes over me, the corners of my eyes burning and I rapidly blink away the tears.

As I begin to set the items back into the bag, I notice a small envelope inside. Leaving the paints and brushes, I pull it out and read my name written across the front of the white paper. I slowly open it, my heart crawling into my throat as I find a small card inside.

On the outside, there are a few decorative swirls and inside there's a handwritten note.

> Eli,
> The world deserves to cherish and appreciate art like yours.
> Paint until your heart is full and your soul is content.
> I'm still waitin' for you to tell me when I get to take you out again.
> Don't worry—I promise it won't be a date ;)
> Your Cowboy

My lips part, a shallow breath slipping from me, the corners of my mouth lifting on their own accord. Blush creeps across my cheeks and I glance around to see if he may be lingering somewhere, watching.

He's nowhere to be found, but that doesn't put a damper on my mood. It doesn't take away from the excitement that's running through my veins. A giddiness settles inside as my stomach does its own acrobatic routine.

He continues to surprise me and threatens to obliterate any belief I've had about other people. I know who I can trust in my life. My circle may be small, but I can count on the few people I have for anything Chloe and I could possibly need.

Cole Wild has been the most unexpected thing in my life. His kindness and generosity continues to supersede any expectation I could ever have of someone who's simply a friend. There's no ulterior motive to the things he's doing.

With Jacob, I was young and dumb. I craved an escape and love from someone so desperately, I was willing to take whatever I could get. I looked past the red flags that were blatantly waving directly in front of my face. With him, I was powerless. It felt like I had no control over my life. Like I had no say in what was happening.

Cole is the greenest flag I've ever met and it terrifies me. I'm skeptical of everyone I meet—constantly questioning who they truly are. How can I possibly question someone who hasn't shown me one inkling of a darkness inside of him?

He's tearing down my walls, one paintbrush and pink toy truck at a time.

He remembers everything I say to him. About the paints, about not wanting to go on a date. He never fails to forget the most minor details, as if he's hanging onto every word I say to him.

How can I continue to fight against someone who is the actual definition of good?

I watch Chloe for a moment, my smile widening as she tries to whistle at a bird perched on the small dogwood tree in the yard. In her hand is the small pink truck Cole gave to her.

She deserves the best things in life… and perhaps I do too.

Grabbing the bag, I bring it with me to the steps and sit down on the top one with it sitting next to me. Chloe runs past, chasing a butterfly with a string of giggles drifting through the air. I lift my coffee and take a sip as I reach into the front pocket of my robe for my phone.

I open my messages and start a new one, typing his name.

ELLA

You're sneaky.

He responds in less than a minute.

COLE

I don't know what you're talkin' about.

My mistake. It must have been the other Cole I know who decided to leave a bag of paint supplies on my front porch.

COLE

You know another Cole?

I stifle a laugh. I don't actually know anyone personally with his name, but his reaction is amusing.

COLE

It wasn't him.

So it was you then.

COLE

Yes. It was me.

You didn't have to do that.

COLE

Did I get the wrong things?

No, they are right. I would feel better if you'd let me pay you back for them.

COLE

That's not how this works, El. When someone gets you somethin' as a surprise or a gift, you don't pay them back.

You got the most expensive kind.

COLE

I know. You deserve the best ones they
have.

Cole...

COLE

You won't be payin' me back, El. If I want to
spend every last dollar I have on art
supplies for you, that's exactly what I'll do.

Well, that would be pretty senseless.

COLE

Tell you what... if you wanna pay me back,
you can.

You can pay me back by not going on a
date with me.

Deal.

I don't tell him I already planned on wanting to ask him if he wanted to go out again. When he left the other night, I told him I would let him know when I wanted to see him again. What I failed to tell him was that I never actually wanted him to leave.

I wanted to see him the very next day.

Cole Wild has been working his way under my skin and I'm afraid once he's under it, there's no way I'll be able to get him out. I've been trying to keep him at arms length but I can feel my resolve slipping. It's growing weaker with every interaction with him

COLE

What are your plans this evening? There's
somethin' I'd love to show you if you have
time.

What is it?

COLE

Well, that would ruin the surprise.

You didn't say it was a surprise.

COLE

It is now.

Remi and I are both off tonight so I take a chance and text her to see if she would be able to watch Chloe for a few hours. She doesn't bother to ask why, probably because she knows why.

REMI

Let me know what time and I'll be there.

ELLA

You're the best.

REMI

I know 😁

I switch out of her message and tap on the thread between Cole and I.

ELLA

I'm free tonight.

COLE

I'll come by and pick you up at six. Does that work for you?

ELLA

That's perfect.

COLE

See you tonight, El.

"Momma, wook!" Chloe calls out as she points up at the sky. I tilt my head back, looking up at the clouds she's pointing at. "A heart!"

A smile creeps across my lips as Chloe comes running over to me with a handful of weeds. There's a smudge of dirt across her cheek and I wipe it away before pulling her onto my lap.

A sense of doubt creeps into my brain, traveling down my torso before sinking into the pit of my stomach. The peace that has settled into my life feels too good to be true. There isn't a single thing that has been going wrong.

I'm happy.

I'm hopeful.

And I'm waiting for the other shoe to drop...

CHAPTER TWENTY-ONE

COLE

"Remember, our toys do not go in the fish tank!"

I tilt my head to the side as Ella pulls the door shut behind her and turns around to face me. Her eyes meet mine from where I'm standing at the bottom of the steps and a smile lifts her lips.

"Trust me, you don't wanna know," she admits with a soft laugh and a shake of her head. She lets out a soft breath before telling me anyway as she starts to walk towards me. "Somehow toys keep ending up in the fish tank and no one seems to know how they are getting in there."

"It could be worse, right?" I offer, raising my eyebrows as I hold my arm out for her.

Ella slips hers through mine, letting me lead her to my truck. "It can always be worse."

I walk her out to my truck, pulling open the passenger side door for her. Ella slips her arm from mine and gets inside. I shut it and make my way over to my side before getting in next to her.

Ella turns to look at me as she buckles her seatbelt. "Are you gonna tell me where we're going?"

"Now, El…" I start, my voice trailing off for a moment. I start the engine and turn to look at her. "Didn't I tell you that would ruin the surprise?"

She stares at me with an unreadable expression and I watch as a touch of worry washes over her eyes. "Well, yeah, I know, but since this isn't technically a date, I don't know if a surprise is really needed." She stops and lets out a breath before she continues through her ramble. "I'm not really a big fan of surprises and not knowing what is going on or where we are going gives me a little bit of anxiety and—"

"Sweets, stop," I say, my voice soft and gentle as I reach for her hand. I didn't mean to cut her off mid sentence, but hearing her spiraling into her panic has my heart breaking. "Take a deep breath. We're just going to the marina. I thought we could go out on the water and stop to get dinner along the lake."

Her expression softens, the panic immediately vanishing as her eyes return to their normal size. "I'm sorry. I didn't mean to ruin it, it's just better for me knowing what's going on." Ella directs her gaze away from me, turning her head as she stares down at her lap.

"Hey," I start, releasing her hand and reaching for the side of her face. I pull her back to look at me. "Don't you dare apologize. I'm sorry for not knowing." I pause, offering her a soft smile. "No surprises, okay?"

She smiles back at me, although it doesn't come close to reaching her eyes. "Okay."

I resist the urge to pull her into my lap. I want nothing more than to wrap my arms around her and tell her it's okay, but I don't feel like it's my place. With her, I have to dip my toes in slowly. I can't scare her away, especially when it's clear that she's on high alert.

And if there's one thing I do, it will be to show her it's okay to let her guard down.

It's okay to let people in.

We fall into a comfortable, safe conversation on the way to the marina. Ella asks me about the ranch and minor details about my life, not diving in too deep, yet not keeping things too superficial. I give her what she wants, although I don't do the same. I don't want to poke and prod, especially after the way our evening started.

When she's ready to let me in and open up, she will. And dear god, I don't care how long it takes. I'll wait a lifetime for this woman to share her life and her secrets with me.

Ella looks out the window as I drive through the gates to the marina. It's tucked away along the shore near the base of the mountain and you need access to get inside. There aren't many people here since it's in the middle of the week so I find a parking spot easily. Ella reaches to undo her seatbelt and I turn off the engine before unbuckling my own. I move quickly, getting out of the truck to meet her at her door as she goes to open it.

She lets out a soft breath, her eyes flashing to mine. I pull it open and hold my hand out to her. "Cole…" she says quietly, almost as if she's saying my name as a warning.

I tilt my head to the side, not moving my hand away. "It's not a date, remember?"

"This feels like one."

"Says who?" I question her, my eyebrows pulling together. "Is there a rulebook that says what does and doesn't count as things you are supposed to do when you take someone out on a date?"

Her gaze drops down to my hand and she slowly slides her soft palm against mine as she lets me help her out of the truck. Electricity travels up my arm, erupting across my chest, but I release her as soon as she's standing upright and shut the door behind her. "You're right," she agrees, a soft smile dancing across her perfect lips. "I forget that you're such a gentleman."

I can't help myself.

I lean closer to her, my hand brushing her hair away from the side of her neck and my mouth dropping to her ear. "I am, but if there's ever a time you don't want me to keep bein' a gentleman, all you have to do is say the words, darlin'," I murmur, my lips brushing against her.

Ella inhales sharply, her chest rising abruptly as she holds her breath for a beat. I ease away from her, watching the hues of pink spreading across her cheeks as she stares at me wide eyed. Her nostrils flare and I don't miss the flames burning in her gaze.

"Shall we?" I question her, holding my arm out for her to take again.

She swallows hard, her slender throat bobbing as she pulls her lips in between her teeth and nods. She doesn't speak a single word and I can't help but smile at the irony of her being rendered speechless right now. If only she knew the very things she does to me every time I'm in her presence.

Ella threads her arm through mine and I feel her soft skin warm against my flesh as I pull her with me, leading her towards the docks with boats. We walk past a row, taking the first right down another one with different boats in their slips. We get to the third to last one and I stop in front of it, Ella stopping beside me.

She looks at the boat and glances at me. "Is this Austin's boat?"

I smile, shaking my head at her. "His boat is over there." I point back in the direction we came from. "This one is mine."

"He finally convinced you to get one?"

Not him—you did.

"Somethin' like that," I smirk, the corners of my lips lifting. She didn't exactly convince me I needed to get one, but that one day when I was at the bar with Austin and we were discussing boats… He made a valid point and she was the one who pointed that out to me.

Honestly, it did make the most sense and it was time for me to finally get my own. Plus, now I can take Ella out whenever I want to.

"Did you name it?" she asks me as she cranes her neck, trying to see the side of it. "That's what people do, right? You have to give it some kind of a name."

I let out a soft laugh and motion for her to get on board with me. She lets me help her onto the boat and I follow behind her. "Yeah, most people do. I haven't come up with a name for her yet." I move around the boat, getting it ready to move away from the dock. "Maybe you can help me."

A nervous laugh escapes her and she drops down onto one of the bench seats, crossing her leg over her knee as she watches me. I don't miss the way the bottom of her dress shifts and reveals a few extra inches of her thigh.

"Let me think about it and I'll get back to you," she says softly, smiling at me as I move to the seat by the steering wheel. She directs her gaze out to the water and I start the engine before carefully moving the boat from the slip.

Ella looks peaceful and content with her arm against the side of the boat and her face turned to gaze at the horizon as we head across the water. The vessel bobs over the small waves and I watch the way her blonde hair drifts through the air. She's absolutely breathtaking, it's hard for me to look away.

It's only a three minute boat ride to the restaurant we settled on for dinner tonight. We find a spot out back and dock the vessel. Ella watches me as I move around, ensuring everything is where it needs to be. After I finish, I walk over to her, dropping down onto the bench seat next to her.

"We have a few options for dinner," I start while pulling my phone from my pocket. "We can go inside and eat, order take-out, or they will serve us here on the boat."

Ella chews on the inside of her cheek for a moment. "Which would you prefer?"

"The choice is yours, El," I say, the corners of my lips twitching in amusement. "I wanna do whichever you'd like."

She gives herself a second to think before her eyes shine like the sun setting in the distance. "Can we get take-out, but eat it here on the boat?"

"Of course."

"Are you sure?" A wave of uncertainty passes over her expression. "I thought if we got takeout, then we don't have to stay here if we don't want to. Or we won't have anyone interrupt us."

"It sounds like a perfect plan," I assure her, nodding eagerly. I don't want to make her feel any negative way about her seeking some kind of approval. Bad habits die hard, but it's one I intend on erasing from her memory.

We go over the menu and place an order online. Ella asks about the restaurant as she admits she's never been here before.

"Where else haven't you been?" The question tumbles from my lips before I get the chance to review the sentence.

Ella's eyebrows pull together, but she names a few of the restaurants and bars that she hasn't been to. I make a mental note of every place, storing them in my brain for a later date.

"Why do you ask?" she asks as I notice someone in the distance carrying a bag of food in our direction.

I smile at her before rising to my feet to retrieve the food from the servers. "So I can make sure I take you to each place."

My heart skips a beat in my chest as I turn back around and catch her staring at me. Her expression is unreadable, yet her eyes are filled with so many emotions, swirling within the flames burning in her irises.

"There are some cushions I can bring up so we can sit out here and eat."

Ella's lips part and a soft breath escapes her and I walk past her, heading down into the cabin. I reach the bottom of the steps and hear her light footsteps behind me. I walk over to the table, setting the bag down before turning around to face her.

"Ella." My head tilts to the side, my eyebrows drawing together. "Is everything okay?"

Conflict sweeps across her expression, her slender throat bobbing as she swallows hard. My heart thrums inside my chest, anticipating humming in my veins as she moves away from the steps. She closes the distance between us, her tortured expression dissipating as it's washed away by determination.

Want. Need. Desire.

The air leaves my lungs in a rush as she enters my space, her delicate hands slipping around the back of my neck. She lifts onto her toes, her eyes searching mine, as if she's seeking assurance once again.

The corners of my lips lift and I lower my face to hers, stopping as my lips almost touch hers. She inhales sharply, her grip tightening on the nape of my neck. I don't kiss her.

Instead, I wait.

I wait for her to take exactly what she wants.

And she does.

CHAPTER TWENTY-TWO

ELLA

Cole doesn't hesitate as my mouth collides with his. His arms are around my waist, pulling my body flush against his as his lips move with mine. Any possible thought I have is floating out in the cool air, completely vacant from my mind. He consumes me, enveloping me with his heat as he kisses me back with a fervent need.

The moment belongs to us and no one else. We're tucked away in the cabin of his boat, our food growing cold as he steals the air from my lungs. Cole kisses me with a tenderness that has me melting into a puddle by his feet.

This isn't something I would normally do, but I couldn't help myself. We've had far too many moments that have led us to this same place. There's been a burning tension, growing and spreading between us. I'm only human and sometimes our walls come crumbling down in a rush.

I've denied myself the simple pleasures in life for too long. I've spent too much time walking around, glancing over my shoulder, making sure I'm not taking too many risks or putting myself in harm's way, but I'm tired. I'm tired of running and not getting to enjoy myself and life.

I'm tired of not allowing myself the opportunity to enjoy him.

I break away from Cole, suddenly feeling like I crossed a line without asking him. My actions were out of character and I think I shocked both of us by kissing him like that. He's out of breath, his chest rising and falling in rapid succession as his eyes search mine.

"I'm sorry," I let out in a rush. "I don't know why I did that." I start to feel panicked and the confidence I was feeling is quickly waning. "I shouldn't have—"

"Do it again."

My heart skips a beat in my chest and my eyes widen. "What?"

"Do it again, Ella," he urges, his grip tightening on my waist. "Stop being so cautious. Stop being afraid of everything." He pauses, his eyes burning holes through mine. "You are safe with me. You don't have to be cautious and you don't have to be afraid." His nostrils flare as he stares at me with an intensity that infiltrates my bone marrow. "You. Are. Safe."

My heart crawls into my throat as my chest constricts around the emotion his words illicit inside me. He's never made me question my safety. It's always been me being cautious and afraid, but I know I don't have to be with him.

Cole has never made me feel anything less than everything. He's attentive and gentle. Tender and soft. He makes me feel confident and more sure of myself than I've felt in a long time. He takes the fear inside of me and molds it into something else. Something that resembles hope and all the dreams I've never thought I'd be able to reach.

I'm safe with him.

"I'm not afraid—not of you," I admit, my voice barely audible as I begin to push back up onto my toes, entering his space once again. Cole lets out a groan and the sound vibrates through my own body as his mouth captures mine. My eyelids flutter closed and I give in to everything I've been fighting against. I take the plunge, diving in head first, unsure of what is going to happen in the end, but I know it will be okay.

Cole Wild is worth the risk.

His mouth is soft and slow as he kisses me with a sweetness that has my soul shimmering. His tongue slides along the seam of my mouth and I slowly part them, granting him access as he deepens the kiss.

Tentative hands slide down my torso, stopping as they reach the backs of my thighs. Cole bends his knees, gently lifting me upwards before setting me on the small table in the cabin. His mouth never leaves mine and I part my knees, allowing him to step into the space between my legs. His hands find the sides of my face, soft and gentle as his fingertips caress my skin.

His tongue tangles with mine, caught in the slowest dance together. My hands abandon the back of his neck and slowly begin their descent along his shoulders. His body warms my palms as I move them along the rigid planes of his arms. My fingertips dig into his flesh and I kiss him back with an intensity.

He doesn't match my urgency, instead kissing me with a sweetness that has my heart fluttering in my chest. His movements slow, his tongue leaves my mine, and his lips close as he kisses me tenderly. Cole slowly pulls away, allowing me the opportunity to come up for air as he presses his forehead to mine.

We're both breathless and my heart pounds in my chest, threatening to break through my ribcage. My body tingles as my head feels like it's floating into the clouds. I'm not sure what reality I've stepped into, but I'm certain I never want to leave.

"The food is going to get cold," Cole says quietly, his voice hoarse and gravely as he forces the words out. His hands are still on the sides of my face and he lifts his forehead from mine, softly pressing his lips above my eyebrow. "We should eat."

"We should," I murmur, agreeing with him, although I'm not so sure I have an appetite for food any longer. "We don't have to though."

"We do," he says, tilting my head back to look up at him. His eyes burn holes through mine, warming my soul in a way that sends a bolt of electricity down my spine. "I'm tryin' to be a gentleman here, El."

My throat bobs and I swallow. "You don't have to be."

He groans, his nostrils flaring as closes his eyes for a moment. The muscle in his jaw tightens and his eyelids lift as the intensity grows within his irises. "Yes, I do," he tells me, the sound of his low voice scratching against my eardrums. "My self-control is waning and this is where I gotta draw the line. If I don't stop myself now, we'll be entering territory you aren't ready for yet."

His assumption pricks my skin. My nose scrunches, my eyebrows pulling together and I tilt my head to the side. "You don't know what I am or am not ready for, Cole."

"Oh really?" The corners of his lips twitch as his expression softens. Amusement and mischief dance within the flames in his eyes. "So, are you ready for me to bend you over the side of my boat while I bury myself so deep inside you, you forget your own name? Are you ready for me to fuck you into an oblivion on every surface of this damn thing?"

My breath catches in my throat, my heart tumbling over itself. There's a lightness in my chest, coupled with the tingling that instantly builds in between my legs. My stomach flutters with excitement over the prospect, although there's a touch of uncertainty.

I'm caught off guard by the words he spoke. I'm rendered speechless.

"That's what I thought," he says softly, a smile dancing across his lips before he kisses the tip of my nose. "And that's okay. I will never rush you or make you feel pressured. I have no desire to fuck you until you're ready for me to."

"I—um—" I pause, letting out a nervous laugh as he slides his hands down my arms. A part of me feels a twinge of rejection, but I also appreciate his honesty. "I want to be ready," I admit, my voice barely audible. I let out a ragged breath, staring back at him, reveling in his warmth that envelopes me. "I want to let you in."

"I'm not in any rush." The smile falls from his lips and he slowly shakes his head at me. "Can you do somethin' for me?"

"Of course," I say, without any hesitation.

"When you're ready to make the move from friends to somethin' more, I need you to be the one to ask for it. I need you to be the one to take what you want."

Insecurity floods me even with his assurance. "What if I take too long? What if you get tired of waiting?"

What if you decide I'm not worth the wait?

"Ella." His voice is soft, but my name rolls off his tongue with purpose. "When it comes to you, I have all the time in the world." Concern washes over his gaze and he frowns as his forehead creases. "Who hurt you, El?"

My throat constricts, my chest overwhelmingly heavy with emotion as I inhale sharply through my nose. I was able to evade his question before, but I'm exhausted. I'm so tired from constantly keeping my walls in place and keeping him out.

"He did," I whisper, my voice barely audible. I taste the bitterness on my tongue before I say his name. "Jacob did."

His nostrils flare. "Your ex?"

I draw my lips between my teeth, clamping down to keep my tears and emotion at bay. I nod. "He wasn't abusive or anything like that. He destroyed my self worth. He constantly cheated and something like that really takes a toll on you mentally." I pause, letting out a ragged breath. "It makes it hard to trust anyone."

The words fall from my tongue, although I don't dive into the deep details of it all. Cole doesn't say anything, but the muscle in his jaw ticks.

"I left him when I found out I was pregnant and when I told him, he refused to accept that she was his."

"He didn't want anything to do with Chloe?"

Oh, no, there it is. The question I was hoping I would be able to avoid. I can't tell him the truth. I can't have him knowing that Jacob denied the possibility of her being his.

I shake my head, not speaking the words, but still not telling him the full truth, nonetheless.

Cole scoffs, the anger evident in his expression. "I would love to fuckin' meet him."

Thank god that will never happen. At this rate, I'm sure he's forgotten about me. He's forgotten about my existence and has moved on in life.

I can only hope.

"I promise one day I will tell you the whole story."

Cole stares at me, his lips parting as the anger dissipates from his facial features. For a moment, he appears shocked. "Whenever you're ready, El," he tells me, his voice tender. "And if you decide to never tell me, that's okay too. It changes nothin' between us."

My eyes widen as his words settle inside my brain. How he can say something that heavy with such a declaration is beyond me. He knows my past isn't great, yet he sees past it.

He sees me.

CHAPTER TWENTY-THREE

COLE

"Remind me why we decided to do this today."

Austin glances at me as he slows his horse to a stop. "No one else wanted to go with Cash, remember?"

"Right," I laugh, shaking my head. Cade turned Cash down when he asked him. Amber was preoccupied with cleaning stalls. And he asked me to come with him so we could hangout.

When he saw Austin pull up, he ended up roping both of us into his mission. He was convinced there was a spot along the south side of our property that the fence needed fixed. Taking on the responsibility of the entire ranch has been a struggle for all three of us.

There's so many moving parts, so many things to do to keep the entire business afloat. Between the cattle and the horses and Cash on the road for rodeos, it's a lot and sometimes I wonder if we've bitten off more than we can chew.

We manage and we do get things handled, but at some point, we're going to need to bring in some additional help.

Our horse training business has taken off and is beginning to feel a bit overwhelming at times.

I see Cash in the distance, turning around on his horse as he waves for us to follow him.

"Look, over here!"

I dig my heels into the sides of my gelding, sitting deep in my seat as he immediately rocks, breaking into a lope. Austin clucks his tongue to the dappled mare he's on, breaking into the same gait as we head in the direction of where Cash is sitting on his horse.

Cash slides his feet from his stirrups, throwing his leg around the withers of his horse before sliding onto the ground. He walks over to the suspicious looking post and begins to wiggle it.

It moves in the ground and when it does, it creates just enough space for a calf to slide under the rails.

"This must be where he got out from."

I glance around, pulling out my phone to mark the exact location. Reaching into my saddle bag, I pull out a red ribbon and hand it to Cash to tie around it.

"Let's keep them out of this field for now," I tell Cash, glancing around the pasture. "We can get it fixed tomorrow."

Cash shakes his head. "I can get it today, that way we don't have to worry about it anymore." He walks back to his horse, grabbing the reins in his left hand as he grabs onto the horn. He slides his left foot into the stirrup, grabbing the back of his saddle with his right hand as he hoists himself back into his seat.

"We'll all get it," I say as we begin to ride back toward the barn. I glance over at Austin, mischief dancing in his eyes. "I'll race you there."

Cash erupts with laughter, immediately leaning

forward on his horse as he squeezes her body with his legs. "It's on!"

We all break out into a gallop, our horses kicking up dust as we race across the hollow. My gelding's legs stretch, his stride long as he carries me ahead of my brother and friend.

The wind whips past me, pushing my hair from my forehead and stinging my eyes as we all race to the barn. My reins are loose and I let my horse go at the pace he wants. Austin's mare inches closer, but my horse refuses to let them get past us.

We all race until we're reaching the edge of the field and I beat the two of them by a furlong.

"You cheated!" Cash yells, his horse slowing from a gallop into a lope and finally a jog. "You got a head start."

"Don't be a sore sport," I retort, rolling my eyes at him. "I didn't cheat."

"Come on, boys," Austin interjects. "I don't want to be out here all day, so let's get this done so we can go get food."

I hop off my horse, kicking open the gate and my brother rides past me, giving me the middle finger. I give it back to him, before laughter spills from my lips.

Typical Wild brother behavior.

And I wouldn't have it any other way.

Austin leads the way as we walk through the front doors of the restaurant. We end up at Harvest by the base of the mountain and head out to the veranda where they're serving lunch. One of their hosts seats us at a table on the far side with the best views of the mountain. We sit and order our drinks before browsing the menu.

It doesn't take either of us long to settle on what we're ordering and when the server comes back with our drinks, we tell her what we both want. Austin lifts his glass, taking a sip of the mixed drink before washing it down with a gulp of water.

"I wanted to ask you about Vera's gallery," I start after following suit and taking a sip of my own drink. It's strong and burns my throat as the liquor slides down. It's a little earlier than I'd prefer it to be to drink, but it's only one.

Austin's cousin Vera is a world renowned art dealer with one of the biggest galleries in the country, right in the heart of Wyoming. People come from all over the world to see the art she showcases in her gallery.

Vera's parents divorced at a young age, so half of her time was spent in Silverspur Springs and the other half was in the city.

She stumbled into the art industry after she went to school for sculpting. She was a talented artist herself and her brand originated and grew from the sculptures she created.

Austin and Vera have always been close. Her mother lived with his family for a few years while we were kids, so in a sense, they were more like brother and sister than cousins.

"What's up?" He questions me, tilting his head to the side. "Are you looking for a painting or something?"

"I'm not," I say, shaking my head. "Although, I have met an artist I think Vera might be interested in."

Austin lifts his drink, taking another sip before raising an eyebrow at me. "Oh really? Who is it?"

I swallow roughly. "Ella," I admit, my voice low. "She's

been painting as a hobby, but her work is breathtaking." I pause, pulling out my phone to find the pictures I took that night at her house. She saw me take them, but I think she thought they were so I could look at them another time. I hand it over to Austin, watching the way his face transforms as he flips through the different painting pictures.

"Holy shit." Austin's eyes flash to mine before looking back at my phone. "These are incredibly realistic, yet still whimsical and artistic. Does she only do landscapes?"

I shake my head. "She has some portraits, but I wasn't able to get any pictures of them."

Austin narrows his eyes on mine for a moment. "Does she know you took these pictures?"

"Yes and no." I let out a soft laugh. "She saw me take a few pictures, but she has no idea I'm talkin' to you about them."

"Do you think she would be interested in doing a showcase of some sort? Vera has a slot she needs to fill since someone ghosted her." He pauses for a moment as he pulls out his phone and taps on the screen a few times. I see Vera's name on the screen as he puts it on speakerphone and sets it down. "I know she won't say no to these."

"People ghost Vera?" I ask him, raising a curious eyebrow. According to Austin, Vera has made a name for herself in the art industry and is very well known. Her gallery draws in a lot of people from all over the country, especially when they have high profile artists or work there.

"Oh, all the time," he says, shaking his head as he rolls his eyes. "You'd be surprised how many don't want to be the center of attention or don't want any public recognition."

I stare at him for a second, our conversation pausing as our server comes back with our plates. I wait until she leaves again and play his words over in my mind. Ella isn't the type of person who wants any attention drawn to herself. She's filled with self doubt and her confidence is only now starting to bloom. I hadn't considered the possibility of her not wanting to do anything like this.

"Hello?"

Vera's soft and elegant voice sounds through the speaker.

"Hey V," Austin says, taking another sip of his drink. "You remember my friend Cole?"

"Sure, what's up?"

"So, he's seeing this girl who paints and you're going to want to see this." Austin looks at me. "I'm gonna have Cole send you some pictures."

I hand Austin my phone and he selects the photos, typing in Vera's number before sending them to her. He hands it back to me and I watch on the screen as it changes from message delivered to read.

She's silent for a moment. My heart thrums away inside my chest, picking up the pace before Vera finally speaks. "I want her."

"I knew you would," Austin chuckles.

"I don't care what you have to do to make it happen, Austin." She lets out a breath. "I have many clients who would pay top dollar for paintings like this."

"So, I haven't told her that I was going to show these to either of you," I admit, breaking into the conversation. "Let me talk with her," I tell Austin and Vera. "I don't want to spring this on her without her being okay with it."

"I have to get back to work, Austin, but I'll send you the openings in the schedule for shows. If any of the dates work for her, let me know and we'll get her in the gallery."

"Sounds good," Austin says to her, smiling at me from across the table. "I'll keep you posted."

Vera ends the call and Austin's eyes scan his phone. "Vera has an opening next weekend." He looks at me. "Do you think she'd want to do that?"

"Let me text her now." I glance at the time on my watch. "That way if she's not able to, you can tell Vera now." I'm not sure what time she goes in today, but hopefully I can catch her before she is working.

> Hey you. Are you busy right now? I wanted to ask you about something.

ELLA

I just walked into work. Is everything okay?

> Everything is great. Remember Austin's cousin I was telling you about who owns a gallery?

ELLA

I do...

> Don't hate me, but I showed Austin some of your art and he talked to Vera and she wants to bring you in to do a show next weekend.

ELLA

You're joking.

> I told you your art belongs in a museum. This is just the first step, El.

ELLA

I have to see if I can get someone to watch Chloe.

> Chloe can always come.

ELLA

I'm not sure if I have enough pieces to
bring.

One would be enough.

ELLA

I don't know, Cole. I'm not sure if they're
good enough to be featured somewhere
like VT Galleries.

I never mentioned the name of the gallery but she
must have done some digging on the internet after I
mentioned Vera's name.

Ella, stop it. You're more than good enough.
Vera wants you there for a reason.

I need you to believe in yourself the same
way I do.

ELLA

But what if no one else wants them?

But what if everyone does?

ELLA

I've never done anything like this before.

Then there's no better time to take the
plunge.

ELLA

Okay, I'll do it.

"She's in."

Austin smiles at me from across the table. "Wonderful.
Vera wants her email address so her assistant can get in
touch with her."

Good decision.

Send me your email so they can get all the
information to you.

She sends me her email and I pass it along to Austin.
He doesn't hesitate to send it to his cousin. Knowing Ella is
probably feeling anxious from all of this, I send her one
last reassuring text.

I promise you won't regret this.

ELLA

I hope you're right.

I know I'm right. This is the moment she needs. It's
time for her to see she's capable of anything. Her dreams
aren't unattainable. All she has to do is push through her
self doubt.

Because there isn't a single thing this woman can't do.

CHAPTER TWENTY-FOUR

ELLA

"This one has to go to the gallery."

I slowly turn around to find Remi holding up one of the paintings I finished while Chloe was still a baby. I found serenity in painting after she was born. It allowed me the opportunity to escape from the hardships of life. All my emotional baggage was checked at the door as soon as I stepped inside my little painting room.

Over the course of a few months, I painted until my hand was cramping. It was always in the middle of the night, after the rest of the world had gone to sleep and Chloe was tucked away in her crib. Thankfully for me, she was an excellent sleeper. During that period, we were in the cycle of sleeping a few hours at a time. I would sacrifice some of those hours to lose myself in my art.

My eyes scan the small square, taking in the angry reds and emotional yellows smeared across the canvas. I remember that one specifically. It was the last one I painted, right before Chloe turned a year old, until I started again a few months ago.

We were nearing Chloe's first birthday and I was filled with an unsuspecting rage. A rage toward myself for my life ending up the way it did. I wasn't angry that I left Jacob or that I was doing everything as a single mother. I was angry at that naive young adult who fell for him.

So, I stayed up until the wee hours of the morning, before the birds began to chirp. I painted and cried and mourned and fought the urge to rip it all to pieces.

"I don't know if that one should go," I say, half cringing at the thought of showing such raw emotion to other people. "That one isn't quite like the others."

It's still a landscape, but it's messy. It's chaotic and unorganized. It oozes pain.

"I think that's what makes it stand out," she says, her voice encouraging as she looks at the painting once more. "There's so much emotional depth to it." She looks back at me and her lips part as if she's going to ask, but she doesn't have to.

She already knows enough to understand where it came from.

"I'll leave it here, you still have a few days to decide. Maybe you'll change your mind."

"Okay," I agree, nodding as I glance about the room once more. I pull out my phone, looking at my email once more to see what they are asking for. Vera, Austin's cousin, is the one who ended up sending the email, not her assistant. And she didn't specify what type of paintings to bring. She simply said they would showcase whatever I wanted to submit.

"Do you want to take a break?" Remi asks me as she moves away from the stack of paintings. "I promised Chloe we would go get ice cream this afternoon."

Chloe's in the other room coloring. I shake my head at

Remi. "Can you take her? I want to finish getting this stuff ready."

Remi looks concerned, but doesn't comment on it. "Yeah, sure. We'll be back in a little bit."

"Take your time." I force a smile onto my lips as she exits the room. My eyes scan the perimeter again, taking in the various stacks of paintings on the floor and the ones hanging on the walls.

We've been at this for two hours and I think there are a total of four sitting by the door. Decisions like this create an unease inside me. Self doubt has already proven to be one of my downfalls and a situation like this is not helping.

I walk around the room, running my fingers over the paintings hanging on the walls. There are two that I think they would maybe like, so I take them off and put them over in the pile we have. A part of me wonders if I should take everything and whatever they don't want can go in my car.

A wave of nausea rolls in my stomach as I'm flooded with anxiety. I don't know what to wear. I don't even know what I'm supposed to do. I've never been to an art show before and I've certainly never been to an event where there are people in attendance to see my work.

My phone vibrates and I pull it from my pocket, my eyebrows tugging together when I see it's an unknown number. I don't have time to deal with telemarketers. I ignore the call, returning my attention back to my work.

Stepping in front of the stack on the far side of the room, I sink to the floor, sitting cross legged in front of them. The front door shuts and I know I'm safe from Chloe or Remi coming in to find me in the middle of breaking down.

My heart picks up the pace in my chest, beating erratically. I can feel the pounding inside my ribcage and my bounding pulse in my neck. It feels like my entire body has a heartbeat at this point. I'm acutely aware of my breathing and I have to focus to keep it steady. My head swims and the walls of the room feel like they're closing in on me.

I force my eyes shut, blocking out the now harsh light, dropping my head into my hands.

"I'm okay. Everything is okay." The words become somewhat of a chant or a mantra and I attempt to calm myself. This isn't the first anxiety attack I've had, but it's been a while since I've had one. The experience is jarring.

My phone vibrates again and irritation prickles my skin for a moment before relief washes over me when I see a message from Cole on the screen.

COLE

Do you need any help getting your stuff
together for this weekend?

My forehead creases and the thought of him sends another jolt to my heart. He's going to be there this weekend, looking at every single painting, every single emotion I've felt over the past few years. It's a vulnerable feeling, one I'm not familiar with and my stomach suddenly feels like it's going to fall out of my butt.

COLE

I'm sure you don't, but in case you do, I'm
here.

I suck in a shallow breath, unable to get my lungs to expand enough to inhale deeply. Emotion washes over me, mixing with the anxiety, and my body shakes as I let out a rush of air.

"I'm okay."

I'm not okay.

I can't do it.

COLE

Is everything okay?

You shouldn't have said anything to Austin.

COLE

Ella, what's going on?

I just can't do it.

When Cole doesn't respond, I lock my phone and set it back down on the floor. I close my eyes, burying my face in my hands once more. I stay in this position for at least ten minutes, trying to get myself together. Agreeing to this show was a mistake. My paintings are garbage. I'm not good at being the center of attention. Nothing about this was a good decision.

"Ella, are you in here?"

My head springs up, instantly feeling a rush of dizziness as everything feels distorted from the adrenaline overload in my body. I didn't hear a knock or the front door opening.

"Ella?"

What the hell is he doing here?

My eyes are wide and I stare at the half open door, completely mortified about him finding me like this. Cole Wild steps into my line of vision and I want to crawl into a hole and pretend he was never here.

His eyebrows pull together, his head tilting to the side as he pauses in the doorway. "Hey." His voice is soft and gentle and he quickly steps into the room, closing the distance between us. He bends his knees, crouching down in front of me on the floor. "What's goin' on?"

"This was a mistake, Cole." I shake my head, my voice quivering as I half laugh. "My paintings aren't what they're looking for. The thought of being the center of attention has me so nervous already. I don't know what I was thinking, agreeing to something like this."

"Ella, darlin', look at me," he says in a hushed voice as he reaches for me. "You are amazing. Your paintings are exactly what they are looking for. You can do this." He moves into a seated position, spreading his legs as he pulls me between them. I don't fight him as he guides my body closer to his. "Tell me something you can feel."

I focus on his words, feeling my hands on his forearms. His skin is soft and warm beneath mine. "You."

"Tell me something you smell."

I swallow hard, inhaling his familiar scent through my nose. Leather and cedar. "You."

"Tell me something you see."

Emotion washes over me as my heart begins to steady. My breathing is more controlled. I look into the depths of his blue eyes. "You," I whisper. "It's you."

"Good," he says softly, his eyes burrowing through mine as he pulls me flush against him. "If you don't want to do this, you don't have to. No one will be mad if you decide to change your mind."

My body relaxes into him as conflict momentarily engulfs me. I know this is a great opportunity, but the thought of failure is paralyzing. Jacob used to tell me that being an artist would never be a viable career. That it was only ever a hobby.

And there was a part of me that hung onto that. No one wants to be a starving artist. No one wants to put themselves out there and deal with the rejection that comes with it.

But, I know deep inside that I will be okay if it doesn't work out the way I'm hoping it does. Cole grounds me, giving me the opportunity to look at things clearly.

"This isn't something I should pass up."

"I agree, but it doesn't mean it can't happen another time."

My eyes bounce back and forth between his. "I want to do it. I don't want to keep second guessing things and myself. I don't want my self doubt to continue to hold me back."

Cole stares at me. "So, what happens next?"

I let out a ragged breath, still feeling the aftershocks from my anxiety attack. Cole was able to distract me enough to get myself under control. He didn't make it go away, but he helped me through it.

"Will you help me decide which paintings to take?"

A tender smile spreads across his face.

"I'd love to."

CHAPTER TWENTY-FIVE

COLE

"Do you want to stay for dinner?"

I glance over at Ella as she's going through the last of her paintings. After I found her in the middle of an anxiety attack, I wasn't sure how the rest of her afternoon was going to go. She asked me to stay, so I've been sitting in here with her trying to figure out which pieces I think Vera might want.

Remi took Chloe to get ice cream and when she called afterwards, Ella asked her if she could take her to the park to give us a little more time.

"I don't want to impose," I say, offering a soft smile. The last thing I want is for her to feel like she has to ask me to stay when that's not what she wants. I know her daughter will be home soon and I should go before she is.

Ella rises to her feet, straightening her pants before she offers me her hand. I slide my palm against hers, letting her guide me to my feet. I stand in front of her, my chin tipping towards my chest and my eyes find hers.

"It's not imposing if I invited you," she tells me, her voice soft as she raises an eyebrow.

"What about Chloe?"

Ella tilts her head to the side, scanning my face before settling on my eyes. "She's already met you once before and we have run into you a few times in town. I think it would be okay if she saw you again."

The air leaves my lungs in a rush as my heart picks up the pace, stumbling over itself a bit. This is a huge step for Ella. Even if she doesn't want anything to do with me besides being friends, she still trusts me enough to be around her daughter. She wouldn't offer something significant like this if she didn't see me somewhere in her future.

I smile at her, the intensity of the moment permeating my soul. "I would like that."

"Perfect," she responds, her smile lighting up her face. "I should see what we have that I can cook."

My hand reaches for the side of her face, my thumb trailing over her skin. "Today has been a long and stressful day. Let's get delivery." I pause for a moment, my fingertips lingering over the pounding pulse in the side of her neck. "I do wanna cook for you one night, though."

She inhales sharply. "I might have to let you do that."

"Good," I murmur, my fingers trailing beneath her chin, tipping her head back farther, revealing her slender neck. "There are a lot of things I want to do for you… and to you."

She bats her eyelashes at me, her nostrils flaring as she closes the small amount of space between us. My heart kicks into overdrive, blood rushing through my veins. She steps closer and anticipation builds in the pit of my stomach. Her chest brushes against my torso as her hands find the sides of my waist. Her lips part, and she begins to lift onto her toes.

"Honey, we're home!" Remi calls from the front door

as it shuts behind her. It opened quietly enough that neither of us heard her at first.

I groan and Ella falls back onto her flat feet, her shoulders sagging as she closes her eyes. She opens them, the hues of blue dancing within her irises as she lets out a soft laugh.

"I wasn't expecting them already," she says in a hushed voice. She takes a step away from me as the footsteps in the hall grow louder. Her eyes search mine. "If you want to stick around after dinner, perhaps we can finish what we started."

Oh, shit.

I wasn't expecting her to say anything remotely close to that.

"Momma!" Chloe's voice echoes in the room as she comes bounding through the door, running directly to Ella. Ella bends down, sliding her hands beneath Chloe's arms and lifts her into the air before tucking her against her body.

"Hi baby. Did you have the best time with Aunt Remi?"

Chloe nods eagerly, her smile bright and her eyes filled with amusement. She giggles and the sound drifts through the air, tangling around my soul. She looks like a replica of her mother. The softest features with the brightest eyes. Her smile lights up the entire room.

"Did you get everything figured out?" Remi questions her as she walks through the doorway. She half pauses, her eyebrows raising as she sees me standing in the center of the room. "Oh. Well, hello."

"Hey Remi," Ella starts as a blush spreads across her cheeks and she motions toward me. "Cole stopped by to help me and we were just talking about getting dinner from somewhere."

Remi purses her lips with mischief dancing in her eyes. She knows we were doing a little more than that, judging by the look on her face, but she doesn't call either of us out. "I am actually going to head out. My mom called and asked me to come help her with her new plates."

Remi makes a face at herself and shakes her head, shaking it off before smiling at the two of us. "I'll talk to you tomorrow, El."

Ella bites back a grin and nods at her friend before she disappears from the room. Then she directs her attention back to Chloe in her arms. "Can you say hi to Cole?"

"Hi Co."

A soft laugh rumbles in my chest. "Hi Chloe," I smile at her, giving her a small wave.

"Do you remember Cole? He gave you the little pink truck."

Chloe nods eagerly as she squirms in Ella's arms to let her down. She runs out of the room, the sounds of her little feet padding on the hardwood floors as she heads into the other room. Ella abandons her art room, stepping out into the hallway before going to see where Chloe went.

I follow after her, anticipation and excitement filling me as we stop in the doorway of Chloe's bedroom. She has the pink truck in her hand with a few other toys in her other hand. She walks right up to me and I crouch down in front of her to get to her eye level. She opens her hand and I catch a small plastic elephant from her fingertips before it falls onto the floor.

"Dis for you."

"For me?"

Chloe nods eagerly and her smile is infectious. "Yes,"

she half giggles as she glances at her mother and then back to me.

"Well, thank you so much, Chloe," I smile, lifting the elephant up to inspect it. "Does it have a name?"

"Ella."

Ella snorts from behind me. "I told you she needs a new name, Clo."

"I think it's perfect," I wink at Chloe and curl my fingers around the elephant. "I promise I will keep her safe."

Chloe lifts her hand and pats me on top of my head. "Good boy."

This earns a hearty laugh from her mother and I can't help myself as a string of laughter falls from my lips. "Okay, who's hungry?"

***

The sun sets in the distance, casting hues of yellow and orange across the horizon. I lift my tea, taking a sip as I stare out at the colors mixing together. Contentment settles in my soul and I adjust in my seat, setting my foot down on the ground, planting both feet and gently rocking back on the bench swing.

We ended up ordering takeout from the bar and hung out in the backyard until it was time for Chloe to go to bed. I didn't want Ella to feel like she needed to finish what we started earlier, but the moment I suggested I go, the disappointment in her facial expression told me everything I needed to know.

She wanted me to stay.

"Hey, cowboy." Her voice slides like silk across my eardrums and I turn my head to look at her over my shoulder. She changed into a different pair of cotton shorts and has an oversized t-shirt on. Her long hair is pulled up in a bun on top of her head. She's truly the most beautiful piece of art I've ever laid my eyes on.

"Hey darlin'."

Ella walks over and sits down next to me. Her leg is warm as it presses against the side of mine. "Thank you for today."

I turn my head to look at her, taking in her side profile before she looks over at me. "You don't have to thank me, El. I'm glad I was close enough to get here quickly. Thank you for inviting me into your home."

She stares at me for a moment, her expression unreadable as she lets out a soft breath. "I'm sorry about that. Sometimes I get easily overwhelmed and that's when I really start to overthink and second guess everything." She pauses for a moment, chewing on her lip before releasing it. "In a way, life has become easier since Chloe because I've been forced to make the hard decisions, but sometimes, things just feel like too much, you know?"

"You're trying to juggle a lot, Ella," I say. "I admire your strength. You're the best mother that little girl could ask for and it's clear in how you handle things. If you weren't havin' a breakdown every now and then, that's when I would be concerned about your mental health."

She lets out a quiet laugh, shaking her head at me. "It's not easy, trust me. I've found that things are easier to shoulder if I try to remain positive. I want Chloe to know that not everything in life is always positive, but you can get through anything if you keep your head up."

My eyes trail over the planes of her face, memorizing every inch of her. "You're absolutely right."

"Will you come to the show with me?"

My chest cracks wide open, inviting her into the home she's been constructing within the confines of my heart. Her eyes are filled with hope—with a light I never want to see extinguished. I will go anywhere this woman asks me to go.

"You don't even have to ask."

CHAPTER TWENTY-SIX

ELLA

There are two small flecks of the darkest of blues hidden in the hues of his eyes.

My eyes slowly cascade down his face, landing on his mouth. Cole watches me, his tongue darting out to wet his lips as his nostrils flare. Tension brews within the air between us and there's a spark of electricity connecting the molecules.

"Ella," he half growls, half groans. His throat bobs as he swallows hard. "You've gotta stop looking at me like that."

Excitement dances in my stomach as confidence soars inside my soul. He makes me feel confident in myself. He makes me want to take a chance—to take a risk. To do something I wouldn't normally do. "Like what?"

"Like you wanna finish what we started earlier."

I pull my legs onto the bench swing, tucking them under my body, rising onto my knees. My hands find his shoulders and I throw one leg over his body. I lower myself onto his lap, straddling him. "What if I do want to?"

Cole's nostrils flare, his eyes darkening as he grabs my

hips. His fingertips dig into my flesh and his eyes probe mine with an intensity that ripples down to my toes. "What about Chloe?"

"She's sleeping," I assure him, lifting my hands to cradle the back of his head. His dirty blonde, wavy locks of hair feel like silk between my fingers. "She was exhausted, so I don't imagine she'll be waking up anytime soon."

His hands abruptly find the sides of my face and he pulls me down to him. I inhale sharply as my mouth crashes into his. My mouth melts against his as he kisses me gently at first. His lips are soft and warm, moving against mine slowly as he takes his time. There's no hesitation from me as his tongue touches the seam of my mouth. I instantly part my lips, letting him in.

The kiss deepens and he cups the back of my neck with one hand as the other slides down my neck, over my arm, and down my torso. He's deliberately slow and always the gentleman. There's nothing rushed about the way he moves, almost as if we have all the time in the world.

And my god, I wish we did.

His tongue slides against mine, tasting and teasing as his hand ends up on my thigh. I kiss him back with a need to feel him closer. To feel more of him. My fingers are tangled in his hair and my tongue moves with his. It's a careful art of taking and giving and Cole never takes more than he gives.

I've never met a man more gentle or more attentive. He continues to put me ahead of himself, constantly lifting me to heights I never dreamed of being able to reach.

I can never thank the universe enough for bringing him into my life.

My movements become hurried and I kiss him back with a fervent need that's spilling into my veins. My body has a mind of its own as I press myself against him, feeling how hard his cock is beneath me. This is the closest we've been and my inhibitions are already dissipating. My self control is waning and I find my hands dropping down to the waistband of his pants.

"Ella," he murmurs as he abruptly breaks away from me. He lets out a shallow, ragged breath and my heart runs rampant in my chest. "Not like this."

Rejection hits me in the center of my sternum. "Why?"

"You have no idea how badly I want to strip you out of these skimpy fuckin' shorts and have you sink down on my cock right here." He lets out another breath, his voice as strained as his cock is against his pants.

"Oh," I breathe as warmth builds in between my legs. These feelings are all foreign to me, yet they feel right with him. I've never had anyone make me feel like this before… not even Jacob when we first met.

"When this finally happens, I want to take you on a real date. I want us to have an entire night of time carved out where I can take my time with you and we won't have any interruptions."

My heart swells inside my chest as my throat simultaneously constricts. "That sounds perfect," I say, my voice quiet, not fully trusting myself.

"You deserve the world, Ella," he says with genuine honesty shining in his eyes. "I have no intention of givin' you anything less than that."

I'm beginning to form a habit of finding myself speechless around this man. A cool, gentle breeze drifts past us and I instinctively shiver against it. Cole abruptly rises to his feet, swiftly lifting me into the air and supporting me with his arms.

"What are you doing?"

"Takin' you inside where it's warmer," he says matter-of-factly. My heart triples in size and I wrap my arms around his neck, pressing my face to the side of his, breathing in the smell of leather. He's familiar and comforting and I revel in the sense of security I feel with him.

Cole carries me through the house and into the living room where he sets me down on the couch. He walks away, grabbing a blanket from the basket in the corner. He drops down next to me and instead of sitting there, he grabs me, pulling me with him as he lies down on the couch.

I settle against his side, my face pressed against his chest as he throws the blanket over both of us and wraps his arms around me. "Do you want to watch a movie?" I ask him, slipping my arm around his waist.

"If that means I get to lay here for a few hours holdin' you, then yes."

A buzzing sound comes from somewhere in the distance, past the blanket of sleep I'm wrapped up in. I squeeze my eyes tighter, settling into the warmth that encapsulates me. I start to drift back asleep and I'm toeing back into the dream I was in as the sound grows louder.

The warmth beside me stirs and I'm pulled back into my dream.

Except it isn't a dream.

My eyelids slowly open and I blink a few times, settling into my reality. My arm is wrapped around his waist and my head is still on his chest. He holds me tightly against his side and he breathes evenly, his chest rising and falling as he's still asleep.

There's a soft glow from the silent TV as the movie ended hours ago. Cole fell asleep with me on the couch. Sunlight is already beginning to poke through the windows as the sun begins to rise, changing the colors in the sky.

The vibrating sound starts again and that's when I realize it's my phone on the coffee table. The screen lights up for a third time and I lift myself up, reaching over Cole for it. My eyebrows pull together as I see Remi's name. It's six-thirty in the morning. Panic instantly floods me.

"Hello?"

"Ella. Shoot, I'm sorry to wake you." Her words are hurried and her voice sounds like she's been crying. "We think Mom had a heart attack. She called me around five with symptoms that woke her up in the middle of the night. I brought her into the emergency room and they're talking about taking her in for a procedure."

I quickly sit up, my knees knocking into Cole. His eyes flash open and he blinks the sleep away as he stares at me with confusion. "Is she okay? Are you okay?"

"I'm fine. Honestly, they said it could be a lot worse, so I think that's a good thing?"

Cole is alert with a look of concern as he watches me quietly. He moves out of my way and I climb off the couch in a haste.

I start to pace. "I'm going to wake up Chloe and we will be there as soon as we can."

"Ella," Cole interrupts as he walks over to me. His arms find my biceps and he holds me for a second. "Just go. I'll let my brother know I won't be coming today, they can handle things at the ranch. I'll be here with Chloe."

"I can't ask you to do that." I shake my head as tears prick the corners of my eyes. Iris isn't my biological mother, but she's the closest thing I've had to one in years.

She's Chloe's grandmother. She took me under her wing when Remi picked me up from the airport, completely terrified and pregnant.

Iris helped heal me.

"Who is that?" Remi asks, but I half ignore her and stare at Cole.

"I'm tellin' you, you can. We will be fine, El, I promise you." He pauses, gently squeezing my arms. "Go be with Remi and Iris, I'll take care of Clo."

Tears fall from my eyes and my throat constricts. "Are you sure?"

"Yes. I am more than sure."

I let out a harsh breath. "I'll be there as soon as I can, Remi."

"Okay, I'll be here. Thank Cole for me, too."

The corners of my lips twitch and I nod. "I will."

We end the call and instinctively, I step to Cole, wrapping my arms around his waist, burying my face in his chest. "Thank you. I really appreciate you staying here with her."

"You don't have to thank me, Ella," he says with a softness in his tone as he holds me tightly and presses his face against the top of my head. "I am here for whatever you need, whenever you need me. Go be with them and make sure Iris is okay."

Emotion washes over me, overwhelming my senses and I revel in the way he feels wrapped around me. He's surprised me more than I ever imagined. When I first saw him again, I wasn't looking for anyone. I didn't need any kind of distraction. I was fine on my own, doing my thing with Chloe and knowing I never needed another person to complete me. A relationship wasn't something I planned on getting into any time soon, especially when I was still trying to nurse the wounds that Jacob left.

Cole Wild helped me to heal. He showed me that not everyone is like Jacob Evans. There is good to be found in people. There is hope in the world. He has changed my view on so many things, but he also helped me to look at myself differently. There's still a lot of work to be done, a lot of internal habits and thought processes I need to change. But now there is a confidence within me that I never knew I possessed.

I'm starting to believe in myself more than I ever have before.

I'm starting to believe in this... in us.

"I don't know what I did before you," I murmur, my voice barely above a whisper. My nostrils flare, tears pricking at the corners of my eyes. Now that he's in my life, I can't imagine it without him. I don't want to imagine it without him.

Even if he is only a friend.

"You did what you had to do, El," he whispers, his hand stroking my head as he runs it over my hair and down my back. "But now I'm here to lift some of the burden from you. I'm here to do the heavy liftin' for you."

"I don't need you to do any of that." I pull away and peer up into his eyes. "I don't want you to ever feel like you're taking on any of my problems or anything like that."

He lifts his hand to cup the side of my face. "Then just let me be here by your side. I'm here to support you, to lend a helping hand. I'm at your disposal, Ella Daniels. Whatever you need, I'm your guy."

I lift up on my toes, pressing my mouth against his as

my lips melt against him. Cole holds onto me as he kisses me gently before pulling back.

"Go," he says, moving me away from him. "Take your time. Take the entire day. When you come home, we'll be here."

The words linger on the tip of my tongue, but I don't dare speak them out loud. "Thank you, Cole."

"Anything for you, El."

CHAPTER TWENTY-SEVEN

COLE

I'm in the kitchen when I hear her soft feet coming down the hallway. Turning around, I wipe my hands on the apron I found hanging in the mudroom and find a sleepy little Chloe standing in the doorway. She has a stuffed elephant tucked under one arm and the other has a soft pink blanket draped over it with more than half of it dragging on the floor.

"Hey Clo," I say softly, a smile breaking out across my face. I walk over to her, crouching down to her level. Her blonde hair is a tangled mess on top of her head and she raises one fist to rub at her left eye. She looks like she could go back to sleep still and I can tell there's a touch of confusion in her expression. "Your mommy had to go see Aunt Remi, but she'll be back later today. You and I are going to hangout and do some fun stuff."

I don't bother telling her where Ella actually went. At her age, she won't understand and the last thing I want to do is cause any anxiety or for her to get worked up at all. Chloe doesn't say anything and nods, her eyes assessing me like she isn't sure whether or not she's okay with it. I don't want her to freak out and I know I'm still a little bit of a stranger to her, so I need to find a way to ease into this to make her feel comfortable with me.

This isn't exactly how Ella or I planned on me getting to know Chloe, but I couldn't leave her hanging this morning. Ella needed to go make sure Iris is okay and be there for her friend. I didn't hesitate to jump in and help and it made my heart soar when Ella agreed to it. It was a leap of trust I wasn't sure she was ready to grant me.

"Do you like pancakes?" I ask Chloe.

I already know she does, but this is a way for me to get my foot in the door with this tough little critic.

Chloe nods her head, half craning her neck to see what I have going on at the stove.

"Have you ever made pancakes before?"

She purses her lips and nods her head. "Momma wets me help."

"Well, since she isn't here, do you think you can help me? I don't know if I'm doing it right."

Chloe's face cracks the slightest and a smile breaks through as she moves past me, walking over to the dining room table. I watch her as she grabs one of the chairs and the sound of the legs scraping against the floor echoes in the house as she pushes it over to the oven. I walk over, trying to help her, but she gives me a look that is exactly like one her mother would give if she didn't ask for help.

I can't help but smile as a chuckle rumbles in my chest. She climbs up onto it and I move over to her, making sure I'm there to catch her if she needs any help. She hands me her blanket and stuffed animal and I set them on an empty part of the counter before standing by the stove with her. Chloe picks up the spatula and tries to replicate what she's seen her mother do.

She doesn't fully know what she's doing but her confidence is admirable. She's reluctant to accept my assistance, but by the third botched pancake, I have her accepting my help. We work together and end up with a hefty stack of pancakes on a plate. Chloe climbs down from her chair and I carry it over to the dining room table before setting everything else out for breakfast. I help her into her seat and give her a smile before putting a pancake on her plate.

"Thank you for your help, Chloe," I smile at her and put some food on my own plate.

"You welcome," she says in her soft little kid voice, offering me a kind smile. I laugh at her words and she gives me another look before she starts to eat. She doesn't dare tell me how good they are, but I don't think they would taste as good as they do if I wouldn't have had her help. She's like a mini Ella who encapsulates all the good pieces of her. She told me she wanted to raise her daughter to be strong and fierce and I think it's safe to say she is succeeding.

<hr>

After breakfast, I help Chloe get into the outfit she picked out and we head into the bathroom for her to finish getting ready. She's extremely independent and insists she can brush her teeth herself. I stand in the doorway, watching her as she proves herself right and manages to get it all done independently. The only thing she asks me for help with is to get the lid off the toothpaste and to squeeze the perfect amount onto the bristles for her.

Chloe grabs a brush and attempts to get through her tangled locks. I can see the frustration on her face as she tries to stretch her arms to get the back of her head. She misses a few of the knots and the defeat hangs in her shoulders before she turns to look at me. "Co, help!"

Her question catches me off guard while simultaneously making my heart constrict in my chest. "Of course. Let me see the brush."

She hands it to me and comes to stand in front of me to brush her hair. I try to do it as gently as possible and it takes a little longer than it should, but we manage to brush through all the knots and then I end up trying to pull her hair back into a pony tail so it's out of her face. It's the first time I've ever done it, but I don't think it looks too bad.

Chloe looks in the mirror, turning her head from side to side. "My momma do it he-uh," she tells me, pointing up toward the top part of the back of her head. "Dis okay."

"I can try and fix it."

She smiles and shakes her head. "All done."

I smile at her, accepting it as it is and we head out of the bathroom to the living room. I glance at the watch on my wrist, internally cursing when I realize what time it is. I had a mile long to-do list for today and am supposed to meet with one of the owners of the mares I've been training.

My phone is sitting on the coffee table and I pick it up, noticing I have three missed calls and a few text messages. I forgot to call him earlier in the whirlwind of Ella leaving.

The missed calls are all from Cade so I quickly call him back, letting him know that I got tied up at Ella's but will be at the ranch soon and that Chloe's tagging along. There's a text from Wyatt, saying he tried to get ahold of Ella to tell her he's on his way to the hospital.

I quickly text him back to let him know that I'll text her. When I text Ella, she quickly responds, letting me know she already talked to him. She sends another thank you after I let her know Chloe's going to the ranch with me.

"Okay, Chloe, we need to find your shoes so we can go do some fun stuff."

Her eyebrows pinch together. "Wike what?"

I didn't really think this through.

"Do you want to go see some horses?"

Her face lights up and she nods eagerly. I don't know if she really knows what she's agreeing to, but she doesn't give me any issues as we find a pair of little boots and she slides her feet into them. I check my phone to read three more messages I missed before we leave the house. There's one from Cade, saying he got the owners to reschedule and there's two from Ella.

> **ELLA**
>
> Thank you again for watching Chloe. I hope she is being good and I left her car seat on the front porch in case you need to go anywhere. She'll tell you what she needs and doesn't need, but let me know if you have any issues. She usually takes a nap around two, but she's been fighting it a lot lately.
>
> Also, Iris is doing really well, so I can come home whenever you need me to.

I smile, reading over her messages twice. I ask Chloe if she has a bag she takes along and she nods before walking over to the front door and grabs a backpack. I open it up, finding some snacks packed inside, along with extra clothes and anything else she might need.

Is there anything we need, other than what is in the backpack?

And take your time, please. We're going to the ranch for a little bit, but I will make sure to have her home for nap time.

ELLA

The backpack should have everything.

Thank you, Cole. You're amazing and I seriously owe you.

COLE

I'll see you when you get home.

Chloe's little hand is in mine and we walk along the field, her eyes moving back and forth as she looks at the horses that come to greet us by the fence. She raises her other arm, pointing at the big bay mare who reaches her nose towards us.

"She's a big horse, isn't she, Clo?" I ask her, scooping her into my arms.

"So big!" She exclaims, her infectious smile spreading across her lips. I take her hand in mine, holding it out with her fingers protected.

"Here, let her smell you first," I say as the mare reaches towards us, inhaling the scent of Chloe's hand before blowing out a breath through her nostrils.

Cade comes walking from somewhere behind the horses, raising an eyebrow as he sees me holding Chloe in my arms. "Since when do you have a kid?"

"You didn't know about her?" I joke, chuckling and rolling my eyes at my brother. "This is Chloe, Ella's daughter."

"Oh, shit," he laughs, a smile drifting across his lips. "I mean shoot. Well, hello Miss Chloe."

"Chloe, this is my brother, Cade."

"Hi Cade."

Cade chuckles, giving her a soft, tender smile. "It is so nice to meet you." He looks back at me. "What exactly are you doin' with her here?"

"I brought her to come see the horses," I say with a shrug. I wasn't really needed for anything today, since I was giving the horses the day off and Cade got the owners to reschedule. "We're going to head to the lake to collect some rocks after we're done here."

Cade stares at me for a moment before walking up to the mare and pulling her away from the fence. He slides the rope halter over her head and leads her through the gate with the leadrope. I walk over to him with Chloe, letting her pet the mare.

Chloe's fingers dance through the mare's mane and she giggles as the horse turns her head, blowing a soft breath against Chloe's cheek.

"I think she likes you, Clo," I smile, watching carefully as the mare nuzzles Chloe's neck. It's a tender moment between a massive animal and the smallest little girl.

I keep my eye on her like a hawk, just in case. I have faith and trust the horses, but you never know. All it takes is one little thing…

Moving away from the mare, I adjust Chloe against my side, tucking her close to my body. She looks over my shoulder, pointing out to the pasture as she watches one of the other horses rolling in the dirt.

"You know, I never imagined you with kids, Cole,"

Cade says quietly as Chloe pays no attention to us. "But now I think I can."

"I never put much thought into them and honestly, I'm not even sure I need my own," I say, adjusting Chloe in my arms. "I'd be perfectly content with having the two of them in my life."

"You're fallin' for her, aren't you?"

I stare at my brother for a moment and let out a deep breath. The realization hits me like a ton of bricks. I swallow roughly, over the lump lodged inside my throat.

I don't know how or when it happened. All I know is it happened fast–faster than I thought was possible–and I know there's nothing I can do to change the way I feel about her now. She's nestled herself in my chest beneath my ribcage. She took my heart and made it a home.

"I think I am."

A smile lifts his lips. "You deserve to be happy."

I turn to look out at the mountains in the distance. "So does she," I say softly, not only telling him but also myself.

Ella deserves everything good that there possibly is, whether I'm the one who gives it to her or not.

Although, I do hope she'll let it be me...

CHAPTER TWENTY-EIGHT

ELLA

Pausing outside the front door, I take a deep breath, my chest rising with my inhale before letting it out. Today started out rougher than I had imagined, but now that I'm home, I feel like I could break down and cry. The emotion is overwhelming, especially after the scare Iris gave us this morning. When Remi called me, I instantly went into panic mode. I was expecting the worst and wasn't sure how I was going to handle any of it.

I was terrified I was going to have to come home to my daughter and shatter her entire world. Iris is the only grandmother Chloe has. She's the only person in her life who has assumed that role. Losing her would be devastating to all of us.

Unfortunately, she did have a heart attack in the early hours of the morning. Thankfully, it wasn't a bad one and since everyone acted as quickly as they did, they were able to implement the interventions to minimize the damage to her heart. When I arrived at the hospital, they were taking her into the O.R. to put in a stent. After her procedure was done and she was in recovery, they told us that it was something that will be able to be managed. She's at high risk now because it has happened once already, but her future isn't bleak.

It's manageable and she will still be with us for hopefully many years to come.

When something like this happens, it has a way of affecting every part of your life. Chloe is a happy and healthy little girl, but that doesn't mean accidents can't happen. Our time together can easily be cut short.

If anything, the jarring experience with Iris reminded me how fleeting life is. How time is a thief and how important it is to cherish the time we have with people because tomorrow isn't guaranteed. In the blink of an eye, it can all go away. And one day when we're old, we'll look back and wish we would have had more time than we did.

I wipe a tear away from my cheek, collect myself, and turn the doorknob to the right before slipping into the house. The soft sound of classical music plays from the kitchen and I inhale the scent of something similar to soy sauce coming from the same direction. I kick off my shoes and let my nose lead me to where Chloe and Cole are hovered over the stove.

Chloe has an apron that is far too big for her wrapped around her waist. It looks as if Cole folded it a few times so it wouldn't hang around her feet, creating a tripping hazard. She's wearing a little chef hat and I'm not sure where it came from, but I can't help myself as I smile at the sight of them. Cole's wearing a baseball hat that's backwards on his head and he has an apron of his own tied around his waist.

"What's going on here?"

Chloe whips her head around to look at me, her face lighting up as soon as her eyes settle on me. "Momma!" She exclaims, attempting to climb off the chair. Cole reaches for her, gently setting her down on the floor before she comes barreling at me. I scoop her up, wrapping my arms tightly around her holding her close to me, reveling in her warmth and familiar smell.

I lift my face from her hair and catch Cole watching us with a wistful grin on his face. My heart soars in my chest as my gaze rests on his. He's warm and welcoming, safe and steady. Emotion wells inside of me, the waves crashing against the shore. I'm done keeping him at arms length. I've tried to pretend that Cole Wild isn't deep inside my heart but goddammit, he is.

He's nestled himself inside my ribcage and I'm tired of trying to eradicate him.

"I hope you're hungry," he says with a smile before turning back to the stove. I hold Chloe in my arms and walk over to him, looking at what appears to be a stir fry in the wok and a pot full of rice. "Chloe said you really like vegetables."

I stifle a laugh as Chloe giggles in my arms. "I wonder what else she's told you."

"Nothing bad," he tells me with a wink before finishing up the food. I head over to the dining room table, finding that he already has three places set for us. I set Chloe down, helping her to take off her apron, but she insists on wearing the hat as she sits down in her seat. Cole walks over, setting everything in the center of the table before he heads back into the kitchen once more to grab a pitcher of water.

Making sure Chloe can't reach any of the hot stuff, I

follow him over to the counter and he almost runs into me, water sloshing over the edges of the pitcher as he turns around to face me. "Hey darlin'," he breathes, a smile pulling on his lips.

"Hey cowboy," I say, smiling back at him. Without another word, I slide my hands around the back of his neck, pulling his face down to mine. His lips brush against my mouth, stealing the air from my lungs as he kisses me with a tenderness that pulls at my heartstrings. There's nothing rushed about the way his lips move with mine. It's like he has all the time in the world...

All the time for me.

"What was that for?" He says breathlessly as we break apart. His eyes are hopeful as they search mine with an intensity that seeps into my bone marrow.

I shrug, feeling the heat creep up my neck. "I just wanted to kiss you."

"Well," he says, his lips pressing against mine before he pulls away again. "You can kiss me anytime you want."

"Okay," I whisper as the corners of my lips lift in the slightest.

"Well, this is interesting."

My stomach drops. I forgot Wyatt was stopping by before heading home.

Cole's arms don't leave my waist as he looks past me at my brother. "Hey Wyatt."

"Wild," he says with a tense tone. I move in Cole's arms, turning to face my brother. He stares at the two of us, his eyes drifting between Cole and I before settling on Cole's face. "El, can you give us a minute?"

I slowly pull away from Cole, my gaze moving to his face and then back to my brother's. "Sure. Chloe and I will be waiting for you two at the table."

I grab another plate and set of silverware before disappearing into the dining room. I strain my ears, trying to hear whatever my brother and Cole are talking about, but I can't. I know I'll have to wait until later to find out what was said between the two of them.

That is, as long as my brother doesn't chase him away.

CHAPTER TWENTY-NINE

COLE

Wyatt steps deeper into the kitchen, stopping directly in front of me as he backs up to the counter and leans against it. He's silent, studying me as if he's trying to measure what has changed between us.

I don't speak a single word. There's nothing for me to defend here and I'm sure as hell not going to apologize for what he just saw. Instead, I stand there, waiting for him to connect the dots. It takes less than thirty seconds for him to speak.

"You're in love with her," he finally says, his voice low as he tilts his head to the side.

There's no sense in lying to him.

I roll my lips between my teeth, bobbing my head. "I am."

He falls silent, his jaw flexing slightly. He blows out a breath. "For how long?"

My throat bobs and I swallow hard. "For a while."

He inhales deeply. "This isn't just a…" He waves his

hand, releasing the breath. "A moment or a phase or something, is it?"

"No," I admit, shaking my head. "It's not."

His eyes fall to the floor for a second. "You know, you could have told me," he says softly, his eyes flashing back to mine. "When you took her to dinner, you could have told me there was more behind it."

"There wasn't at that time," I admit, my voice low. "I didn't want to say anything to you until I knew she was ready for this. Until I knew she was ready for something more with me."

He stares at me for a moment, studying me before he finally nods. His movements are slower and he lets out another breath. "I'm not mad," he admits. "I'm honestly not even surprised by it."

I blink twice. "You're not?" This isn't the reaction I expected.

"No," he says, shaking his head as he pushes away from the counter. "I see the way you look at her. You're the only guy I would trust with her. You're not stupid enough to mess her up." He pauses. "Or that little girl."

Emotion catches in my throat and I force it away. "I don't wanna screw any of this up." I pause, swallowing over the lump. "I'm letting Ella lead. I'm letting her decide how far she wants to take things and how quickly."

Wyatt's eyes search mine. "You haven't told her, have you?"

My heart pounds in my chest. "No, not yet."

"Don't wait too long," he says, giving me one last searching look. He closes the distance between us, clasping his hand around my bicep. "You never know how much time you have."

There's a heaviness in his tone and I know he's thinking about their parents.

"I plan on telling her when she's ready to hear it."

Wyatt slowly nods. "Good. I trust you to do right by her, and by Chloe." The corners of his mouth twitch. "You have my blessing."

"Thanks, Wy."

"Sure," he says, releasing my bicep before slapping it. "Just know, I'll burn your ranch to the ground if you break her heart."

He lets out a chuckle and I laugh along with him, but I don't miss the darkness in his eyes. Wyatt means it. Those two are the only real family he has left and even though he doesn't live close by anymore, he'll still protect Ella and Chloe in whatever way he has to.

Wyatt leaves without another word, heading into the dining room to Ella and Chloe. I follow after him and Ella's gaze immediately flashes to mine.

I give her a smile, a gentle tip of my chin, and watch as her expression visibility relaxes.

She has nothing to worry about, just like her brother…

CHAPTER THIRTY

ELLA

Cole and I stand on the front porch, waving to my brother as he climbs into his truck for his journey home. Cole's hand lingers against my lower back and I revel in the way he feels here with me.

In a way, he's still the same kind and gentle boy I remember growing up, but in other ways, he's different. He's grown into an admirable man. Strong and solid, loyal and dedicated.

He makes me feel seen, he makes me feel heard. It's like the things I say matter. My dreams are real and attainable. His support is unwavering and it's something I can see me losing myself in.

Cole Wild slipped between my ribs and burrowed deep inside my heart. He's the light in the darkness. The salve that soothed my wounds. He helped me find myself—my voice—and helped to piece me back together.

He breathed life back into me.

And I know with him, it's okay to fall, because I can trust him to catch me.

Chloe abandons my leg and instead sandwiches herself

between Cole and I, wrapping her arms around both of our legs.

I watch as Cole's other hand reaches down to her head and Chloe looks up at him, smiling brightly. I've never felt this contentment before, but it's everything I wished for.

This peace, this happiness...

It's a sanctuary I've never experienced until now.

We're safe.

<hr>

After seeing Wyatt off, I get Chloe tucked away in bed and find Cole sitting on the couch flicking through the channels on the TV as he waits for me. When he sees me enter the room, he pauses, his eyes meeting mine in a rush. I let out a sigh, exhaustion mixed with relief and sit down next to him.

"What did my brother say to you?" I question him after a moment passes between us.

Cole turns to look at me, a smile drifting across his face. "He's okay with this, El. I promise you, there's nothin' to worry about." Cole hands me the remote. "I don't know what to put on TV. I don't watch it much."

Relief floods me and I take the remote. Instead of finding something, I toss it onto the couch behind me and climb onto his lap. His eyes widen as I settle on him, my hands finding the sides of his face. I stare into the blue depths of his shimmering irises.

"You know, when we were younger, I had a huge crush on you. But when I saw you again, I wanted nothing to do with you," I start, my voice quiet as he stares back at me with that intense look that tangles itself around my soul. "After Jacob, I didn't want a relationship. I swore I would never put myself in a vulnerable position again. He may not have broken my heart in the typical sense, but he still left me damaged. I became dependent on him and in our relationship, I felt powerless. He changed my life for the worst and I swore I would never do it again. I never wanted Chloe to think something like that was normal."

Cole doesn't say anything, he's patient and kind as he waits for me to continue.

"When we started to talk and the seed of our friendship was planted, I knew it would never remain like that. I tried to keep you out of my heart. I tried to keep my guard in place and resist the feelings that were slowly chipping my walls away." I pause, tears pricking the corners of my eyes and I stare down at the man who holds my entire heart in his hands. "I never stood a chance against you, Cole Wild. You came barreling into my life with your sights set on my heart."

"And they still are."

"You are my calm after the storm," I say, my voice breaking around the words as tears fall from my eyes. "When the clouds break apart and begin to separate. The sun shines through the cracks, urging them away from each other as the sky transforms into the most beautiful showcase of colors. Hues of oranges, yellows, and pinks dancing across the bright blue sky."

Emotion dances within the depths of his eyes as they shine back at me. "The calm." He lifts his hands to catch my tears as they fall.

"I can't deny my feelings for you any longer, Cole." I laugh softly, shaking my head. "I thought it was a little crush that would go away, but I was terribly wrong. It's not just a crush and these feelings aren't going anywhere. If anything, they've only become more intense."

He stares at me for a moment as he slides his hands underneath my jaw. "Say the words, El. I need to hear it from you."

"I think I'm falling for you."

His nostrils flare and the corners of his mouth twitch." It took you long enough."

Without another word, without another chance to breathe, he pushes up off the couch, his mouth claiming mine. He steals the air from my lungs, kissing me without a single beat of hesitancy. His lips crash against mine like the waves against the shore from a storm surge. His fingers trail along my jaw, savoring every touch, every inch of skin he strokes.

His lips are soft and he tastes sweet as he traces the seam of my lips with his tongue. This is what I want. He is what I want. I part them, letting him in as his tongue slides across mine. I'm lost in him, caught in the undertow as he pulls me deep into the depths of his soul. He surrounds me, consuming me, and overwhelming every single sense.

My tongue tangles with his and I memorize the way he feels and smells. My heart pounds erratically in my chest, but I can barely feel it hammering away. All I can feel is him. He kisses me with a reverent need and what started with no urgency, quickly transforms into something completely different. He pulls the air from my lungs, drinking me in and I let him. God, do I let him...

His hands are soft and attentive as they slide down the sides of my neck, tracing their way to my collarbone. My hands are at the bottom seam of his shirt, pushing it up his torso, his warm skin beneath my fingertips. My hands explore every inch of his abdomen, memorizing the dips and the curves, imprinting the way he feels beneath my palms inside my brain.

"El," he murmurs against my lips as I push his shirt up farther. I pull away from him, sitting up straighter in his lap, reaching for the bottom hem of my shirt and pulling it up over my head. I toss it onto the floor. "Fuck, Ella," he breathes, his voice hoarse with a burning desire.

My breath catches in my throat and there isn't a single part of me that feels uncomfortable under his gaze. I got lucky with my pregnancy and only have a few stretch marks around my belly button to show for it. From time to time, I feel self conscious of them, but with the way he's looking at me, all those feelings are instantly chased away.

He trails the tips of his fingers over the scars, staring at them before his eyes meet mine in a rush. "Goddamn, you're perfect." He lets me remove his shirt, his eyes searching mine as he watches me reach around my back. I unclasp my bra and the cool air brushes across my breasts as I slide the straps down my arms and toss the undergarment onto the floor with our shirts.

Cole's throat bobs as he swallows roughly and it's as if he's frozen in place. I reach for his hands, lifting them up to my breasts until he's cupping each one. His cock presses against my center with only our clothing separating us. I'm taking a chance. I'm taking all my chips and putting them on Cole Wild. He groans, the sound half strangled as he presses against me, his hands wrapping around my breasts.

"Ella, darlin'," he breathes, his face contorting. "Are you sure this is what you want?"

Pulling my bottom lip between my teeth, I nod. "I want this," I admit, letting out a shallow breath. "I want you." I pause, his gaze penetrating mine. "Love me, Wild."

"Fuck," he groans before his mouth crashes back into mine.

CHAPTER THIRTY-ONE

COLE

I n a matter of seconds, I'm on my feet lifting her into my arms before carrying her down the hallway to her bedroom. Her hands are in my hair, her lips trailing down my neck as I find her room and step inside. I kick the door shut behind me and Ella murmurs against my neck.

"Lock the door," she says breathlessly as she nips at my bounding pulse. "I don't want Chloe to walk in on us."

Dammit.

The thought of her daughter has me freezing in place. My movements are slow as I turn back to the door and reach for it, but Ella immediately breaks the moment between us. She shimmies from my grip, dropping down to her feet as she half covers her naked chest from me.

"If you don't want to do this, we don't have to," she offers, her voice dejected and small. "You're a single man without kids. I get it if you don't want to get involved with an emotionally damaged single mom."

Her words are like a blow to my chest and I instantly feel regret for making her feel like she was anything less than everything. I lock the door behind me, immediately stepping into her space, grabbing her wrists and pulling her arms away from her body. "Let's get two things straight, El," I start as I back her toward the bed. "Number one, don't ever hide yourself from me." She stops as the backs of her legs hit the mattress. "Number two, Chloe is the cutest kid I've ever met and you being a single mom changes nothin' between us. It doesn't make me want you any less. It doesn't make me want this any less." I pause, my eyes searching hers as I cup the sides of her face once more. "I want you and I want her."

"What made you pause then?"

"I just wanted to make sure it didn't matter that she's here."

Her lips part slightly and she looks momentarily conflicted. "She's asleep. She has a white noise machine so she won't hear anything."

A chuckle rumbles in my chest. I like the way she's thinking... worrying about anyone hearing her. "Good." I start to lower her down on the bed, hooking my fingers under the waistband of her pants and panties, swiftly removing them. "When is the last time someone made you feel good, Ella? When was the last time someone other than yourself made you come?"

Blush instantly spreads across her cheeks. "It's been a long time."

"So you don't mind if I go ahead and make you come then?"

"Be my guest," she tells me, her voice hoarse as she stares up at me.

I move away from the bed and stand at the edge. Her legs part, her knees falling to the side as my eyes scan every inch of her body. "Goddammit, look at you," I groan, my cock straining against my pants. "I could stare at you like this for the rest of my life."

"Take off yours too," she says, her voice urgent as she tries to reach for me. I chuckle again, undoing my pants and pushing them down with my boxer briefs. Ella's eyes instantly land on my cock. "Holy shit." The curse word on her lips makes my dick twitch. "You're big. Like big, big."

"Don't worry El," I murmur, lowering myself onto the bed. "I promise we can make it fit."

She reaches for me, wrapping her hand around my length as she lets out a strangled gasp. Her fingers trail across the barbells on the underside of my dick. "Are these piercings?"

"They are."

Her eyes flash to mine, shock mixing with curiosity. "You're full of surprises, aren't you?"

"Hmm," I murmur again, my voice catching in my throat as I move away from her touch, lowering myself down onto my stomach between her legs. Her pussy is right in my face and I groan as I run a finger along her center, feeling how wet she is already. "You're fuckin' soaked," I breathe as she writhers beneath my touch. "You're ready for me, aren't you?"

"Yes," she moans as she lifts her head. There's a touch of anxiety in her eyes and I want to chase every fear away.

"Can I taste you?"

Worry crosses her features. "I don't–it's been a long time since anyone has ever gone down on me." Her voice drops lower. "What if I don't taste good?"

"Why don't you let me be the judge of that?" I question her, dying to run my tongue against her. "If you want me to stop at any time, tell me."

"Okay," she breathes, nodding at me before lowering herself back down onto the bed. "Okay."

My face dips down between her legs and I hold her legs apart with my arms, running my tongue along her. A low groan rumbles in my throat and my cock simultaneously throbs as I taste her. She tastes like the sweetest thing I've ever had the honor of divulging in and I'm ready to eat her alive.

I lick her pussy, circling my tongue around her clit before lapping at her once more. Alternating between tasting and teasing, I fuck her with my mouth before pushing my tongue inside her. She surprises me as her hands dive through my hair, gripping the locks tightly against my scalp. I continue to move against her, deliberately slow as I move against her clit over and over again. This is what has her bucking her hips, pressing her pretty cunt against my face.

Holding her in place, my fingers dig into her flesh and I swirl my tongue again, flattening it, applying more pressure. All her inhibitions are lost. She's a mess of moans, bucking against my face, withering on the bed beneath my touch. She's so close to coming apart at the seams and I'm ready to fuck up her entire life.

She shifts her hips and presses her cunt to my mouth and I devour her. A smirk pulls on my lips and I grin against her as I continue to work against her clit. Her legs shake beneath my arms and she pushes against me in an effort to close them. I know she's close to coming so I pin her down, my tongue lapping at her over and over again.

"Oh my god, Cole," she moans, her voice crumbling around the words. "I'm so close. I'm going to come."

"Come for me, El," I groan against her cunt, my

tongue swiping her again, swirling around her clit. "Fuck my face until you come on my tongue."

Ella's grip on my hair tightens and she holds on for dear life as she's on the brink of ecstasy. One roll of my tongue is all it takes to have her orgasm tearing through her body. She cries out my name, the sound penetrating my eardrums. I pin her down, ravaging her sweet cunt, finding myself swirling into a treacherous addiction. I'm addicted to the way she tastes, to the way she feels coming on my face.

Goddamn, she is absolute perfection.

I slow my movements as she begins to ride out the waves of her orgasm. I lap at her, licking and tasting every drop until she has nothing left to give. Ella's lost in the aftershocks and I pull away. Moving up her body, I crawl until I'm hovering above her face. Ella looks up at me, her lips parting with a ragged breath. She lifts her legs, wrapping them around my lower back as she begins to pull me closer to her.

"Ella," I groan, the tip of my cock pressing against her dripping wet cunt. "Are you sure this is what you want? I need you to tell me before I fuck you."

"Yes, Cole," she breathes, her eyes glazed over. "I want to feel you inside me." She pauses, her voice softer. "If you're worried about not having a condom, it's okay. I have an IUD."

A moan creeps up my throat as I slide the tip inside of her. "Thank god," I murmur, pushing inside her in one fluid movement. Her hands are instantly on my back, her nails digging into my flesh as her lips part. Her eyes are wide, her cunt stretching around me as I fill her to the hilt. "That's it, El, you can take it." I groan, pressing deeper into her. "I told you we would make it fit."

"Jesus Christ," she breathes, her voice getting caught in her throat. Her chest rises and falls as she sucks in another rapid breath. "I've never been with someone this... big. Or pierced."

"Good," I smirk. "And you're never going to be with anyone else after this. I'm going to ruin you for any other man, Ella." My lips capture hers in a hasty kiss and I move my hips. "You take me so fucking well. Your cunt is so tight around my cock. I don't know how long I'm going to last."

She moves her hips with me, lifting them to meet me as I begin to move inside of her. The barbells along the underside of my dick massage her insides and I pump my cock into her, sliding in and out, filling her to the brim with every thrust. My balls smack against her, the sound echoing in the room around us as it mixes with the soft moans that escape her.

She continues to stare up at me, her lips parting slightly as breathless moans fall from her lips. I hear my name rolling off her tongue as I pound into her over and over. I love seeing her like this right now. She clenches around me, her tight cunt sucking me in with every stroke. My movements slow as something shifts in the air between us. As much as I want to fuck her into oblivion, I want to love her even more.

Ella pulls my face down to hers, our mouths crashing into one another and I rock into her again. Her legs tighten around my waist and she lifts herself, wanting as much as I can give her. "Don't you dare stop, Cole Wild," she breathes against my lips before kissing me deeply.

"Tell me what you want, El."

"I want you to fuck me until you come. I want to feel you deep inside of me as you make me come again."

Goddamn.

Her words only fuel me more and I pound into her harder. I thrust into her over and over until we're both a mess of moans. Until she's crying out my name and coming apart at the seams. She loses herself around my cock, her orgasm thrusting her into a different universe as I lose myself inside of her. I fill her with my come, pumping my hips until neither of us have anything left to give. Only after she's fully satiated do I slide out of her and pull her into my arms. She nestles against my side, her face pressing against my chest as she wraps her arm around my waist. I bury my face in her hair, breathing in the scent of her before I press my lips to her head.

"You feel so good," I murmur against her hair, her arm tightening around my waist. "I love you here, like this." I pause, letting out a slow breath. "How are you feelin'?"

She slowly rolls her head, propping her chin on my chest. I watch her lips as the corners lift, her eyes glazed over, eyelids heavy. "Amazing," she breathes, letting out a soft laugh. "That was unlike anything I've ever experienced before."

I stare at her, my breath catching in my throat. "I wanna make you feel good, El. In bed, out of bed. Wherever you are."

Her eyebrows lower, her throat bobbing as her eyes grow misty. "You do," she says softly.

Reaching for her face, I brush a stray hair away from her cheek, tucking it behind her ear. "I don't know what you're doin' to me, darlin, but goddammit, I love it."

"Yeah?" She asks me quietly, her voice barely above a whisper. "The feelin's mutual, cowboy."

Leaning forward, I press my lips to her forehead before pulling her back against me. She nestles in, her walls remaining lowered, her face turned to the side against my chest.

She has finally let me in and I have no plans of ever letting her go after this. As much as I thoroughly enjoyed losing myself inside of her, I want her to know that she's more than that. She will never be someone I only want to fuck. Even if that's what we're doing, I want her to know it's something deeper. It's always something more.

Above all things, I want Ella Daniels to know that she's loved.

And that I'm the one who loves her.

CHAPTER THIRTY-TWO

ELLA

I stand in front of the gallery, my head tilting backwards as I look at the sign above. My stomach is in knots and excitement runs rampant through my body. I'm a nervous ball of anxiety mixed with a touch of anticipation. This is the first time I've ever done anything like this, so there is a part of me that is excited. But the part of me that is surrounded by self doubt doesn't think I can do this.

It's hard to convince myself that I won't be a total failure.

Cole helped me bring all my paintings here to Vera's gallery the other day and they said everything would be handled before the show. All that was required of me was to show up a little bit before it opened so I could get a feel for things and then it was showtime. I have no idea what to fully expect. I don't know how many people will be here.

"Hey darlin'," Cole's voice slides against my eardrum as his hand touches the small of my back. I resist the urge to melt into him, to seek safety and comfort in his arms as he presses his lips to the side of my head. "Are you ready to go inside? The team is in there waitin' for you."

I slowly turn around to face him, my eyes scanning his features. "What if this doesn't go well? What if this entire thing is a flop?"

"El, we talked about this." He shakes his head, offering me a small comforting smile. "I will never set you up for failure and if I didn't believe in you and your work, I never would have presented any of it to Austin."

I hang onto his words as they infiltrate the crevices of my brain. I don't know how he manages to do it, but every time I feel myself beginning to spiral, he has this way of grounding me. He has this ability to pull me back to reality and present things to me in a clear, more optimistic fashion. He chases away the scaries in my mind. He shows me what it feels like to have someone on your side, someone who wants to lift you up instead of keeping you from reaching your potential.

He's the calm.

"Okay," I tell him, the facade of confidence rolling over me. I straighten my spine, pushing my shoulders back as I nod at him. "This is going to be great. Even if only a few people show up, it will still be amazing."

He stares at me for a beat. "Even if no one shows up, *you* are still amazing."

Emotion lodges in my throat and my lips part as a ragged breath escapes me. Behind me, the doors push open, cutting through the moment between Cole and I. He directs his gaze past me and I slowly turn around to see who it is. It's Vera, who's smiling at both of us with her bright red lips reaching towards her deep green eyes. Her sleek auburn hair is styled in a bob stopping below her cheeks. My eyes roam across her white suit jacket and pants and suddenly I feel underdressed.

Remi insisted we go shopping yesterday in preparation for the show. I found a black gown that hugged my curves before fanning out around my feet. I wasn't sure what I was supposed to wear to an event like this and Remi suggested I dress up as if I were going to a gala or something. The dress isn't as revealing as Vera's suit jacket that has a cutting V that goes to the bottom of her sternum.

Regardless of how she looks, I still feel beautiful in the dress I'm wearing.

"Ella, people will be here within the next half an hour, so we would love to have you come inspect the set up before they begin to arrive."

I glance at Cole and he gives me a reassuring smile before he looks at Vera and nods. Vera holds the door open for me and I glance back at Cole when I realize he isn't following me inside. "Aren't you coming?"

"I am. I have to run out to my truck quickly and then I will be here before everyone arrives."

My eyes widen as panic licks at my heart. "Don't make me do this alone."

"You'll never be alone, darlin'," he tells me, his voice soft and warm like an embrace. "I promise I will be right back."

I let out a ragged breath, nodding as the anxiety melts away. I know I can do it without him, but I don't want to. The thought of doing something out of my comfort zone alone has my skin tingling as if it's going to break out in hives. Cole would never set me up for failure—he said so himself.

He walks around the corner of the building, heading in

the direction we both parked and I find Vera patiently waiting for me. She smiles, motioning for me to enter the gallery. As we step inside, the air leaves my lungs in a rush as my heart crawls into my throat. The walls have been stripped of any art that isn't mine. My paintings are positioned on the walls throughout the gallery, each one showcased separately so it has its own moment of being in the spotlight.

Tears prick at the corners of my eyes. This has always felt like a pipe dream for me. Never in a million years did I think my art would be the center of a show in a gallery. Never once did I think people would come to purchase the pieces I painted from the emotions that were swirling inside of me.

"What do you think?" Vera questions me as she steps up beside me. Her eyes are on the painting in front of us as she assesses the strokes of oil across the canvas. "Does everything look okay to you?"

"It's amazing," I say, my eyes scanning the wall before I look at her. "It looks great. Thank you so much for doing this for me."

Vera shakes her head. "Thank you for creating timeless pieces like this. We're always looking for new artists and I showed some of your work to a few of our clients who will be in attendance tonight. You bring a freshness that we haven't seen in quite some time."

My heart is in my throat and I swallow hard over the emotion, nodding at her. Words fail me and at this moment, I'm not sure I even trust myself to speak. The emotions swirling inside of me are encapsulated with an intensity that threatens to make me a sobbing mess before the night even begins.

"Are you okay with being on the floor during the show?" She glances over at the door as it opens, but I don't turn to look. "Usually the artists will mingle, walk around and talk about their art with patrons."

"I'm okay with that."

Vera looks behind me again as the sound of footsteps grows louder. "I'll check in with you before things start." My eyebrows pull together as she turns to walk away with a knowing smile pulling on her lips.

I feel his presence before I turn around to look at him and my heart melts at the sight of Cole standing in front of me. In his hand is a bouquet of the most beautiful flowers I've ever laid my eyes on. The tears that threatened to fall before are definitely falling down the sides of my face now. I blink them away, a soft laugh escaping me as I lift my hands to brush them away from my cheeks.

"These are for you," he says softly, handing me the massive bouquet. "I know it isn't much, but I want you to know how proud of you I am. This is completely out of your comfort zone and you're here. You're doin' it. I think that alone speaks so much of how you have grown in the past few months." He pauses for a moment, his lips pulling upwards in a smile. "You're the most amazing person I've ever met and I know you can do anything, El. I hope tonight helps you to see that."

Another laugh falls from my lips and Cole steps closer, his hands cupping the sides of my face as he wipes a few stray tears away. He lowers his face to mine, his lips claiming mine in a slow, tender kiss that has my toes curling. Our surroundings fade away as his tongue slides against mine and I forget for a moment that we have an audience. Only when someone starts to slow clap, do I remember that we're in a gallery with other people.

Cole chuckles, his gaze colliding with mine as he pulls away from me and presses his lips to my forehead.

"That was movie worthy," Austin calls out, clapping slowly as he walks up to the two of us. "Seriously, you deserve an Oscar for that entire performance, Wild."

Cole rolls his eyes, moving to the side of me as he wraps his arm around my lower back. I melt against his side, my hand coming to his chest as I let him hold me against his body. "Maybe you can learn a thing or two." Cole looks back at me and winks.

"Yeah, right," Austin says as he mimics Cole and rolls his eyes before he looks at me with a playful grin and winks. "Good luck with this one."

"Alright, everyone," Vera cuts through the conversation as she begins to clap her hands. "People are outside and we're opening the doors in two minutes. Is everyone ready?"

Anxiety rolls through my stomach once more and Cole gives me a gentle squeeze, taking the flowers from me as he turns to face me. His mouth drops down to my ear. "You've got this, El. You can do this." He presses his lips to my temple before pulling away from me. I suck in a shallow breath, nodding, letting his confidence in me wash over my body.

I can do this.

"Okay, it's showtime!" Vera calls out as she walks over to the door, her heels clicking on the floor. I move away from Cole as someone hands me a glass of champagne and I take a hearty sip just as the doors open and people begin to file inside. A smile pulls on my lips and I take another deep breath and head toward the crowd of people by the far wall.

I am doing this.

"Damn, little sis," Wyatt says softly as he wraps his arm around the tops of my shoulders and pulls me close against his side. "I'm so proud of you."

I slide my arm around his back, half hugging him as we stand in the center of the gallery. My eyes scan the walls, finding them all bare. "I can't believe I actually did it. I can't believe people bought all my paintings."

"I can," Wyatt says, kissing the top of my head. "You're an insanely talented artist, El. Mom and Dad would be proud of you for chasing your dreams."

My heart crawls into my throat, lodging itself there as my breath catches in my chest. I swallow hard, shoving down the emotion as I blink away the burning sensation in the corners of my eyes.

"I hope they would be," I say, my voice quiet, turning my head to look up at him. "Thank you for coming tonight. Thank you for everything."

Wyatt was able to get a week off from his residency program because of Iris being in the hospital so he's been staying with her since she got home two days ago.

"That's what I'm here for, El," he tells me, a tender smile lifting his lips. "I know I'm not around like I should be, but I promise to be better with my time and make more of an effort."

"It's not just you," I admit, my throat bobbing. "I could have come to Cheyenne more to visit you." I pause. "And I will. Let's both make more time for each other, when we can, of course."

Wyatt releases my shoulders and holds his hand out. I reach for it, sliding my palm against his before we seal it with a firm shake. "Deal."

Vera walks up to the two of us, her smile reaching her eyes as her gaze follows mine. "You did so well, Ella," she says quietly as she looks back at me and then at my brother. "Can I borrow her for a few?"

Wyatt tips his chin at her. "Absolutely. I should head back to Iris' in case Remi needs any help with her or Chloe." Wyatt pulls me in for a hug. "Love you, El. I'm so proud of you."

"Love you too," I say against his chest, hugging him tightly before we break apart. Wyatt pats the top of my head, like he used to when we were kids and leaves with his laughter filling the air.

I direct my attention back to Vera and she's watching me with a grin spreading across her lips.

"We have clients who requested to be on a list to see anything else you paint in the future."

My jaw hurts from the emotion lodged in my throat and I swallow it back. "I don't even know what to say."

"You did this, Ella," she tells me, her voice filled with encouragement as she beams at me. "You say thank you and you go find that handsome cowboy of yours and go out to celebrate."

My eyes drift over to the door, where I find Cole engaged in a conversation with Austin. All of the patrons have since left and it's only a few of us still here. Vera watches her assistant as she writes something down in her notebook at the front desk.

My heart is so full, it's overflowing with love and adoration from everyone tonight.

Cole walks up to me, a smile spreading across his entire face. "I'm so proud of you, El," he tells me as he stops in front of me. "I know it's getting late, but since neither of us have eaten, do you want to go get dinner with me?"

I shake my head at him. His eyebrows pull together and he waits for me to explain. My throat bobs and I swallow. "Do you remember that date you talked about taking me out on?"

His eyes widen and excitement washes over his irises. "I told you if I took you on a date, it would be proper and planned."

"Are we limited to only one date?"

He smiles brightly. "Absolutely not. I'll take you on as many dates as you'll allow."

"Okay, good," I say, smiling as I look up at him. "I think I'd like to go out on a date with you tonight."

He stares at me for a moment. "You think or you know?"

"I know."

I do know—I know it's him.

And it will always be him.

CHAPTER THIRTY-THREE

COLE

Ella's back presses into the door and I plant my palm alongside her head, pushing it against the wood, caging her in. My mouth drops down to hers in an instant and I drink her in, stealing the air from her lungs. Her hands tangle in my hair and she holds my face down to hers as my lips move against her mouth. Gone are the soft and tender kisses. Instead, we're both caught in an intense race to the top. To the abyss of euphoria when I dive deep inside of her and slam into her until she's screaming my name.

Her fingers tug on my hair and I nip at her bottom lip, urging her to open her mouth with my tongue. She doesn't hesitate and kisses me back in a bruising, demanding manner. Her teeth clash against mine as she strips me bare. I've never been more vulnerable and exposed than I am with Ella Daniels and I don't even fucking care.

I'll gladly bare my entire soul, stripped of skin and bone for her. She can have every last piece of me. I'm beginning to fear I'm nothing without her.

"We should probably go inside," Ella breathes against

my mouth, only breaking our kiss to murmur the words before her tongue slides against mine once more. We're tangled up in one another, completely consumed and completely lost. I want to drown in her.

"Or I can bend you over the railing and fuck you right here," I quip.

Ella laughs softly against my mouth as she tugs on my hair once more. "I don't think your brothers would appreciate a show like that."

"Fuck them," I growl, nipping at her bottom lip. "I dare them to look at what's mine."

She lets out a ragged breath. "Is that what I am?"

"Damn right," I murmur, sliding my hands under the straps of her dress before pushing them down her arms. "Let me get you inside and show you just how much you are mine."

Ella turns around in my arms, taking my keys from me and drops her hand down to the doorknob as she unlocks it and pushes the door open. She turns back around to face me, an intense need burning deeply in her eyes as she reaches for me. She grabs my tie, pulling me towards her as she pulls me into the house and kicks the door shut behind me.

She leads me into the house and I don't protest as I tell her where my bedroom is. My steps don't falter and I follow after her until she releases her grip on my tie as she steps into the room. I pause in the doorway, my eyes glued to her as she slips out of her dress, letting it fall onto the floor. A groan rumbles in my chest. She's not wearing a bra or any panties. Ella glances over her shoulder before she moves to stand by the bed.

My hand drops to my pants and I quickly undo them, pushing them down to the floor before I step out of them. I reach for the buttons of my shirt and unbutton them as fast as I can as I watch Ella turn around to face me. Mischief dances with lust in her eyes and she watches me with a hooded gaze as I strip down until I'm completely naked.

I reach her, my hand sliding along the nape of her neck, lifting her hair. "You're so goddamn beautiful, Ella."

Her eyes search mine as she lifts her hands to my chest. Her lips part as if she's going to say something, but I silence her with my lips, stealing the words from her tongue. She plants her hands against me, spinning me around so I'm the one whose back is to the bed now. She breaks away from me, giving me a gentle shove until I'm flush against the mattress.

"Scoot up to the headboard," she instructs as she bends for a second. I don't protest or dare question her as I move to exactly where she tells me to go. A smile lifts the corners of her lips as she holds up my tie and begins to walk toward me. "I want to try something. Can we do that?"

"You can do whatever the hell you want to me, El," I breathe, my chest expanding as she climbs onto her knees on the bed. "I'll never tell you no."

"It's something I've never done before," she tells me as she lifts one leg over my body and straddles me. My hands begin to move toward her hips but she quickly intercepts and grabs me by my wrists. "Hold your hands above your head."

I raise an eyebrow but I don't question her any further and do what she says. "Good boy," she murmurs quietly, her eyes meeting mine as my already hard cock throbs. She positions both of my wrists together and begins to wrap the tie around them, securing both of my hands together with a knot. The ache in my shoulder is nonexistent at this point.. Her mouth tips up as she lifts them toward the headboard and ties me to the wooden post.

"I want to fuck you."

Jesus Christ.

My mouth is instantly dry and my cock feels like it's going to immediately explode. Frustration grows inside of me as I tug against the restraints that keep me from touching her. Ella's nostrils flare and she stares down at me with so much power rippling off of her. Seeing her like this has me so goddamn turned on. I want her to exercise her control. I want her to be in charge.

"I'm at your disposal, El," I say, my voice gravely and hoarse with need. "You're in charge here, so I want you to do whatever you'd like."

She inches down my body, her hand finding my cock as she grips the shaft. Holding it up right, she stares at me for a moment as she wets her lips. My heart crawls into my throat and I don't even get a chance to breathe or think before she wraps her lips around the tip of my cock and inhales my length. She takes it as far as she can, until her mouth reaches her hand wrapped around the base. I groan, my hips instantly bucking, her tongue wet and warm against the barbells on the underside of my dick.

"Jesus Christ," I moan, my hips moving again as she bobs her head, moving her mouth up and down my cock. I don't know what her angle is here and I don't know that I even care. "Sit on my cock, El. Climb on and fuck me."

Her head slowly lifts, sucking my cock before she releases it with a pop. She stares at me for a moment, pumping her hand along my length. "I'm in charge here, cowboy. I'll ride your cock when I think you're ready for me to get on."

My heart stumbles over itself inside my chest. I don't

know where this version of Ella has been hiding, but goddamn, I'm in love.

I'm in love with every version of her.

Ella wraps her lips around my dick again, playing with my piercings with her tongue as she sucks me harder. She takes me deeper into her throat until she's gagging around me. Saliva drips from the corner of her mouth as she breaks away from me once more and she wipes it away with the back of her hand. Her eyes meet mine once more and she grips my dick as she straddles my waist and begins to lower herself down. Her tight cunt surrounds me, squeezing me as she impales herself with my entire length, not stopping until her body is flush against mine.

"You were made to take my cock," I rasp, jerking my hands against the tie, trying to reach for her again. Instinctively, I growl, pulling harder as she smiles down at me and shakes my head.

"If you're a good boy, I'll let you touch me."

My nostrils flare and I lift my hips in an attempt to top her from the bottom. "What do I have to do to be a good boy?"

"Let me fuck you until you come," she moans as she rolls her hips, her hands planted on my chest as she sits up straight on top of me.

"Deal."

Heat builds in the pit of my stomach and I stare up at her, watching her as she bounces up and down, riding me like she was made for this. She lifts her hips up before sinking back onto me again. I want my hands free, but I want to come. I want to watch her come. I want to be a good boy for her so we can both reach the stars.

"Fuck, you feel so good," I moan, my head tipping back as my eyes roll in my head. "Don't stop, El."

She intentionally begins to slow her movements and I lift my head to look at her. A sinister look dances in her irises as she stills on top of me. "Ask nicely."

"Please don't stop," I murmur, the words coming out half in a plea. "Please fuck me until you come.

Her hips shift again and she begins to work the muscles in her thighs, bouncing up and down on me. I curl my hands around the tie, pulling swiftly as I get one hand free. Ella inhales sharply, raising an eyebrow at me as my hand slides between us, my fingers rolling over her clit. She doesn't say anything and instead my movements earn me a hearty moan as she tips her head back.

I play with her pussy, rolling my fingers over and over across her clit as she continues to move up and down, stroking the length of my cock with her soaked cunt. Planting my heels against the bed, I lift my pelvis, slamming up into her every time she sinks down. She moans out loud, her movements becoming rushed as all her inhibitions are out the window. She fucks me and I fuck her back, feeling the barbells along my dick rubbing inside of her.

"I'm going to come, Cole," she breathes, moving her hips once more, her ass slamming against the tops of my thighs as I thrust my cock deep inside of her. She's filled to the brim and I can feel her quickly approaching the edge of the cliff. I flatten my palm against her pubic bone while I work my thumb over her clit. Applying more pressure, I start to roll it in circles, giving her exactly what she wants.

"I can feel how close you are," I breathe, pushing harder as we become a mess of thrusts and moans. "Come for me, El. Make me come."

"Fill me with your come," she moans as her eyes roll back in her head. "Oh god." Her legs tighten as her cunt clenches around me, sucking me in deeper. Her body begins to shake as an earthquake tears through her body. She's engulfed in the flames of her orgasm, my name falling from her lips as she continues to ride me. The walls of her cunt shatter around me, the vibration sending me over the edge with her.

Heat erupts through my body, spreading through my veins like wildfire as I lose myself deep inside of her. I pump my hips a few more times, emptying myself into her before she collapses against my chest. We're both breathless and I wrap my arm around her back, holding her warm body against mine, reveling in the way she feels on top of me. This is where I always want her--right here with me.

She's fucking perfect.

And all mine.

CHAPTER THIRTY-FOUR

ELLA

Cole looks up at me from where he's lying in bed as I pull my dress back on. "Can't you just stay here the rest of the day?"

"I wish," I smile at him, shaking my head, glancing at the clock on his nightstand. I ended up spending the night here last night and Cole somehow convinced me to spend most of the day in bed with him while we ordered food delivery and spent our time wrapped up in one another. "Wyatt has Chloe at Iris' with him and he's bringing her home around dinner time, so I want to go get a shower and change my clothes."

"Shower here," he says with a playful grin as he rises from the bed and pulls his own pants on. "Shower with me."

I laugh softly as he walks up behind me, wrapping his arms around my waist as he pulls my back flush against him. He buries his face in my neck, his lips trailing along the side of my throat. I spin around in his arms, throwing my own around the back of his neck. "Do you want to come over for dinner tonight?"

"I would love to," he tells me with the softest smile before pressing his lips to mine. "Does that mean I get dessert afterwards?"

I kiss him back before pulling away. "If you play your cards right, cowboy," I smirk with a wink.

"What if I come over now instead, and we can shower together at your house?"

I tilt my head to the side, mulling over the idea before I step away from him. "I like that idea better."

"Perfect," he grins and I want to store the picture of him looking at me like this for an eternity. "I should swing by the barn to make sure everything is okay and then I will be right behind you."

"Even better."

"Such a dirty girl," he laughs, pulling me back to him as his mouth claims mine once more. "I like you greedy like this."

"Well, a certain someone has opened my eyes to a lot of things. This is all still new territory for me, but I don't want to have my guard up with you. I want to be able to act freely without overthinking everything."

Cole's eyes probe mine. "Well, you got an A+ for last night."

Blush creeps across my face at the memory of how I acted with him. Taking charge isn't something I've ever done before, but he gives me a sense of security, like I can do those things with him and not be afraid of it. "Get out of here," I giggle, swatting at him before pushing him away again. "I'll see you in a little bit."

I blow Cole a kiss before leaving him in his bedroom to deal with the mess of clothes and sheets everywhere. A stupid smile is stuck on my face as I head out to my car and start my drive home. I head off the ranch and across town, stopping at the two different red lights I hit before pulling into my driveway. I turn off the engine and stare at the house for a moment, my heart soaring outside of my chest from the past twenty-four hours with Cole.

My footsteps are light as I walk up onto the porch and make my way to the front door. I reach for the doorknob, accidentally turning it before sliding my key into the hole when it opens anyways. My eyebrows pull together, conflicted for a moment. Yesterday was such a whirlwind between getting ready for the art show and actually going there. I know I usually lock my door when I leave the house, but perhaps it slipped my mind yesterday in the frenzy of trying to leave early enough.

I push open the door, my eyes scanning the foyer and living room, finding nothing out of the ordinary. The panic in my stomach begins to dissipate and I let out a sigh of relief, shaking my head to myself as I push the door shut. I need to stop being so paranoid all the time. It's gotten better over the past few months, but that feeling of an impending threat still looms above.

Setting my purse on the table in the foyer, I kick my shoes off and slide my feet into a pair of pink fluffy slippers. The house is quiet and I walk through the living room, opening all the curtains to let the sunlight spill in. It's late in the afternoon, but the sun is still hanging high in the sky outside. My footsteps are soft and I start to hum a song from the radio as I walk into the kitchen. I walk to the sink, pulling the curtains open farther. Cole will be here in a little bit, so I want to clean some things up before he's here and before Chloe gets home later.

As I turn away from the counter to walk to the fridge, the air leaves my lungs in a rush and I'm frozen in place. My spine straightens as a shiver of fear cascades down my vertebrae. There he is, sitting at my dining room table. He looks as I remember, his jaw set in a straight line. He's aged a bit, more gray hairs speckle his naturally dark locks.

"Hello Ella."

Fear lodges in my throat and I don't know what the hell to do. I don't know how he got inside my home or what the hell he's doing here.

The facade of safety I've been living in comes crumbling to the floor around me.

"This is a lovely home you have," he muses with a bite lingering in his tone. "It seems like you've built your own life here for you and your child." He pauses, his eyes slicing to mine. "I'm not here for her."

"You broke into my house, Jacob. I could call the cops right now and have you arrested."

"The door was unlocked, so I let myself in. That's not breaking and entering, Ella." He levels his gaze on me. "I've tried calling you and stopped here twice now. It seems like you were too busy with that cowboy boyfriend of yours to be here when I needed to talk to you."

"What could you possibly need to talk to me about?" I scoff, half spitting the words. Inside, I'm shaking, but I refuse to let him see it.

"Our divorce was never finalized."

My eyes widen and I watch in horror as he rises from his seat at the table. "What?"

He walks over to where I'm standing, reaching in his back pocket to pull out a folded paper. He unfolds it and lays it down on the counter. "You missed a signature." He pauses, letting out a sigh. "It went unnoticed, until recently."

I stare at the paper, my eyes wide and heart sinking into my stomach. "We're still married?"

"Yep," he says, popping the P sound at the end. "I wonder what your boyfriend would think if he knew he was sleeping with a married woman?"

My eyes flash to his. "You have no room to say anything remotely close to that, Jacob. We both know the things you did during our relationship. And as far as anyone is concerned, we aren't married."

"Well, according to the courts, we are." He narrows his eyes on mine. "I need you to sign the papers. I'm sure you can imagine the shock both my fiancee and I experienced when we found this out."

My breath catches. "You're engaged?"

"Mhm," he murmurs, pulling a pen from his pocket and clicking the top of it. "We have a two and a half year old and another on the way, so we'd really like to get this over with."

My stomach falls onto the floor. "You–" I pause, my face contorting. "You have a child?"

I don't bother doing the math because at this point, it doesn't even matter. That means she was pregnant when I was. We got pregnant around the same time… to the same man.

Except I was married to him and she was not.

"It's her, isn't it?"

The woman my brother saw him with. The last woman he cheated on me with.

"Does it really matter, Ella?" He half snaps at me. "I just need you to sign the damn papers so I can move on with my life."

I can feel myself curling inward. My efforts to remain strong are being tested past what I thought I could handle. But I know I can't break. I can't fold.

If not for me, I have to stay strong for Chloe.

"You need to leave before I call the police."

"Ella? What's going on?"

My shoulders sag the instant I hear his voice. I glance over my shoulder, seeing Cole as he walks into the kitchen. His eyes are glued to Jacob, who has now directed his undivided attention to Cole. "Everything's okay. Jacob was just leaving."

"Ah, you're the boyfriend," Jacob laughs, tilting his head to the side. "This is fun. You get to find out the news too."

Cole's expression doesn't change. "What news?"

"Turns out, Ella and I are still married." He smiles. "You've been sleeping with a married woman."

Cole narrows his eyes. "She's not your wife. Legally, maybe. In every other capacity? Absolutely not." Cole looks at me from the corner of his eye. "Did he break in?"

I nod slowly, looking past Cole to Jacob and then back to Cole. "He did. I told him I was going to call the police."

"The door was unlocked," Jacob chimes in.

"Call them, El."

"There's no need," Jacob says, raising his hands in innocence. "I need Ella to sign the papers and I will see myself out."

"I need to look them over with my lawyer before I'll sign a damned thing." I narrow my eyes on him, my heart racing inside of my chest. "I don't know what those papers are and I need to make sure they are legitimate and I'm not signing some random papers from you."

"Do you think I would do that?"

"I don't know, Jacob," I say, lowering my voice, shaking my head at him. "There are a lot of things I didn't think you'd do, but I was wrong."

Cole levels his gaze on Jacob. "You need to leave. Now."

"This is Ella's home, not yours."

"And she already asked you to leave." Cole takes a step forward. "You've broken into her home and now this is bordering on the line of harassment." He stops as he reaches Jacob. "You have three options. You leave yourself, Ella calls the cops, or I remove you myself."

Jacob's lips part, like he's going to say something to get himself in trouble, but he pauses and looks at me. "I'll have my lawyer send all the papers to yours."

He moves forward, brushing past Cole as he walks through the house, acting like he owns the place. He walks through the living room, Cole following behind him, with his shoulders pressed back and chin high, like he hasn't just cracked open the worst parts of me in front of someone who's actually worth something.

I climb to my feet, following after the two of them. As Jacob reaches the threshold, Cole stops in the center of the room. His voice drops, low and sharp. "You come back here uninvited, it won't be words next time."

Jacob glances over his shoulder to look at him, a smirk lifting his lips. He snorts, shaking his head and pulls open the front door. Without a second glance in our direction, he walks out, letting the screen door slam hard behind him. A picture falls onto the floor, the glass shattering across the surface.

Silence settles in the air around us. For a long, awful moment, all I can hear is the pounding in my chest. My gaze drops to the floor and I stare at the lines in the wood, bracing myself for the sound of Cole's voice.

For the judgment. The disappointment.

For that step in the wrong direction.

Instead, I hear the sound of his boots on the wood floor as he closes the distance between us. The toes of his boots stop by mine and I lift my eyes, finding him standing there, his hands gently curling around mine.

"You okay, El?" he asks, his voice low and calm, like I haven't just had my world flipped upside down again.

I nod, but it's shaky. "I didn't know. I thought it was done—I thought we were done."

"I believe you," he says without hesitation, shaking his head.

Tears sting at the corners of my eyes, but I blink them away. "You're not... upset?"

He shrugs, eyes steady on mine. "I'm not thrilled he showed up like that, but this doesn't change how I feel about you. He's your past, Ella. I'm here for your *future*."

The air leaves my lungs in a rush. I swallow roughly over the emotion lodged in my throat. Cole reaches for me, pulling me flush against his chest without another word.

He wraps his arms around me, like he's anchoring me back to solid ground. Back to the present moment.

Back to him.

And for the first time in a long while, I let myself lean into someone—really lean.

Because for once, I'm not standing alone.

CHAPTER THIRTY-FIVE

COLE

Ella pulls away from me, the sudden distance shocking and cold. She moves to stand behind the couch, turning her head to look at me. Unreadable emotions dance in her irises as she swallows. "I'm sorry about that," she says, her voice barely audible as she shakes her head. "You were never supposed to meet him. He was never supposed to come here."

"I'm sorry I didn't get here sooner," I retort, a frown pulling my lips downward.

She stares at me for a moment. She pulls her lips in between her teeth, biting down as she nods in agreement. "Thank you for coming. I've never had someone break into my house like that. I've never had to threaten calling the cops on anyone before."

"I'm proud of you, Ella," I say, my voice firm, yet there's a tenderness to it as I step up to her. She shrinks backwards as I reach for her and I immediately freeze. It's a blow to my chest and I know it's the lingering feelings from the events that happened this afternoon, but that doesn't soften the blow at all. My breath catches in my throat and I immediately drop my arms to my sides. "I'm sorry. I didn't mean to overstep."

It's such a mind fuck and my face contorts as I'm overwhelmed with conflicting feelings. I want to go to her. I want her to know she's safe with me, but I don't want to cross any boundaries that she's not comfortable with. And at this moment, it doesn't seem like she even knows what she wants. She's shook from her ex and from the reality he brought down upon her. We're both stuck in a weird spot and I don't know what I'm supposed to do at this moment.

"No, I'm sorry," she apologizes again, a frown sitting on her perfect lips. I hate seeing her like this. I want to make her laugh, to chase all her worries away. I want her to be light and happy, not bogged down by the bullshit from her past. "I think I need some time alone. I need to get my head straight and process everything that's going on."

My head tilts to the side, pain rippling through my entire body. "Okay," I concede, not wanting to push too hard arguing with what she said. "If you need anything, I'm only a phone call away. Whatever you need, whenever you need it, I'm here for you, sweets." I pause for a moment, collecting myself, concealing the emotion from my expression. I know I'm doing a shit job when her eyes scan my face and they glisten with tears. "I'm nothing like him, Ella."

Her throat bobs as she swallows roughly. Her nostrils flare and two tears streak down the sides of her face. "I know you're not." She lets out a breath, her forehead creasing. "You're everything good in the world. You're the best person I've ever met. But you can't fix everyone's problems. This is something I have to deal with on my own."

Her words are like a blow to my chest. "I want to fix this for you."

"You can't."

Conflict tugs at my heart. I know I can't do anything about her situation, but goddamn, I want to. It's my natural instinct–to protect and be the one who handles things.

But this situation… it's completely out of my hands.

"Okay," I say, finally agreeing with her, resisting the urge to go to her. The corners of my eyes sting and I blink the sensation away.

Her lips part as if she's going to say something, but she quickly clamps them shut. Her face looks like she can break down at any second and fuck me--it kills me to walk away from her right now, but she thinks that's what she needs. And maybe it is.

Maybe right now, she doesn't need me.

"I don't want to leave you alone," I admit, my voice low. "I don't like the thought of you being here by yourself after he was here."

Her throat bobs and she nods slowly. "Wyatt is coming to bring Chloe home soon. I'll be okay until he gets here."

"El," I start, my voice trailing off as she shakes her head at me.

"I'm a big girl, Wild. I appreciate your concern, but I'm not a damsel in distress." She pauses, letting out a ragged breath. "I got me."

Goddamn.

That last statement hits my chest like a ton of bricks. I know she's felt powerless before and I imagine Jacob invading her space has her sense of control feeling threatened.

I have to walk away. I have to let Ella stand on her own two feet right now.

My eyes search hers one last time, memorizing the flecks of gray in her icy blue irises, the freckles peppering the bridge of her nose and the tops of her cheeks. This might be the hardest thing I've ever done. A sad smile lightly lifts the corners of my lips and I give her one last longing gaze before I force myself to turn around. I can feel her eyes on my back as I reach for the door.

It takes everything in me not to look back at her as I slip outside. A ragged breath escapes me, my entire lungs deflating as my shoulders sag.

I'll give her what she wants... even if it's breaking my heart in the process.

***

Sitting on the dock, I stare out at the water with my hands planted on the wooden surface and my fingers wrapped around the neck of a beer bottle. After leaving Ella's, I ended up heading to the marina, unsure of what the hell I'm supposed to do. I still have to keep moving forward, even if it's not in the same direction as Ella.

Having to step away is something I'm not used to. By nature, I'm a fixer. If I see a problem, I want a solution. If I see someone who needs help, I want to help them. Seeing Ella like this and knowing she doesn't want my help is literally killing me. There's still so much I don't even know about her situation with Jacob and maybe that's for the best.

I never expected her to tell me, nor did I push for the knowledge because at the end of the day, it doesn't change the way I feel for her. It changes nothing between us, so if she doesn't want to talk about it, she reserves that right. It's her past, not mine. She needs to untangle herself from this mess without me. Ella can't live in the past and that's exactly what she's doing right now. She's been trying to outrun it this entire time and you can only run so far and so fast before these kinds of things catch up with you.

She has no choice but to deal with it head on now.

And she made the choice to do it on her own.

"I had a feeling I'd find you out here."

I glance over my shoulder at Wyatt as he walks down the dock toward me. My best friend tilts his head to the side when he reaches me, taking in my disheveled appearance and tired face.

"What are you doing down here?"

I lift my beer, taking a long swig. "Watching the water."

His eyebrows pull together and he motions for me to scoot over as he sits down on the wooden surface with me. "Ella said you were there with her when Jacob showed up."

I stare out at the water, avoiding his gaze. "I should have gotten there sooner."

"To do what, exactly?" Wyatt questions me, his voice low.

I lift my shoulders, letting them fall quickly. "I don't know. Probably somethin' that would have put me behind bars." I look at him. "Where is Ella?"

"She's at home with Chloe."

My spine immediately straightens. "You left her there alone?"

Wyatt levels his gaze on mine. "Yes, Cole. I left her home alone, with her daughter. She's been doing this by herself for long enough, she knows how to take care of herself."

"But what about Ja—"

Wyatt immediately cuts me off. "He's not coming back, Cole. And even if he did, she would call the police or call me." He lets out a breath. "She's fine."

I let out a ragged breath, clutching the beer bottle in one hand and running my other through my hair. "I just–" My chest deflates. "I know I can't help her, but I want to. I want to take all of this away from her."

"I get it," Wyatt says, his voice low and understanding. "You have to let her do this alone. It's all out of your control right now." He pauses, his hand hand lifting to squeeze my shoulder. "Ella is strong and independent and believe it or not, she doesn't need you."

"I know she doesn't," I agree, my voice gruff. "I hate this helpless feeling."

"Well, get over it," Wyatt says, his hand dropping from shoulder. "All of this will work out in the end, you just have to trust her. Let her get this all straightened out and let her come back to you."

A harsh laugh rumbles in my chest. "How can you be so sure that that will even happen?"

"Because she loves you, Cole." He speaks the words as if it's a fact. "And even though this is my sister we're talking about, a good guy like you deserves to get their happily ever after." The corners of his mouth twitch. "And you're the best person for her."

His words play over in my head and I attempt to hang on to every syllable, letting it seep into the fibers of my heart. I hope he's right because I can't imagine a life without her and Chloe. And I don't want to.

I can't imagine a future that doesn't revolve around my girls.

CHAPTER THIRTY-SIX

ELLA

Exhaustion settles in my bones as I take my paint brush and sweep the bristles across the canvas once more. It's already the middle of the afternoon and Chloe went down for her nap an hour ago. This is how I've been spending my time these last few weeks, letting the emotions pour from me, mixing with the oil paints. Life has been a bit of an overwhelming, emotional whirlwind since I found Jacob sitting in my kitchen.

There's a soft knock on the door and I divert my gaze, lowering my paintbrush. "Come in."

The door opens slowly, Wyatt stepping into my space. "Hey," he says softly, walking over to stand next to my easel. "Sorry to interrupt. I just finished installing the cameras and wanted to show them to you."

After Jacob's unexpected drop by, my brother, along with Iris and Remi, decided that I needed to get a doorbell cam installed, along with some other cameras around the exterior of the house.

"Of course," I say, climbing to my feet. I look down at my paint laden hands as we slip out of the room and head down the hall. My feet carry me to the kitchen sink and I run the warm water over my hands as my brother walks over with my phone.

He already knows my passcode and unlocks it, opening the app he downloaded. "I put a camera by each door and installed the doorbell camera. All three are linked to this app," he explains as he shows it to me.

I work a lather with soap in my hands, scrubbing my fingertips, listening to him explain how to operate them. Wyatt goes through the entire thing and I rinse and dry my hands.

"Thank you for doing that," I say, a tense smile on my face. "I never would have thought I would need this, but here we are."

"Everyone only wants you to be safe, El," he tells me, his voice soft. "I'm not here and it doesn't make me feel great all the time. I don't even want to think about what may have happened if Cole weren't here with you."

Cole.

The sound of his name alone sends an electrical current through my veins.

"Yeah, me too," I admit, my voice barely above a whisper. "I'm glad he was here–that I didn't have to face Jacob alone."

"You know, sometimes it's okay to let other people in, right?" Wyatt says, his voice quiet. "I know you don't want to get hurt again. You're the strongest person I know, but letting someone in, letting someone help you… it doesn't make you weak."

I stare at him for a beat, swallowing over the lump lodged in my throat. "But it can make me dependent."

"It doesn't have to," he says. "You can depend on someone, without being dependent on them."

I let out a breath, a heaviness tightening around my chest. "Maybe."

Wyatt shrugs with indifference, although there's emotion in his eyes. "You deserve to be happy, El." He pauses. "You got the paperwork, right? Your divorce was finalized?"

I slowly nod. Iris' lawyer helped me to get everything sorted. Since Jacob and I had been legally separated for the past few years, the divorce was granted without any issues. We didn't have a waiting period before signing the paperwork. Things are different in each state, and thankfully the state we were married in finalizes within seven to ten days.

I am finally free from that man.

"Good," he says softly, his chin dipping. He steps closer, wrapping his arm around my shoulders to pull me closer to him. "Everything will be okay, little sis."

I hug my brother, my eyelids falling shut as I hold on to this moment with him. Wyatt has always been the biggest supporter in my life and I know he means what he says. "Thanks, Wy. Thanks for always being here for me."

"I always will be. Even if I'm not here in person all the time, I'll always be here for whatever you need."

I spend the rest of the afternoon with my brother before he heads back to Iris'. After Chloe goes to bed, I find myself back in front of my canvas. I spend the rest of the evening painting, well into the middle of the night until I'm past the point of exhaustion, falling asleep with a paintbrush in my hand. When I finally resurface from my work, I realize Chloe will be up in a few hours and then it's time for us to start our routine all over again.

At least I have her... I'll always have her.

"There's my little sweet pea," Iris smiles, reaching her arms out for Chloe.

Chloe releases my hand and sprints through the living room, climbing up onto the couch with Iris before slipping into her arms.

Iris has been doing well and so far, everything has been going on schedule with her healing.

"Rose said as long as everything is good, I can leave a little earlier tonight, that way I'm not late coming to get Chloe."

My brother walks into the living room, tucking his hands into the front pockets of his shorts as he leans against the doorway. "She's fine, El."

I look at Iris, watching her love on my little girl, before looking back at my brother. "I know. I just don't want it to be too much, you know?"

Although Iris has been home for a couple weeks now and seems back to normal, I don't want Chloe to hinder her healing. Wyatt's been coming back to help with Chloe when Remi can't watch her and even though he's the one technically watching her, I don't want it to be overstimulating for Iris.

Iris' eyes flash to me. "She never is," she assures me, wrapping her arms tightly around my daughter. "Plus, Chloe loves being here with Grammy Iris, don't you, sweet pea?"

Chloe nods her head eagerly, burying her face in the crook of Iris' neck. She's been missing her, somethin' fierce and I know the two of them being together like this is probably better for Iris' mental health.

A smile works its way across my lips. "Okay, well if you need me to come earlier, I can."

Wyatt walks over to me, squeezing my shoulder. "We've got it, sis."

Walking over to Chloe, I press my lips to the top of her head before doing the same to Iris. "Thank you for everything," I whisper to her, my eyes slowly searching hers.

Iris reaches for my hand, giving it a gentle squeeze. "You've always been like a daughter to me, El. I love you and Chloe, even Wyatt like you are all my own. You never have to thank me for doing what feels right and natural to me."

Tears prick the corners of my eyes and I swallow over the lump lodged in my throat. "We love you too."

Iris gives my hand one last squeeze and I blow kisses to the three of them before leaving a little piece of my heart in her living room. Emotion encapsulates me on my ride to work and I'm so grateful for everything in my life.

There were so many times I doubted I could have this, but here I am.

Surrounded by love.

Safe and secure.

***

The bar isn't as busy tonight and Rose has been handling the few tables we have while I bartend. We're already past the dinner rush and things are starting to quiet down with only a few people occupying the barstools. I say goodbye to a couple as they rise from their seats and thank them while I begin to collect their empty glasses and wipe down the counter. As I'm moving the cloth over the surface, a familiar face sits down in front of me.

"Hello, Ella."

My heart stops in my chest and Vera lowers herself into the seat directly in front of me. Kennedy, her assistant, sits down beside her. Since the incident with Jacob, I've been ignoring every call from them both.

"Hi, Vera. Hi, Kennedy."

Kennedy gives me a soft, gentle smile and Vera simply tilts her head to the side. I haven't had a lot of interactions with the two of them and Vera has never been anything less than pleasant and nice. She has a colder, more up tight exterior than Kennedy does. Between the two of them, Kennedy is definitely the sunshine of their party.

"How are you, Ella?" Kennedy adjusts her ponytail as she smiles brightly. "We've been waiting for you to bring some new work into the gallery!"

Vera glances at her from the corner of her eye. "You've been evading our calls. Are you not interested in us representing your work anymore?"

Kennedy instinctively grabs Vera's forearm, giving it a gentle squeeze. Her hand lingers, her thumb trailing over her skin as she stares at her for a moment. Vera blows out a breath, her shoulders melting as Kennedy remembers I'm standing there. Her gaze meets mine and she pulls her hand away from her boss's arm, a blush creeping across her cheeks as she swallows.

"I apologize for being blunt and crass," Vera forces out the words, smiling apologetically. "This week has been stressful and as my therapist has said, I need to stop projecting. What I meant to say is, we've been trying to reach you and haven't gotten a response."

"That's my fault," I tell the two of them, my voice sounding stronger than it has in the past. I'm really working on channeling Ella who is learning to stand up for herself. The same Ella who took control in the bedroom with Cole. "Life has gotten a bit messy the past few weeks and I've been easily overwhelmed by things. I have been painting and I did plan on calling you back... eventually."

"We work with artists all the time and understand the creative process," Kennedy offers, smiling at me as she reveals the dimples in her cheeks. "We are also human and understand life happens."

"Well, I have been painting, despite everything going on."

Vera's face lights up and she looks very pleased with my truth. "Well, this is great news. Are you interested in selling any more of your work?"

I nod slowly, grabbing two napkins and setting them in front of the ladies. "I am. I'm very interested in trying to pursue this as a career."

"If only convincing you was this easy," Vera mumbled under her breath to Kennedy. Kennedy's eyes sliced to the side of her face, but she quickly recovers and brushes away the awkwardness. I'm not sure what that was about. Vera looks back at me. "Our clients will wait. You have my number, so please call us as soon as you finish some projects and would like to talk about things."

"Thank you," I smile, a lightness spreading through my chest. It's a breath of fresh air, knowing I have this opportunity whenever I am ready for it.

I can only hope Cole waits the same way Vera will.

"Can I get you both something to drink or food perhaps?"

Vera nods. "I'll take a dirty martini and I'd love to look at the menu." She glances at Kennedy, waiting for her to respond.

"I'll have what she's having."

I smile at the two of them, grabbing two menus and handing them to both Vera and Kennedy before I walk to the center of the bar to prepare their drinks. After handing them their drinks and taking their food order, I move around to the other patrons, stealing glances at Vera and Kennedy together while I work. I'm not sure what their relationship dynamic really is, but I don't miss Kennedy's tender gaze as she stares at her boss. Vera is a little more closed off, but she is visibly more relaxed around Kennedy.

All I can do is make assumptions and, considering that Vera is Kennedy's boss, I don't think they have a relationship they're sharing with the world. There's stolen glances and secret, gentle touches that almost feel like I'm invading their privacy by witnessing it. There's something blossoming between them, even if they haven't decided to let everyone in on their secret.

The trust they have is palpable and I can't help but feel a twinge of jealousy inside. They're comfortable and safe with one another.

It's everything I had with Cole. And everything I still want with him.

I can only hope he'll be understanding and that he'll still be waiting for me after I get my life straightened out.

After I put my past to rest and can focus solely on my future... and him.

CHAPTER THIRTY-SEVEN

COLE

It feels like I'm reliving the day of her art show, except this time, I'm not here with her.

Standing outside of the front door, I watch through the window as people move about, all of their heads tipping back as they look at the different paintings hanging on the walls. When Wyatt called me earlier to tell me about Ella's new show at the gallery, I didn't hesitate to show up. It's been a little over a month now since I last saw her or spoke with her and the time apart hasn't gotten any easier. I've been spending my days working on the ranch and busying myself with my boat, although nothing seems to be enough to block out the thoughts of her.

I've resisted every single urge to text or call her, simply out of respect for her wishes. A part of me has been feeling like a damn psychopath on the verge of giving in to my temptations. I want to hear her voice. I want to feel her next to me. Not only do I miss Ella, but I miss Chloe too.

I guess watching El through the window like a damn stalker is good enough for now.

"Are you planning on coming inside or standing out here like a weirdo?"

I turn my head to the side, seeing Wyatt as he walks out of the gallery and comes to stand in front of me. "I don't know what I'm doing. I want to come in, but I feel like I'm imposing."

Wyatt frowns as he remembers what I told him earlier. He was in town to visit and check in on Iris. He called me about the show, thinking Ella had told me. Only when he realized my surprise was genuine and I told him what happened did things click in his brain. "Maybe this is your chance to talk to her again. This is a neutral place for both of you."

That right there is exactly why I've been avoiding going to the bar. Before Ella, it was one of my regular places and after Ella, it became the only place I went for a drink or dinner. That place is hers, not mine. Showing up there while she was working felt invasive, like I was crossing a boundary she had set. She wanted space and time, so I am giving her as much as she needs.

Although, I can't help but wonder if she's been working to forget me instead.

"This is a public space, Cole. You and I are friends and she knows we're bound to see each other while I'm in town." He pauses, his nostrils flaring as he sets his jaw. "Either come inside or head back to the ranch. You've been lingering out the front for long enough now, and it's only a matter of time before someone questions who the psycho staring through the windows is."

"Fuck you," I chuckle, giving him a look and rolling my eyes. "I'll come in."

And if she wants me to leave, I'll be gone, no questions asked.

"Good choice," Wyatt says, nodding as he motions for me to follow him. He pulls open the glass front door, but he steps in front of me. His blue eyes drill into mine. "Keep her safe, Wild."

"I will."

He stares at me for a moment before finally nodding and heading inside. Wyatt doesn't wait for me, walking away to find Ella.

Blending in with the crowd, I walk around the perimeter of the room, my eyes scanning the wide span of paintings hanging on the walls. Some follow the trend as her art before with the differing landscapes. The first few appear darker and stormier but as you continue on, they start to grow lighter until you reach the last painting that is a sunrise with the sun shining brightly as it crests the horizon. A smile pulls on my lips and I walk to the next series, expecting it to be something similar, but I'm shocked when I see what I find.

These are more of a portrait style, as if capturing different moments. A snapshot of memories that have passed. My eyes scan them, taking in the art she created and I feel like I'm looking inside her mind, seeing the moving parts of the world through her eyes. It's almost like a story that transpires in one painting, only to be continued in the next.

As I reach the last one, the air leaves my lungs in a rush. The others were all realistic, the brush strokes so crisp and smooth, it was almost as if someone took an actual photograph. This last one is wispy and whimsical, but it's romantic and sexy. Two visible people are in the center, surrounded by blooming flowers and vines. The vines are intertwined, sweeping around the naked people as all the colors melt together. Their lips are crushed together, their arms wrapped around one another. Each part where their bodies meet melt together, except as you move farther down their torsos, there's no distinction from one or the other.

They are one.

"This one is my favorite."

My heart skips a beat in my chest, my breathing growing shallow as the sound of her voice slithers down my spine. It feels like a vine from the painting wrapping itself around my soul. Turning my head, I glance at her as she steps up beside me and I drink in the sight of her. Her make-up is light, but there's a dusting of sparkles illuminating her high cheekbones. Soft pink eyeshadow rests on her eyelids and her eyelashes are thick and dark with mascara. Her soft dark hair is slicked back in a low bun, revealing her delicate features and bone structure.

"It's mine too," I admit. And as much as I love the painting, I'm not looking at it. I'm looking at her.

A soft smile pulls on her lips as she turns her body to look at me, her long elegant gown shifting around her ankles. "Thank you for coming tonight. I wasn't sure if you would or not."

My eyebrows pull together and I move my body so we're facing each other. "Why?"

"I knew Wyatt was going to say something about it to you, so I didn't tell him we hadn't spoken."

"So you were testing me?" I ask her, feeling a twinge of hurt in my chest. Manipulation isn't Ella's style, so I'm confused by her omission.

She shakes her head, her lips parting as she lets out a soft breath. "Not the way you think. It was more to see if I completely blew my chance with you or not. If you didn't show, I told myself I wouldn't reach out. I would let you go and allow you to move on with your life."

My heart stops in my chest. "Well, that didn't happen."

"It didn't," she whispers, her voice barely audible as her eyes burn holes directly into my soul.

"So, what now?"

"I know we still need to talk." Her throat bobs. "But, I told myself if you came, then maybe I would still have a chance." Her expression softens and she lets out a breath. "I can't help but wonder if I still do."

I stare at her, emotion welling in my throat as I look at the woman who holds my heart in her hands. "You do, El."

Her lips lift, the smile spreading across her face, reaching her eyes as she tilts her head to the side. My heart beats strong and steady in my chest.. I fight the urge to go to her. I've missed the way she feels in my arms and she's so close I could touch her right now.

"Mama!"

Ella's gaze leaves mine and she turns around, looking in the direction of where Chloe's voice came from. She comes running over, pushing past some legs until she's right in front of Ella. I watch her as she bends down and lifts her daughter into her arms, holding her close against her body. It's like no one else is in the room as she focuses her attention solely on Chloe, listening to the little girl ramble about a leaf she saw on the way here.

Remi comes pushing through the crowd of people, her expression a little frantic and she appears to be a little out of breath. She relaxes as soon as she sees Ella holding Chloe and her chest heaves as she lets out a sigh of relief. "You can't run off like that, Clo."

Chloe looks at her, giving her a guilt filled smile as she shrugs. "Sorry, Auntie Remi."

"Are you Ella?" A woman asks as she steps up to her with her arm linked through her husband's. She looks to be in her sixties and I recognize her from seeing her at Vera's gallery before. She's one of their highest paying clients.

"Hi, yes!" Ella beams with confidence and my heart swells as I watch her come out of her shell to entertain the woman. Remi quickly takes Chloe from her arms as the woman calls Ella over to one of her paintings. The one that she said was her favorite. I watch her as she shakes her head and tells the woman she brought the painting to sell, but now she isn't sure she's ready to part with it. The woman frowns, but they move to the next one, diving into the complexities of the piece.

"Thank you for doing this for her."

I turn my head to look at Remi, pulling my attention from Ella for a moment. "I didn't do this."

"Not this show," she explains, shaking her head as she sets Chloe down. Her eyes travel with her, keeping a close eye on her as she steps closer to my side. "Ella has always been overly cautious and always questioning herself. She did a lot of work on her self-esteem after Jacob and was slowly coming out of her shell, but there was still a spark missing. She was still afraid to take the plunge into any kind of unknown."

Remi takes a few steps forward to keep watching Chloe and I move with her, glancing at Ella before looking back at her friend.

"You helped her to rebuild her confidence. You helped show her there is good in the world and in herself. I've never seen her like this before, but she's glowing." Remi smiles, the pride radiating from her expression. "She never believed in herself before and look at her now."

"This version of Ella was always there inside of her," I say, my voice soft as I watch her moving around the room.

"You're right," Remi agrees, nodding her head as her gaze follows mine. "But without you, I don't think she would have fully embraced it. I think she would have continued to diminish the light inside her soul. You gave her the time she needed to deal with the aftermath of Jacob showing up. You didn't walk away when she needed that time." She looks back at me. "So, thank you, Cole. Thank you for making her see and believe."

I stare at the star of the show, my heart soaring through the clouds as she moves with a confidence she didn't have when we first met.

She's the most amazing person I've ever met.

And I have every intention of making her mine again.

CHAPTER THIRTY-EIGHT

ELLA

Sitting on the back steps, I stare out at the lawn, wrapping the blanket tighter around my body. I'm finally free from Jacob Evans. There isn't a single thing tying us together any longer and I haven't heard from him since he showed up unannounced that one day. Life has taken such an unexpected turn and has been overflowing with positivity.

The gallery sold all of my paintings last week and they've already said they're ready for more, whenever I have more pieces available. It's been absolutely crazy to me, having this all happening. The fact that people want my work has almost instilled even more confidence in me.

The only thing missing is Cole. That night at the art show, I was pulled away by someone interested in purchasing a piece and I lost Cole after that. I caught sight of him walking around with Remi at one point but then after that, he disappeared. As much as I wanted to reach out to him, I knew I had to wait.

I needed to wait until I could officially close that door to my past.

My phone feels heavy in my hand and I stare for a moment, emotion lodging in my throat as I attempt to swallow it back. A wave of uncertainty and anxiety rolls through the pit of my stomach, but I ignore it.

I ignore it because I want to see him. I want to talk to him.

I want to let him in, completely this time.

Skipping over the messaging app, I tap on the phone icon and slowly type in his name. I watch, excitement lacing through me and I press my finger, lifting the phone to my ear. My heart pounds erratically in my chest and time feels suspended as it rings. And rings.

Disappointment washes over me as it goes to voicemail and I end the call, staring at my phone again. An impulsive thought passes through my brain and I grab ahold of it, typing out a message to him before I get the chance to second guess myself.

ELLA

Hey. I know it's getting late, but I wanted to see if you could stop by so we could talk.

My eyes widen, and I read over the message I sent, instantly regretting it. It feels too forward, like I shouldn't have suggested something like that. I should have eased into the conversation instead of jumping in head first.

Inwardly, I cringe, but I don't let myself un-send it. Instead, I leave it there in his inbox and lock my phone before setting it down on the ground beside me. Twenty minutes pass before I finally get up, heading back into the house for the night. Cole never responds and I look at my phone once more before setting it down on the counter as I get a drink.

In an effort to chase away the negative feelings, I head

into my art room to find a blank canvas and some jars of paint to lose myself in.

I don't know how long I've been painting for when a soft knock sounds on the glass pane to my right. My eyebrows pull together, confusion and fear pricking my skin. Convincing myself I was hearing things, I direct my attention back to the canvas when there's another tap on the window.

Dread fills the pit of my stomach and I slowly get up from my stool, my footsteps hesitant as I step to the side of the window and peer out through the curtain. It's dark, but I see him immediately as he stands a few feet away with the soft glow from his phone screen illuminating his face.

Relief floods me and my shoulders sag, releasing the nervous breath I was holding. I lift my hands, attempting to speak nonverbally with him. Cole moves his hand, like he's pointing to the front of the house. I nod in understanding, hoping that's what he means as he disappears back around the corner of the house.

Abandoning my painting, I head through the house, my bare feet padding on the wood floors as I walk to the front door. Unlocking the deadbolt, I turn the knob, pulling it open to Cole standing on the front porch, his throat bobbing as our gazes collide.

"Cole," I breathe his name, my heart pounding against my rib cage. "You came."

The corners of his mouth lift. "You called."

My breath catches in my throat and time is momentarily suspended between us. His eyes search mine, doing a sweeping motion from one eye to the other before he closes the distance between us. He doesn't stop until he's entering my space, his hand sliding along the side of my face as he tips my head back.

And then his lips crash into mine.

He breathes me in with a tenderness that has my heart crumbling in my chest. He's in tune with my body and his opposite hand finds my waist as he holds me close to him. My hand instinctively lifts to wrap around his neck as his lips move against mine.

He tastes like chocolate and smells like leather and cedar. His scent penetrates my senses and I inhale deeply, finding comfort and solace in the familiarity. I've always been safe with Cole and he's always made sure I knew it.

My hands grip at the back of his neck, holding him close as his tongue slides along the seam of my mouth. Without hesitation, I part my lips, granting him access. He deepens the kiss, his lips melting into mine. I match every movement. Every taste. Every breath.

His leg presses between mine, pushing me back into the house. I take a few steps back, guiding him along with me as the screen door slams shut. Cole moves, pushing his foot against the main door and it closes behind us. Dropping one hand from his head, I reach around, turning the lock on the knob.

"I won't let anyone get you, Ella," Cole promises as he breaks away from me for a moment. "No one will get to you or Chloe, ever." He stares down at me, earnest and truthful.

The emotion is evident in his voice and he rolls his lips between his teeth, biting it back before he releases them.

"I'm sorry I didn't call you sooner," I rasp, my voice low as he backs me farther into the house until we're walking into the laundry room.

"You don't owe me an apology." He slides his hands down past my ass, grabbing the backs of my thighs as he hauls me into the air. He sets me down on the washer and settles between my legs. "I would have waited however long you needed."

"I would never ask you to do that."

He tilts his head to the side. "You would never have to."

I pull him back to me, his mouth instantly finding mine. My hands reach for his shirt, slowly pushing up the bottom hem as my fingers trail over his back. Cole follows my lead, his hands mimicking mine as he begins to lift my shirt up to my neck.

My arms lift and I break away from him, letting him strip my shirt away. Cold air dances across my naked torso and Cole groans as he watches my nipples harden from the cool temperature.

"Jesus, I've missed you." He pauses as he reaches behind his neck and pulls his shirt up over his head. "In more ways than this," he adds with a wink while tossing his shirt onto the counter behind me. "I know we need to talk, but I need you, Ella."

"I'm yours, Cole." I pause, letting out a ragged breath.

He abruptly pulls me off the washer so I'm standing flat footed in front of him. His hands find my waist and his eyes search mine once more. "Do you trust me?"

"Yes."

I'm caught off guard as he spins me around to face the opposite direction. "Take off the rest of your clothes," he instructs as I glance over my shoulder at him. He's already undoing his belt buckle and jeans. I watch as he pushes them halfway down his legs, dragging his boxer briefs with them. "If you don't want me to fuck you like this, tell me now."

Shaking my head at him, I follow his orders and push down my own pants and panties. They pool around my ankles as Cole begins to push me forward until the front of my body is flush on the counter.

His fingers urge my legs apart and he moves them against my pussy. "Fuck, you're so wet already."

"I've been waiting for you," I rasp, half panting as he presses his cock against my entrance. "For far too long."

Shifting my weight, I rock back against him, earning a groan from him as he grabs my ass cheeks and starts to push inside me. He stretches me, filling me completely in one fluid movement. The barbells along the underside of his cock rub against my insides, sending a shockwave of pleasure through me.

"Ella, darlin', I want to fuck you so hard right now, but I don't want to hurt you."

Excitement washes over me, dancing with the heat in the pit of my stomach. I turn my head to look at him over my shoulder. "You won't hurt me, Cole. I want you to do it."

"You deserve a proper fucking, don't you?"

Pulling my bottom lip between my teeth, I bite down and nod. God, I want him so badly right now.

Cole slides his hand up to my hair, wrapping it around his fist as he pulls my head back. "Then a proper fucking is what you'll get."

He slowly inches out, his piercings hitting all the right spots again before he pauses with just the tip inside. There's a moment of anticipation hanging in the air between us before he slams into me without any warning. His hips shift and he thrusts into me, pushing me against the edge of the washer.

I cry out in pleasure and I push back against him, meeting every thrust. He releases my hair, sliding both hands to my hips as he starts to fuck me harder. There's a haziness growing along the perimeter of my vision and I'm close to seeing stars as he keeps slamming into me.

Thankfully, Chloe is sound asleep and has her noise machine because I'm in an awfully compromising situation. The last thing I need is for her to find me here with Cole like this.

"You were made to take my cock," Cole groans, his movements becoming erratic. He reaches for my hand, pulling it down in front of me as he pushes it between my legs. "Play with yourself while I fuck you."

I inhale sharply, both nervousness and excitement dancing inside of me. "Okay," I breathe, my voice barely audible as I start to move my fingers against my clit. A low moan escapes me, filling the small room as my legs start to feel weak. "Fuck me harder, Cole."

He leans forward, his body warm as his lips graze my ear. "That's it," he groans, thrusting into me harder as he nips at my earlobe. "Make yourself come for me."

Another moan escapes me until they're cascading from my lips, tangling with his name. Feeling him like this is everything I've wanted. I've missed him and his company, but I've needed this closeness with him. This connection. This wildfire that spreads rampant between us.

He thrusts again and my fingers work against my clit faster until I feel myself clenching around him. His hands, his mouth, his cock, and his piercings. All of it combined with my fingers has me catapulting over the edge of ecstasy. He slides his entire length into me, filling me to the brim as I let out a cry.

Our surroundings faded long ago and my orgasm sucks me under. My legs shake, my pussy tightening around him as he calls out my name. His fingers grip my hips and he murmurs against my ear.

"Oh, fuck, Ella," he moans, rocking into me as he spills himself deep inside me. My head falls forward against the washer as my orgasm starts to subside, but my body is still riding out the waves. "Jesus Christ. You're mine, El. Mine, mine, mine."

"Yours," I breathe, my lungs filling with oxygen as my heart spills over with love.

CHAPTER THIRTY-NINE

COLE

"I owe you an explanation."

I glance at the top of Ella's head as she's lying on my chest. I thought she had fallen asleep as her breathing had evened out and she's been quiet the past twenty minutes. After I fucked her in the laundry room when I first arrived, we ended up coming to her bedroom for a second round. She asked me to stay the night and I have no plans of going anywhere... ever.

"For what?" I question her, my voice quiet as she sits up on the bed. She grabs the comforter, wrapping it around her naked body as I move farther up the mattress, sitting with my back against the headboard. I reach for her, pulling her closer to me so she's sitting right beside my torso. "You don't owe me any kind of explanation."

Ella's eyes search mine and she gives me a soft smile as she shakes her head at me. "I feel like I do. I haven't been completely forthcoming about my past with you and I'm ready to tell you about what happened."

My heart crawls into my throat and I slowly nod. "Okay." I never want her to feel like she owes me anything, especially diving into something like this that has caused her so much pain. Since I met her, it was clear to see she was deeply affected by something and she was continually working to get past whatever it was that has been holding her back. I know enough now, but if she wants to tell me more, I won't stop her from doing that.

She feels safe enough with me or she wouldn't have brought it up.

"When I turned eighteen, I really struggled with my identity and what I wanted to do in life." She pauses for a beat, taking a deep breath, as if she's clearing her head before she continues. "Wyatt had things figured out. He was going to school to be a doctor and I was living on a dream that I could make a career out of being an artist. My parents supported whatever I wanted to do, but they made it known I needed to figure something out, other than just painting."

"After Wyatt and I lost our parents, I felt like I lost a part of myself with them." She pauses for a beat, taking a deep breath as if she's clearing her head before she continues. "It was a really rough time for me. You know, Wyatt struggled that entire summer and it was so hard for me to watch. I felt like I became his parent and had to drag him out of the darkness and force him to get on with his life. Our parents would have been pissed to see him wasting away, so I made it my mission to make sure he didn't mess up his life."

Her chest rises, her lips parting as she blinks away her tears. "Losing them was hard. I'll never forget sitting in that hospital and the doctor walking into the waiting room. Our father died on impact. It was 4:07 in the morning and they weren't able to save my mom. They tried everything they could, but there was too much damage and she had lost too much blood." She lets out a ragged breath. "My life was already in shambles at that point and their death changed the trajectory even more."

Words can't even describe how terrible I feel for her, listening to her recount the tragedy from her past. Ella maintains composure, but my heart breaks in my chest. I remember when they lost them and the aftermath, but I wasn't there when they got the raw, brutal news.

"I'm so sorry, Ella," I concur, my voice quiet, emotion washing over me.

She gives me a small smile and essentially waves it off as if it's nothing. "It's fine. It happened and it was really hard to go through, but here I am. I still think about them frequently and I really do miss them, but it's weirdly gotten easier over the years." She shakes her head. "I feel horrible even saying that."

"Time doesn't erase the pain, but it makes it more bearable."

Ella nods before she continues with her story. "I left Silverspur Springs with Jacob because I thought he could help me build a life. He was older and had his life figured out. Wyatt left for college, you were gone and my parents were focused on their lives after spending so much time raising their kids. In a way... I was just kind of left behind. And alone."

Guilt strikes my chest.

"I was working at that old run-down diner on Mustang Way when I met Jacob. I was looking for a way out of here and I jumped at the first opportunity."

My nostrils flare at the thought of her being that young and meeting him. "How old was he?"

"Twenty-eight."

My blood boils. She was so vulnerable and looking for

someone, anyone to help her feel seen... and that's who swooped in. A man who needed a younger, broken woman to feed his ego.

"Things were good with him at first, but it all moved so quickly. We got engaged less than a year after being together and married about a year after that. Jacob was charming and he made me feel loved. He made me feel like I was the most amazing person. It was everything I thought I needed at that time in my life, but I wish I hadn't been so ignorant to the red flags I saw from the start." She pauses, shaking her head as sadness washes over her irises. "I didn't realize that everything he was feeding me, he was also feeding to other women."

My jaw tightens to the point that it feels like my teeth are going to crumble from the pressure.

"I was stuck in a loveless marriage with a serial cheater. The first time I found out was right before we got married. I didn't want to go through with the wedding, but he convinced me that it would never happen again." She pauses, shaking her head. "But it happened again, not long after the wedding."

"I'm sorry, Ella," I breathe, my nostrils flaring as I conceal my anger. There's nothing either of us can do about it now. "I'm so goddamn sorry."

"It's not your fault," she says, giving me a small smile. "He worked all the time and was constantly away on business trips. I know now that a lot of those trips weren't only for business. He was sleeping with multiple different women wherever he went. Every once and awhile he would take me on a trip with him, but even then, he'd still find a way to sneak off, only to come back smelling like perfume and alcohol, claiming I was making something out of nothing."

"The one that was the final blow was the woman he's marrying now. The one who he seemingly turned it all around for." She pauses, letting out a ragged breath. "Wyatt was the one who caught them together. He was leaving the hospital one night and found them on a park bench on his walk home, making out. When he questioned Jacob about it, the woman went frantic and Jacob told her to go to the car while he explained everything to Wyatt."

"It was devastating," she says quietly. "And even after it all, he still begged me to stay. He wanted to have his cake and eat it too." She purses her lips. "I think he was afraid I would take him for everything, but honestly, I didn't want a single thing from him."

"Ella…"

She shakes her head at me. "I found out I was pregnant the day we buried our parents. I refused to raise a child in a loveless home like that. So, I left. Wy, Remi and Iris were all waiting for me when the plane landed"

Pride lifts my heart in my chest. I can't help but feel sad for her that she was stuck with him for years before she finally left, but I'm so glad she was able to get out. I'm glad she was able to see things for what they really were, rather than choosing to stay. "That took a lot of courage, El. I'm endlessly proud of you for making that choice."

"It was a really scary time," she admits, her voice barely audible as guilt washes over her expression. "I wanted out of the marriage and for a moment, it felt like something that could make me feel stuck instead." She tilts her head back, closing her eyes as she takes a deep breath and looks at me again. "The opposite happened. Jacob swore I cheated and claimed the baby wasn't his. He wanted no involvement, whatsoever."

She pauses, tears filling her eyes. "I don't know where I

would have been without my brother, Remi and Iris. They saved me."

"You saved yourself, Ella." I reach forward, wiping her tears away before pulling her into my arms. "They helped to guide you, but you did it. You got out and stayed strong. I am so fucking proud of you."

She pulls away, her eyes searching mine. "I love you, Cole. I'm sorry it took me this long to finally say it. With everything with Jacob and finding out there was an error in the divorce paperwork, I wanted to make sure that was completely behind me so there's nothing that can get in our way."

"I love you," I murmur, cupping the sides of her face as my heart grows ten sizes inside my chest. "God, I love you. I have since the moment I first laid eyes on you."

"I tried to resist you at first because I was scared. I was scared to ever let someone in again. Once I started to fall for you, I never stood a chance. I fell fast and hard and it terrified me." She pauses, laughing softly. "The feelings I have for you still kind of scare me."

"I don't want you to ever be afraid," I breathe, stroking her cheeks with the pads of my thumbs. "You will always be safe with me. Always."

"I know." Tears shimmer in her eyes and the smile on her lips consumes her entire face. "We're safe and we're loved."

"And you always will be."

EPILOGUE
COLE

ONE YEAR LATER

"Chloe, leave the fish in the water!"

She whips her head to the side, her eyes wide as she realizes she's been caught. A slow smile lifts the corners of her lips and she pushes away from the small pond, straightening her body as she wipes her wet hands on her pants. "Sorry," she says sweetly with her little smile' that always gets her her way. "I just wanted to see if it was heavy."

I stare at the little girl for a moment, attempting to make sense of the logic behind her thinking it was a good idea to try to lift one of the koi from the small pond. I mean, I can understand why she would want to see how much it weighs, considering the damn things are huge, but at the same time, what the hell? It's a fish... in a pond.

"Let's just not do that again," I smile at her as I reach for her little hand. She slides her tiny palm against mine, her small fingers wrapping around the side of mine as she walks with me toward the building. "Your mom won't be very happy if I bring you in here soaked from the pond."

"Or with a fish," she adds with a giggle as she half hops.

A chuckle rumbles in my chest and I glance down at the little girl. "Yeah, I don't think she would love that."

As we walk up to the museum, I pause for a moment, staring up at the building. This past year has been a whirlwind for Ella and I. After her divorce was finalized, she came back to me and we've been inseparable since--not that we'll ever be separated. I've practically moved into Ella's now. I'm not sure the last night I spent at the ranch alone and that's exactly how I want things to be.

I've been wanting to propose to her since she came back to me, but I don't want to scare her. I know she's not ready for anything like that and I don't need a piece of paper to tell me what I already know.

Ella and Chloe are mine.

My world. My girls.

Vera is a member of the board for an art museum in Cheyenne and they set up an exhibit to showcase local artists. When she called and asked Ella if she wanted to be a part of it, my girl didn't hesitate to say yes. I'm so proud of her for how far she's come. Even within the past year, she's grown more and more each and every day. She takes every new challenge head on, pushing her way through the uncertainty and discomfort.

"Let's go find momma," I tell Chloe, smiling down at her as we step up to the front door. The glass doors slide open as we reach them and Chloe skips beside me, her little legs keeping up the pace with my stride. I shorten it to accommodate her, so she doesn't have to rush to keep up with me. As we walk inside the museum there's a large banner in the center of the corridor with Ella's smiling face on it. She's being featured with two other artists and their pictures are also there, along with the location of where their exhibit is in the museum.

We make our way up the stairs and reach the third floor. Chloe's little head turns from side to side as we walk through two other exhibits before reaching the part of the building where Ella's is. Today is the first day that they have it open at the museum, so they are having a small event for the artists. They were invited to come hangout for a few hours for a cocktail hour with anyone who wanted to come check out their work.

I see Ella from across the space as we step into the room with her paintings. She's standing off near the corner, sipping a flute of champagne as she listens to someone speak next to her. The woman points at one of the pictures, her finger singling out one particular part and she smiles at Ella who nods eagerly. I keep Chloe at bay, holding her close by my side as we wade through the group of people gathered around.

As Ella finishes speaking with the woman, she sees Chloe and I walking towards her. Her dark red lips lift as her smile reaches toward her eyes. Her dress, the same shade of red, shifts around her calves as she starts to walk. Her strides are confident and elongated and her hair sways behind her back as she meets Chloe and I in the middle. I reach down, lifting Chloe up as she smiles at her mother, but doesn't reach for her.

"Well, there are my two favorite people," Ella beams, kissing Chloe's head before lifting to press her lips to mine. Her mouth lingers as if she's not ready to move away from me, but reluctantly, she does. "There are so many people here, it's crazy."

"As they should be." I smile back at the woman my heart belongs to. "I told you, your art belongs in a museum."

Tears wash over her eyes, creating a glaze of moisture as she smiles back at me. "None of this could have ever happened without you. You're the one who pushed me to keep painting and to go to Vera's gallery. You're the one who has always believed in me, even when I didn't believe in myself."

"That was all you, El," I murmur, pulling her closer to me, wrapping my arm around the small of her back. "You've always had it in you, you just needed someone by your side cheering you on."

A wistful look passes through her eyes. "It's always been you."

"That will never change."

She lifts up on her toes, her lips finding mine once more as she kisses me with a tenderness that has my soul melting. "Good," she murmurs against my mouth as she pulls away. "Because I don't want to ever have to imagine what it would be like not having you by my side."

"You never will."

She stares at me, a smile finding its way to her lips again as she puts her hand over my heart. "Promise?"

"I promise." My arm tightens around her and I pull her to Chloe and I. "You're my heart and my soul, Ella Daniels. You're the only person I want to do this crazy thing called life with. I love you past the ends of the earth, past the stars and the moon. In this life and the next—it will always be us."

"I love you so much," she breathes, wrapping her one arm around the back of my neck as her other circles around Chloe.

"I love you more."

She lets out a soft laugh, her hand swatting at me. "Liar."

"Want me to prove it?" I question her, raising an eyebrow as she pulls away from me.

She leans down, kissing Chloe's head again before she looks at me and winks. "You can prove it to me later."

She blows a kiss at the two of us and I watch as she walks back to a group of women looking at one of her paintings. She's thriving instead of surviving and my god, she's glowing. Pride swells inside my chest as my heart thrums to the beat of her.

Always her.

STAY UPDATED!

Want to know more of what's coming from Cali?
Sign up for her newsletter HERE to stay in the know!

ABOUT THE AUTHOR

Cali Melle is a USA Today Bestselling Author of steamy, swoon-worthy romance novels that will have you feeling like you're the one falling in love.
If she isn't lost in the fictional world she's creating, she's most likely adding a new book boyfriend to her own roster or sitting in the stands at the ice rink, watching her kids play hockey.

ALSO BY CALI MELLE

ASTON ARCHERS SERIES

Make Your Move

Make Your Play

Make Your Save

Make Your Change

Make Your Shot

ORCHID CITY SERIES

Meet Me in the Penalty Box

The Tides Between Us

Written In Ice

Dirty Pucking Play

The Lie of Us

WYNCOTE WOLVES SERIES

Cross Checked Hearts

Deflected Hearts

Playing Offsides

The Faceoff

The Goalie Who Stole Christmas

Splintered Ice

Coast to Coast

Off-Ice Collision

STANDALONES

The Christmas Exchange

The Christmas Rebound

Tell Me How You Hate Me

The Art of Breathing

Love Me Wild

<u>BAR DOWN SERIES</u>

The Plot Pact

<u>SUGAR HILL HOLLOW</u>

Love Tapped